Pure
Inventions

ALSO BY JAMES KING

FICTION
Faking
Blue Moon
Transformations

NON-FICTION
William Cowper: A Biography
Interior Landscapes: A Life of Paul Nash
The Last Modern: A Life of Herbert Read
William Blake: His Life
Virginia Woolf
Telling Lives or Telling Lies?: Biography and Fiction
The Life of Margaret Laurence
Jack, A Life with Writers: The Story of Jack McClelland
Farley: The Life of Farley Mowat

CO-EDITOR
The Letters and Prose Writings of William Cowper
William Cowper: Selected Letters
Early Voices

Pure Inventions

A novel by

James King

Cormorant Books

**Canada Council
for the Arts** **Conseil des Arts
du Canada**

ONTARIO ARTS COUNCIL
CONSEIL DES ARTS DE L'ONTARIO

The publisher gratefully acknowledges the support of the
Canada Council for the Arts and the Ontario Arts Council
for its publishing program. We acknowledge the financial support
of the Government of Canada through the Book Publishing
Industry Development Program (BPIDP) for our publishing activities.

Printed and bound in Canada

LIBRARY AND ARCHIVES CANADA CATALOGUING IN PUBLICATION

King, James, 1942–
Pure inventions / James King.

ISBN 1-896951-94-5
ISBN-13 978-1-896951-94-2

1. Title.

PS8571.I52837P87 2006   C813 .54   C2005-906948-1

Cover design: Angel Guerra/Archetype
Cover image: *Tsukioka Yoshitoshi, Kusunoki Masatsura* from
Selection of One Hundred Warriors (1868). Colour woodcut.
Collection of James King. Used with permission.
Author photo: Pete Paterson
Text design: Tannice Goddard
Printer: Friesens

CORMORANT BOOKS INC.
215 Spadina Avenue, Studio 230, Toronto, Ontario, Canada M5T 2C7
www.cormorantbooks.com

For William Hanley

"The whole of Japan is a pure invention. There is no such country, there are no such people."

— OSCAR WILDE

OVERTURE

MADAMA BUTTERFLY

CHAPTER ONE

1905

THE TURBULENT HEAVING and sighing of the music are irresistible, relentless tuggings on the heart sleeves. As the orchestra swoops in, time after time, the voices of the singers are drowned. Not that their words are of great importance. The story is simple enough: a Japanese courtesan falls in love with an American naval officer, marries him but is soon abandoned by her spouse; she gives birth to a son; years later, the husband and the woman whom he married in the United States, and who cannot become pregnant, return to claim the love child for themselves. Completely accommodating, the courtesan agrees, sends the little boy away with these two people, and then is overwhelmed by feelings of longing, regret, shame and guilt.

The *kamuro* moves with tedious slowness until she reaches her mistress, bows, kneels beside her and assists her to remove the kimono embroidered with large gold carp swimming in and out of bronze-coloured seaweed. Some of the fish can be seen sailing away; on some only their tails are visible, the heads of others point upwards, downwards and sideways. The gold and green are themselves embedded in a heavy purple which gives the mistress's costume a regal appearance. It is her finest piece of clothing, worn only when receiving guests of the highest calibre. After removing the kimono, the *kamuro* is reluctant to leave, as if fearing that her mistress should not be left alone clad only in her white under-garment. But, from the determined flick of her employer's wrist, the servant knows she must leave.

Making sure that her trusted servant has departed, the woman, with customary grace, seats herself on the floor, looks at the knife before her, bursts into tears, summons up her resolve and plunges the weapon into her stomach. Startled by the violence of the injury she has done herself, but pleased to be doing away with an existence that has become unbearable, she falls forward listlessly.

Throughout, from the rapture of *Viene la sera* to the misplaced optimism of *Un bel dì* to the ironic bitterness of *Con onor muore ... Tu? Piccolo Iddio*, the audience is entranced by this performance of *Madama Butterfly*. Just as the opera reaches its tearful conclusion and before tumultuous applause greets the Cio-Cio San of Emma Destinn and the Pinkerton of Enrico Caruso, a tiny Japanese woman in the audience, her eyes filled with tears, turns to her son: "Hiroshi, I have just seen my early life lovingly recreated. Now you have some idea of what the Yoshiwara was like when I was a girl!"

Although he has a very good idea of the history of the place where he was born and spent the first seventeen years of his life, his mother continually insists it has so changed, for the worse, that he cannot possibly conceive of its former glory. He does not bother to point out that the opera is set in Nagasaki, not Tokyo and its infamous Yoshiwara.

During the performance, Hiroshi, looking in his mother's direction, had seen a variety of emotions cross her face — fear, anguish, despair, even anger. As is her custom, she would never confess to such feelings.

On that sultry June night in 1905, Hiroshi and his mother, Yoshiko, are far from Japan. They are in the dress circle at Covent Garden, accompanied by the dour Mrs. Eliot. On the following day, Hiroshi's mother's ship will leave for Yokohama; three days after that, Mrs. Eliot and Hiroshi are to depart for Boston by way of New York.

Well before she ever saw Puccini's opera, Yoshiko had been deeply moved by the *Butterfly* story that, she correctly observed, bore such a strong resemblance to her own unhappy history.

Unlike Cio-Cio San, Yoshiko did not take her own life, but she did have a child — Hiroshi — conceived during a brief liaison and then marriage to Lieutenant Eliot of the American Navy. Yoshiko and Butterfly did share one trait: although they had been courtesans, they had experienced love only once in their lives. Betrayed by Pinkerton, Butterfly killed herself; betrayed by Eliot, Hiroshi's mother carried on with the business of life because, she insisted, her son needed her. For her, Butterfly was self-indulgent. Yet, at the age of thirty-two, Hiroshi was being handed over to his father's widow and emigrating with her to the United States. He had no idea when he would see his mother or Japan again.

Hiroshi's departure from Japan six months earlier was forced upon him. He had become something of a reprobate and had to be saved from himself, through the agency of the two women beloved by Lieutenant Eliot.

For Yoshiko, Hiroshi and Mrs. Eliot, that evening at Covent Garden was filled with far more complicated emotions than those of Cio-Cio San and Pinkerton. As much as she could, Yoshiko attempted to pay attention to the action on the stage and the glorious melodies that filled her ears. Yoshiko is dressed in a simple, almost mannish, brown tailored suit purchased on her behalf by Mrs. Eliot, but is difficult to ignore. Her thin, beautifully shaped eyebrows, the almond eyes of deepest brown, her slightly pointed chin and aquiline nose give ample evidence that she is still a great beauty. Hiroshi, in a black tuxedo, is the embodiment of young English manhood. His skin is translucent white, his eyes appear to be black like his pomaded, glistening hair, and he holds himself as a young courtier. Only when one's attention is fixed on his eyes does his Anglo-Saxon heritage come into question for they are, like his mother's, almond-shaped.

His eyes feast on the colours on the stage and his ears are stirred by Puccini's melodies, but his mind wanders back to the Orient from which he was removed by Mrs. Eliot. His rescuer considers the opera in exceedingly bad taste; she is no great admirer of Puccini and his love of musical melodrama. Despite her disdain for Cio-Cio San, Kate Eliot bears a tender love for Yoshiko and strong maternal feelings for Hiroshi, but she fears that the young man is a scoundrel.

Kate must have been a great beauty as a young woman, although it is difficult to determine that this evening. Her lavender silk evening gown, made for her in Paris by Worth, enhances the impression that she is a troubled woman, one who has retreated into the shadows. She should wear brighter colours, a deep green or blue, that would emphasize her auburn hair, her green eyes and her bow-shaped lips. But Mrs. Eliot cares not a whit for her appearance. She is apprehensive about all that has happened and she is uncertain what will happen to her and Hiroshi upon their arrival in the New World.

PART ONE

THE APPRENTICE

CHAPTER TWO

1854

ENORMOUS AND GAUDY, the two bright red gates were so immense that the girl feared they might fall down on her and crush the spirit inhabiting her tiny body. There were other dangers. The flying dragons perched on the top of each post might swoop down and carry her away. She could just barely see the menacing glances the two monsters exchanged with each other, their eyes aglitter with mischief, as if debating which of them should do the nefarious deed.

She smelt the blossoms before she saw them. So heavy was the air that she laboured to breathe in the thick, comforting scent. Then, looking into the space framed by the two portals, she beheld the cherry trees.

As a child, Hiroshi was fascinated by his mother's account, told to him over and over again, of her strange journey at the age of eight in 1854 to a settlement in the northern part of Edo.

After travelling for three long days and nights by a variety of boats and wagons from Chiba, Yoshiko and her father are set down by the palanquin driver, who is instructed by her father to await his return in about an hour. An observant child, she notices that the gates are the only entrance and exit to what her father had told her would be her wonderful new home. She wonders why a moat extends from the two gates and presumably restricts the movements of all the inhabitants of the little city she is entering. And yet she will be glad to escape her father, whose breath and clothing reek of sake.

A week before, he had informed his motherless daughter that he could no longer keep her. He told her a samurai must be free to carry out his responsibilities. Two days later, he confided that his only hope for advancement was to take up residence in the imperial city of Kyoto, where lived his brother, a monk. In this way, he might become some sort of middleman who could, for example, carry messages between the emperor in Kyoto and the shogun in Edo, the real centre of power. Since the Yoshiwara was in the northern part of Edo, he should easily be able to visit his daughter when he returned there frequently on business.

Even at her young age, Yoshiko doubted her father's sagacity and his truthfulness. After his wife's death the year before, he had fallen apart, not sure of his future. He had adored his wife, but he was angry with her for having abandoned him. He loved Yoshiko, but she recalled his weakness in so loving her mother. Better to rid himself of the all too tangible reminder of his grief. The guard — who worked for the *shirobei*, the guardian of the gates — informs him that to reach the *ageya* he seeks, he and his daughter should walk down the middle street, *Naka-no-cho*, to the end of the second street on their left. As they set out, Yoshiko notices the regular rows of two-storey houses but when they take their turning, she sees that the fronts of all the houses now have slat-enclosed structures, some vertical but most horizontal. She cannot conceive of any reason for such strange-looking rooms, as if they had been built to contain the surly tigers in some of her father's *ehon*, the picture books. She thinks of asking her father about these buildings but decides against it.

Her father seems to know his way about this strange place, even though he has asked directions to a particular address. Before they turn off the main thoroughfare, she notices that the ranks of cherry trees fill the length of the square and the streets are completely deserted. Cages and cherry blossoms and silence. She has no idea why her father has brought her here.

When they reach the end of the street to which they had been directed, father and daughter stand before a building with a plain entranceway. Yoshiko is relieved. Immediately, an elderly man, a *wakai-mono*, whom her father addresses as if the servant were a mere boy of twelve, slides the door open. He bows ostentatiously in the direction of her father and informs him that the *yarite* is awaiting them. The only furnishing in the small room to which he leads them is a huge, spare bonsai. The little girl is delighted by the green hissing dragon embedded in the drab yellow pot in which the tree lives. Yoshiko withdraws to the back of the room and she and her father sit in gloomy silence for what seems an eternity. The little girl can feel eyes prying into her face and body, but she has no idea where those eyes can be.

As has become her custom in the year since her mother's death, Yoshiko gives herself over to daydreaming and is startled when the partition near her father slides open, revealing a small, slim, elderly woman seated only a few feet from him. The *yarite* introduces herself as Takao, bowing ostentatiously at Yoshiko's father while keeping the little girl in her gaze.

Yoshiko can only overhear snatches of the ensuing conversation. After inquiring about the trip from Chiba, Takao observes that the *ageya* she manages is a first-class house, completely worthy of the daughter of a samurai. Her father nods assent eagerly. Lowering her voice, Takao assures him that Yoshiko is even more beautiful than she had been led to believe. Such smooth skin, such a radiant complexion, such gorgeous eyes. Since she does not look like a woman easily pleased, Yoshiko's father blushes agreement. "You will be leaving her with me?" Takao asks and, again, Yoshiko's father bows in consent.

Discreetly and quickly, so the watchful little girl cannot see, the woman removes a small pouch hidden in her kimono and pushes it in the direction of her guest. He thanks her, bows, rises to his feet and is about to leave the room when he notices Yoshiko watching him from her place in the corner. He walks over to her, tells her to rise, and places his hands on her shoulders. Without saying a word, he is gone. Yoshiko is relieved that she will never see him again.

Hiroshi the boy, hearing this story, considers his grandfather a heartless cad.

CHAPTER THREE

———

AS IF HE had been in the room that very day, Hiroshi can see his grandfather leaving it. He imagines Takao walking over to the little girl; she bends down slowly and then kneels to inspect the child's face for tears but finds none. Hiroshi knows he could never have been as stoic as his mother.

Takao's face is criss-crossed with worry lines. Her skin retains a rosy hue not enhanced by the use of any paint, and her lips are chapped and rough-looking. Her eyes, almost black, are insistent, as if she is attempting to penetrate the essence of the child.

She looks down at Yoshiko's lap. "Do you have your *hina* concealed there?" she inquires kindly. The girl tells her she does and slowly presents the costumed doll for inspection. Takao eyes "Yamatoya" for some time and then takes her in her hands for a closer look. She tells Yoshiko that the doll's eyes are beautiful, her kimono exquisite. Bursting into tears, Yoshiko reveals that her mother, during the last week of her final illness, had made the doll's kimono as a keepsake. Takao observes that the fabric has stood up well and the ivory of the face is in perfect condition, but the doll's straw body is on the verge of coming apart. She resolves to repair the doll when the child is asleep.

"You must always treasure Yamatoya," Takao commands. Then she asks what pastimes Yoshiko knows. When the little girl admits to liking the board game *go*, the woman leaves for a few minutes and returns with the board and its wooden pieces. "We shall soon discover how clever you are," she challenges. The child rightly suspects that her new friend is allowing her to win an inordinately high number of games, but she soon forgets her troubles and exclaims with glee and exasperation during the next two hours.

In between matches, Takao tells Yoshiko she will have two responsibilities in her new home. Most days, she will look after the children of the other women who live in the *ageya*. She will also assist the *oiran*, Harushiba, whom Takao calls the soul of the house. "In her all our hopes reside." She pauses: "Ours is a very small establishment, one catering to refined gentlemen. We are all happy here and you will be happy also." Yoshiko wonders if that is a command but when she looks into Takao's eyes all she can glean is tenderness.

Although she slept well, Yoshiko tires easily the following morning when she has three six-year-old boys to look after. The trio, two of whom are taller than she, get along famously for about twenty minutes, quarrel bitterly, make up, and then begin the entire process over again. Yoshiko has to do her best to keep the boys quiet because their mothers, who work late into the night — sometimes until daybreak — are asleep. Since the *ageya* owns only two hobby horses, one of the little boys is always left out. To distract the excluded youngster, Yoshiko suggests a game of blind man's bluff but this invariably leads to tears when the blindfolded child misses his footing and falls to the ground.

In the afternoon, in the absence of Harushiba who is away on a visit to her mother, Takao teaches Yoshiko the essentials of flower arrangement. In *ikebana*, she informs the girl, the flowers have to be placed so that the front view is best; the other angles may suffer. The flowers are always placed to afford the customer the pleasing angle.

The hands of the girl deftly arrange a pink chrysanthemum bud, bamboo and piece of pine. Takao is amazed at how quickly her pupil, after the rudiments are explained to her, shows such remarkable proficiency in this difficult art. The girl seems to have an instinctive understanding of *shoka*, of how the three elements of the design must contrast and harmonize.

As a samurai's daughter, Yoshiko understands the tea ceremony almost instinctively. She knows how to pick up and grip a tea bowl properly, drink in small sips, inhale deeply, and make audible sounds of pleasure. The child is also accustomed to the bitter taste of *matcha*, the ground green tea that children usually loathed.

Hiroshi, boy and man, detests the smell and taste of *matcha*. He would have spat the stuff on the ground if he had been forced to taste the noxious potion.

That long-ago afternoon, Takao is relieved to have found such an apt pupil. Harushiba can be kindly, but she has never suffered a fool gladly.

CHAPTER FOUR

———

WHEN IT TRANSPIRES that Harushiba's mother is dying and that the *oiran* will be away longer than expected, Takao decides to prepare Yoshiko for the tasks that would ordinarily have been left to the most senior courtesan.

The girl has been with her for five days when Takao takes her to see Harushiba's *zashiki* and the adjoining smaller *tsugi-no-ma*. The tatami mats on both floors are fairly new and of the highest quality. So are the calligraphy specimens on the walls, the Kutani porcelain, the clothes horse, the ancient Chinese set of drawers, the cushions and the tea utensils. Yoshiko ignores these. Her attention is first drawn to the musical instruments strewn on the floor, the *koto*, *gekkin*, and *samisen*, but her eyes linger on the novels, magazines, playbills and other reading material scattered everywhere.

"Do you play the *samisen*?" Takao asks.

The little girl shakes her head No. As if to make up for this deficiency, she assures Takao that she is a very good reader. The woman nods with pleasure. This young lady will be a good companion for our beloved Harushiba, she assures herself.

That afternoon she calls the child's attention to the *tsumi-yagu*: the three futons, the quilt, and the mosquito net. The gold thread on the coverlet is inscribed with the *mon*, the emblem of the gentleman who had presented Harushiba with the bedding; her name is also inscribed there.

Eventually Yoshiko, Takao tells the girl, will look after Harushiba's room to ensure that it is always clean and presentable. That is one of a *kamuro*'s chief responsibilities. The other is to attend to her mistress's hair. She will have to follow Harushiba's instructions carefully as to where the large tortoiseshell combs, especially the *kanzashi*, should be placed; to be diligent in making sure her mistress's hair is kept clean; to attend to the various hairpieces that are sometimes inserted; and to apply just the right amount of pomade. There are other tasks. If even the slightest tear or fraying becomes visible in the bedding or on a kimono, it is her duty to mend it — or to send it away for repair. A wad of fresh tissues always has to be present beside the bedding.

A good *kamuro* is diligent, always anticipating that something can go wrong and making sure that it does not. "You will not find your work difficult as long as you are attentive and alert," Takao assures her.

Sometimes, before drifting off, six-year-old Hiroshi imagines himself sleeping, like his mother, in the tiny chamber behind Takao's bedroom. He knows he could have never have been as dutiful as his young mother.

Secreted away, Yoshiko rests soundly, although at first she is awoken by the sounds of drunken revellers in her *ageya* or passersby in the street. But she quickly becomes accustomed to these noises and sleeps through the night.

When she minds the children, Yoshiko frequently takes them with her around the Yoshiwara, which, she discovers, is a very small village of only eight blocks with four main streets. The rows of red lanterns are everywhere. The largest buildings, very European in style with pillared verandas and lofty vaulted entrances, are the proud-looking homes of the Yoshiwara's most prosperous establishments.

She becomes used to the gazing-back willow tree near the entrance (so called because the men leaving the compound of a morning look back at the Yoshiwara with regret that they are leaving paradise), to the guardian shrine, to the white fox stone from which the sculpture of the presiding deity has been carved, to the tea houses, to the various brothels (first, second and third-class), and to the cookhouses from where food is ordered in.

At first, she is nauseated by the smells of burdock root fried in *goma* oil, arame seaweed, fish seasoned with sake, conch stew, and dried bonito.

With the three boys, she wanders down to the low bog, grown over with reeds and rushes, to search for insects and frogs. On such occasions, she becomes very much aware that she is confined by the water, nine feet deep, that surrounds the Yoshiwara.

There are many other objects of interest, such as the eagle constructed of bamboo sitting upon a tree stump near the entranceway, and the nearby half-dozen wax figurines of men and women plucking flowers and strolling by the fountains. One man, having stepped upon a toad, springs back in disgust. A lady stops before a little brook and stands with her kimono gathered up, hesitating to cross, when a coolie runs up and spreads his coat before her.

Yoshiko nods greetings to the other *kamuro* who are also looking after children. Since the boys she is minding are streetwise, she quickly learns the identities of the various peddlers, beggars, hawkers and the *wakai-mono*. She follows the boys' lead, without knowing why she is doing so, in avoiding eye contact with waitresses and other common sorts of women. In fact, she acts as if they do not exist. The boys tell her to show respect to those associated with the first-class houses, especially as theirs was of the second-class. Although Takao never instructed her to do so, she behaves scornfully, as do the boys, towards all those from third-class houses. She is always pleasant to the servants, especially the maids who do most of the drudge work in the Yoshiwara.

Takao never allows Yoshiko out in the evening, but one night she asks her to carry a note to a cookhouse. "Come back immediately you deliver it," she tells her. When Yoshiko leaves the *ageya*, there is a full, resplendent moon, which assists her in getting her bearings. As she heads for her destination, she notices that the cage-like buildings are now filled with bright lanterns and crowded to bursting with women from the third-class houses.

The streets are filled, something which never happens in daylight. She has to edge herself in and out of crowds of men. The omnipresent smell of sake recalls unpleasant memories of her father. The numerous and immense coloured oil lamps shed a softening glow over everything. A few men reach out to catch or fondle her, but she evades them. Anticipating their moves, she dexterously reaches the cookhouse, hands the note over and begins her return trip.

When Hiroshi the boy imagines his child-mother on this errand, he shudders. He could not have been as brave.

The girl avoids ensnarement, takes her time returning, and notices the women in the cages playing cards, smoking pipes, laughing, and joking. Some of them move very close to the edge of their enclosures so that a would-be customer might be tantalized and attempt to grab them. After foiling such men, the tormentors suggest they hire them for an evening.

By the light of the moon, Yoshiko can see the paste-like white substance that covers the faces of these women who are dressed in the gaudiest shades of red and gold and she catches a glimpse of the greasy pink-camellia oil base underneath it, the thickly applied rouges, the blackened teeth, the eyes rimmed in red and soot black, and the thick vermillion lip-paints. The necks and throats of all the women are covered with white powder, calling attention to this part of their bodies. Yoshiko thinks the necks look as if they could be easily twisted off and then broken; it seems the merest pressure on them would make them bleed. For the first time in two weeks, Yoshiko is frightened. When she reaches the *ageya*, she stops, recovers her composure, enters the house and tells Takao the message has been delivered.

That night Yoshiko cries herself silently to sleep. She knows that she has entered a very rarefied world filled with all kinds of class distinctions, but she has no real idea of why her new home was largely a city of women whom men visited in the night. Despite the apparent merriment, the women had looked like caged birds.

Hiroshi the boy is befuddled when he hears this portion of the story. Not yet aware of the secret of the cages, he spends a sleepless night pondering their significance.

CHAPTER FIVE

WHEN HARUSHIBA FINALLY returned to the *ageya*, she remained, to Takao's considerable distress, incommunicado. Her grief at her mother's passing was so great that she needed complete solitariness to begin the process of recovery. An entire week goes by without the door to her *zashiki* sliding open. Yoshiko passes by that entrance several times a day and every time a different image of the beauty behind the door presents itself to her imagination. Would she be remote and austere? Was there the possibility she might treat Yoshiko as a long-lost sister? Would she see her merely as a servant to fetch and carry things? Or would she be cruel, perhaps even torment her? Yoshiko considered all these possibilities without coming to any conclusions. Meanwhile, she plays many rounds of *go* with Takao and looks after her three charges. Hiroshi the child realizes that he is like those boys — bold, inquisitive and demanding. What a dreadful handful those three young ruffians would have been!

Ever the vigilant observer, Yoshiko notices one morning that the straw body of Yamatoya seems miraculously to have replenished itself. She does not even consider the possibility that there has been human intervention. She is certain, both she and her companion are coping well in their new home. At this point in her narrative, a smiling Yoshiko winks knowingly at her son. But he has no interest in the doll. His attention is riveted on Harushiba. What kind of person will she turn out to be?

The head looking down on her is inquisitive. The woman's hair, which flows down her back, is a bit scruffy and oily. From what she can see in her recumbent position, Yoshiko knows that the woman's neck is as graceful as a swan's and that the mouth and the chin are firm and delicate. The nose is pointed. Her deep-set, tiny eyes are all-consuming, as if to feast upon what they behold.

"I am Harushiba," the woman announces, as if her name revealed everything there was to know about her. "And you are Yoshiko," Harushiba adds, in case the child might not be aware of her own name.

Having concluded the opening formalities, Harushiba welcomes Yoshiko as her *kamuro.* "You will find me an exceedingly easy person to deal with," she claims. Next she quizzes Yoshiko about her background. In an attempt to give precise and full answers, the girl occasionally stumbles over her words. Harushiba responds to her assistant's attack of nerves by teasing her mercilessly. "You have never been within the confines of Edo itself. You're nothing more than a country bumpkin!" She manages a sardonic smile or two when Yoshiko confesses her confusion as to why the Yoshiwara exists in the strange state it does. "You will learn more than you wish very soon," Harushiba assures the child.

During the interrogation, the young woman constantly uses sarcasm as a weapon. Realizing she is not the butt of the remarks and, therefore, not the enemy, Yoshiko decides that she quite likes Harushiba, who has the virtue of speaking her mind. That is a quality of mind to which Yoshiko is not accustomed.

As if reading Yoshiko's mind, Harushiba announces: "The truth is a dull commodity." Looking her *kamuro* directly in the eye, she continues: "Especially in comparison to what the imagination can invent." Mockingly, she adds: "That is the only lesson I can ever hope to teach you."

The courtesan then proceeds to relate the history of their house, the Tamaya, one of the oldest in the Yoshiwara. After listing the great courtesans who had been privileged to work there, Harushiba tells Yoshiko that the glory days of the Yoshiwara and the Tamaya have long disappeared. "Once upon a time, being a *tayu* or an *oiran* of the Tamaya placed a woman at the very centre of both power and prestige. The clients were samurai of the highest class or merchants of great wealth. All has changed. Our house is now so small and insignificant that I am not even allowed to call myself a *tayu*."

The last comment is meant to evoke pity from Yoshiko, but the little girl does not really understand the loss of face implied. Suddenly, Harushiba calls a halt to their conversation. "This evening we shall make a procession to a tea house. We shall begin our preparations in the early afternoon." With a flourish of her hand, she takes her leave.

I would have never tolerated such high-handedness, Hiroshi tells himself.

Dressing for a procession is much more arduous than Yoshiko had dared imagine. Hiroshi the youngster is bored to tears by the loving attention his mother bestows to what he considers mere trivialities.

A white cotton undershirt and a white silk underskirt are put on; then white socks; next the robe is slipped on, putting the right side under the left arm and closing it tightly with a waist-tie just below the waist. The robe has to cover the heels. Another tie is made above the waist and an under-sash placed around the waist. The obi is wound about the waist twice. The ends of the obi are tied in the back, making sure the longer end is above the knot. The long end is folded over the obi-bustle and wrapped in a bustle sash. The tie-ends are tucked above the obi. The long end of the obi is folded under into a tube, where the short end is inserted. Finally, once everything has been fastened tight, the obi-tie is placed in the front.

Shortly after lunch, Takao begins assisting Harushiba and Yoshiko. One of her responsibilities as *yarite* is to arrange for the purchase of the expensive fabrics for the kimono, which she insists on calling by the more proper name of *kosode*. Since the *kamuro*'s costumes have to match or closely approximate her *oiran*'s, she has cut tiny samples of leftover material from three of Harushiba's outfits and given them to Koisan, the best tailor in Edo. So that afternoon Yoshiko is given three magnificent outfits: the first, against a background of brownish orange, displayed a lively assortment of leaves, fans and plants; the second, on pale blue-and-gray ground, showed plum trees and architectural fragments; the third, the grandest of all, flaunted a design of geometrically shaped plank bridges, irises and butterflies against deep purple.

Harushiba summarily informs Takao that she will wear her orange kimono; the *oiran* will use four — rather than the customary six — large combs in her hair that evening but will not require a hairpiece; she will paint her lips but will not use any other makeup. Takao nods assent, but Yoshiko can tell she is displeased that so little face paint is being employed. Then, Harushiba dismisses the *yarite*: "From now on, I shall teach Yoshiko everything she needs to know." Yoshiko can see Takao biting her lip as she makes her exit.

As soon as the older woman has left, Harushiba sings her praises. "She may live in the past, but she does an excellent job of managing this house. She is kindness itself to those other three and their brats. She tolerates my outbursts of temper. And she has taken quite a shine to you." All of these observations are made as the courtesan begins arranging Yoshiko's hair, which, she decides, might require a small hairpiece to get it to stand up properly.

Speaking with hints of both irony and reverence in her voice, Harushiba tells her assistant that fifty years before an *oiran* of the Tamaya would have been accompanied by five *kamuro*. If upon reaching the tea house and glancing at her would-be suitor an *oiran* found him unsuitable, she would simply get up and leave. That would be the end of the matter. Even if she found her potential partner worthy, she would meet with him at least three times before allowing him to enter her *ageya*. When that occurred, there was never a promise of what Harushiba deemed the "ultimate" favour, a very strange expression whose meaning escapes Yoshiko.

Now, everything is different, Harushiba continues. Of course, she and the other women of the Tamaya never have to sit behind the slats, but their presence at the tea house is a mere formality, since anyone the owner of the tea house deems acceptable has to be deemed worthy by Takao.

The final favour could not be withheld. Otherwise, the Tamaya would cease to exist. There is enormous competition from the "gold and silver cats," "the singing nuns," "the boat tarts," and the "night hawks." The latter stroll the streets and are available for a few yen. There are, she added, the waitresses at the tea houses, all of whom she labels common as dirt. Yoshiko has no understanding of what Harushiba is talking about. Neither does Hiroshi when he first hears these strange expressions.

When all is said and done, Harushiba blames all the difficulties of courtesans like herself on the geisha, with whom the Yoshiwara is now overflowing. "They are just like us, but they refuse to admit it. They claim that they are only entertainers, experts in the arts of the tea ceremony, dance, music and conversation. In order for me to fulfil my obligations, I have to be better than them at those pursuits, and I have to debase myself. Mind you, most of the geisha debase themselves on a regular basis."

Most of what Harushiba says escapes Yoshiko's comprehension. (Many years later, Hiroshi the child also has no inkling of what the word "debase" means.) That afternoon, the *oiran* realizes this and makes no attempt to inform the girl further. Instead, she shows her some of the prints she keeps in a cedar box lined with silk. Some of them are small. "These are *chūban*; the larger ones are *ōban*." All of the pictures depict scenes derived from life in the Yoshiwara.

The *bijin* of Harunobu and Koryūsai are exceedingly wispy, insubstantial creatures whose lives seemed devoted to pastimes such as picking flowers, playing cards, and tuning their *samisen*. Utamaro's women are more real. Sometimes they even look out at the viewer with sorrowful expressions on their beautiful faces. A *bijin* by Eizan is bent over in sorrow, unable to control the tears bursting from her delicate eyes.

In what is for her patient detail, Harushiba explains to the girl that the prints usually depict only two kinds of subjects: beauties and actors. Although such prints have existed for a long time, they have become especially popular since full colour printing was invented in the 1770s. Some of the publishers in Edo have enormous shops, where wealthy customers — mainly merchants — spend hours selecting souvenirs, most of which they keep concealed from their families. These prints, which are kept in albums, are brought out for the benefit of like-minded friends. Or the "collector" can enjoy them in private moments.

"Those pictures may be beautiful, but they show a world that has not existed for a long time," Harushiba points out to her *kamuro*. The *oiran* knows this fact of life and hopes Yoshiko will learn it; on the other hand, Takao, Harushiba points out, chooses to ignore reality.

Yoshiko's eyes remain fastened to the prints, where she beholds *oiran* clad in their most beautiful kimono. Sometimes the courtesan is assisted by one or two *kamuro*. More often than not, the beautiful heads of these celebrated women occupy the entire area of the composition. These women always look away from the viewer. Yoshiko admires how each has her own thoughts, her own reflections, her own dreams from which the spectator is cut off.

Harushiba interrupts Yoshiko's reverie, telling her *kamuro* that she can look at the prints another day. The next few hours are busily spent. Yoshiko and Harushiba wash each other's hair, set it, and insert the combs. This takes a considerable amount of time, especially as Yoshiko's hair has never been subjected to elaborate control.

Harushiba dresses Yoshiko before allowing the *kamuro* in turn to dress her. During all this, Harushiba talks with considerable authority about the great *tayu* and *oiran* of the past. Fighting cockerels against dark red had been the mainstay in the kimono of the courtesan Utahime of the Matsubaya brothel; Sodenoura of the Tamaya had been reckoned a great intellectual, her poems had even been published!

When Harushiba and Yoshiko are ready, they present themselves for a brief inspection by Takao, who lavishly sings their praises, perhaps a bit excessively the child thinks. Two burly *wakai-mono*, one in front, one behind, accompany them to the Chikahan tea house. On their promenade, Harushiba looks straight ahead, her lips empty of blood. The *oiran* walks in a deliberately aggressive way, her right shoulder thrust so far forward as if to make her gait into a strut. Yoshiko demurely follows in her mistress's wake. Harushiba, taking no notice of anyone, reaches the tea house quickly in less than five minutes and instructs one of the bodyguards to fetch the proprietor.

The thin, elderly gentleman who soon attends them bows low and often to Harushiba and ignores Yoshiko until the *oiran* introduces her formally to him. When their small party crosses the threshold, Yoshiko can feel her breath leave her body. She had not expected to see a pond, shapely mulberry trees, and pine shrubbery placed in the middle of a huge indoor garden; the delicate, white-veneered bridge crossing over to a little island in the centre of the garden gives her further pause as does the cascading water and artfully placed boulders. The old man, acting as their guide, directs Harushiba's group to a small room appointed with tatami mats of the finest quality. He takes his leave with a flurry of bows to everyone in sight. Just after the party has settled themselves, with Harushiba by herself, Yoshiko five feet behind her on the right and the two *wakai-mono* against the wall, a stout young samurai enters the room.

He sits directly opposite Harushiba, studying her silently for perhaps five minutes. He then informs her that his name is Shirai and that he is from Kyoto. As she is supposed to, Harushiba politely asks about the health of various members of his family and about his comfort on the journey to the Yoshiwara. He responds perfunctorily to all her inquiries and finally informs her that he sees no reason for wasting time in ridiculous, old-fashioned preliminaries. He will be at her *ageya* within two hours and orders her to be ready for his arrival. From where she sits, Yoshiko can see the blood rising in Harushiba's face. At first, she thinks her mistress is blushing because she has been shamed, but then she realizes she is a witness to pent-up rage. For what seems a long time but is only a minute, Harushiba considers her response. Finally, she informs the young man that his wish is her command.

On their way back to the *ageya*, Harushiba remains silent. Once they are home, she dismisses Yoshiko for the evening, telling her to go to bed. The *oiran's* usually flashing bright eyes are clouded, her shoulders hunched.

This part of his mother's story worries young Hiroshi. He has no comprehension of why his mother's friend was so upset.

CHAPTER SIX

———

ON THE FOLLOWING morning, Harushiba is in a foul temper. Takao instructs Yoshiko to avoid her mistress as long as possible. "Stay away unless she summons you!" are her exact words. For the rest of the day, Yoshiko mopes. She had been alarmed by what she had witnessed the night before. On the other hand, she is fascinated by this mercurial woman.

Yoshiko has to wait two long days before Harushiba instructs one of the *wakai-mono* to fetch her. Upon entering her mistress's *zashiki* that afternoon, Yoshiko finds her, still in her nightdress, lying prone, face upwards, staring into space. When Yoshiko offers to make tea, she reluctantly agrees to drink some.

While sipping her tea, Harushiba informs her underling that the Yoshiwara is a place of unmitigated treachery, where truth is a banned substance. As evidence of this observation, she instructs Yoshiko to fetch the large album by her bed in the *tsugi-no-ma*.

When Yoshiko has done so, Harushiba turns the album pages so Yoshiko can see that it is devoted to kabuki actors. Sometimes two actors are dramatically posed together, one — an evil figure — hovering over another. In one a distraught man holds a tiny baby, whom he has obviously saved from a terrible death. Harushiba reminds her underling that there are really only two kinds of ukiyoe: portraits of *oiran* and of kabuki performers. "These are the two groups who serve the wealthy merchants who frequent this place. We are play-things for the rich. However, all levels of society crave the prints." She sniggers. "Courtesans and actors are outsiders in Japan. Yet everyone wants to own pictures of us!"

She calls Yoshiko's attention to the page where she has pasted in an *ōban* by Sharaku. Unlike the woodblocks kept in the wooden

box, the child finds nothing remotely glamorous here. Two kabuki actors, rep-resenting Umegawa and her lover Chūbei, walk entwined, each holding firm to the umbrella protecting them from snow. The male stares intently but awkwardly at his beloved, who is a man dressed up as a woman; Umegawa is lost in submissive reverie.

Yoshiko dislikes the picture because there is nothing even remotely handsome about Chūbei and the actor playing Umegawa has a heavy lantern jaw and a huge nose. Yoshiko is aware that only men act in kabuki, but she finds it sinister that Umegawa is so obviously masculine. The two lovers are about to commit *shinjū*, double suicide. Without asking the girl's opinion, Harushiba praises the artist's realism. He had the courage to depict the actors as they actually looked on stage. Such honesty, she reminds Yoshiko, is repulsive to the Yoshiwara. The rumour that Sharaku's honesty had caused him to be murdered is probably true.

According to Harushiba, the Yoshiwara is a place of intrigue and lies. Without a hint of irony in her voice this time, she rephrases her observation of a few days before, "Here in the Yoshiwara, truth is a meaningless commodity. We live in the so-called floating world, where everything is in flux. Once upon a time, the samurai held power;

then they threatened the stability of the shogunate and were made outcasts. Nowadays, rich merchants are in control of Edo and the Yoshiwara. We must sink or swim according to their dictates. The merchants wish the company of beautiful women; they enjoy looking at kabuki while they fill themselves with sake. We are the servants of these horrible men. True, the occasional aristocrat makes his way here. That is a rare occasion and a cause for celebration. Thank goodness, women of our station do not have to service artisans or the poor.

"Everyone trapped in this madhouse lies to herself. Look at Takao. She was once a *tayu* of the Sugata-Ebi-ya. Her mistake was to fall in love with a married man — a rich rice dealer — and to believe him when he told her that he would run away with her. When she learned that he had no intention of doing so, she slashed her wrists, almost killing herself. She was saved, but her reputation was in ruins. Who would want to hire a courtesan who has had the misfortune to fall in love? So at the ripe old age of twenty-eight she became a *yarite*."

She continues: "If you have your wits about you my girl, you will quickly learn to embrace falsehoods and deceit. There is no other way to survive here."

When Yoshiko retells this long-ago conversation to three-year-old Hiroshi, he is frightened and mystified. How can one live an existence based on lies? Both Yoshiko and Takao have taught him that truthfulness is the supreme virtue, the one to be cultivated above all others.

Harushiba, Yoshiko quickly learns, is easily bored. Deliberately styling herself after courtesans of a bygone age, she passes much of her time reading stories and writing poetry. "Not that I have anyone to send my love-drenched verses to," she laments.

When Yoshiko shows an inclination to share her mistress's literary interests, Harushiba rejoices, albeit a bit sarcastically: "Together we can turn the clock back a hundred years."

Yoshiko is an eager disciple, one who longs to discuss the niceties of the revenge drama *Chūshingura* or the writings of Lady Meiji whenever a chance presents itself. Harushiba does not relate stories to Yoshiko, although she is sometimes willing to talk about what they read. Unlike Takao, Harushiba never takes anything at face value. All the stories she reads mean something else — they are never about what they claim to be.

Appearances are always deceiving the *oiran* constantly reminds her *kamuro*. If she does not learn that lesson — however painful it might be — she will suffer the consequences. Removing her woodblocks of *bijin-ga* from their wooden container, Harushiba asks the girl to inspect them again. As Yoshiko looks at image after image, she finds all the women beautiful, one more stunning than the other.

In a woodblock by Eizan, a fashionably dressed townswoman occupies the picture's foreground, a boy and a man fish in the background. The picture is said to be an illustration of Act 2 of the *Chūshingura*. "The picture has little to do with the activities in the *Chūshingura* and a lot to do with the wily woman. Eizan was having a bit of fun. The woman is a fisher of men just as the boy and the man are fishermen."

Pausing for Yoshiko to look at the print and understand the connection to which she is drawing attention, Harushiba continues: "No matter what, you must always look for secret meanings. Don't take anything on trust." In case the girl fails to get the import of what she is saying, she adds: "Be loyal to no one but yourself."

Takao has recently told Yoshiko that members of the samurai class were celebrated for their devotions to others. She had told her that she must be true to her house and her *oiran*. Now, Yoshiko's *oiran* instructs her to do the opposite.

The boy Hiroshi shares his young mother's confusion. How can you be true to yourself if you betray those closest to you, to whom you owe your daily existence?

CHAPTER SEVEN

TAKAO IS A GENTLER, far less turbulent, soul than Harushiba. A motherly soul, she frequently tells the girl stories drawn from her extensive knowledge of myths and legends. Yoshiko's favorite story is one of the *Inari* — fox — legends:

A little girl, out in the woods by herself, became separated from her mother and father. She wandered high and low, frequently calling out to them but to no avail. When darkness descended, she had no idea where she was. Just ahead of her she saw a light. Hoping that it might have been lit by her parents, she marched in that direction.

As it turned out, the fire was in the middle of a glade with no one around. Although she had no idea who or what had started it, she decided to settle there for the night. Her sleep was broken by bad dreams, but she awoke refreshed in the morning and resumed her quest to find her mother and father.

She had been walking in the woods for about five minutes when she came across a tiny male fox cub at the bottom of a huge elm. The little creature's eyes were filled with terror. He could not run away from her because he had been wounded in one of his paws. He was obviously apprehensive she would attack and, perhaps, kill him. The girl decided to ignore the animal and continue on her way. She had gone for a minute or two when her conscience pricked her. The animal would die if she did not assist him. She was torn. If she went back, she might lose valuable time. Besides, the animal might bite her even though she tried to help him.

Remembering that all animals are part of existence and deserve veneration, she retraced her footsteps until she came upon the fox. When she knelt beside him, she could hear him growl in warning. He was so frightened that he could not conceive of her assisting him. Throwing caution to the winds, the girl grasped the animal's damaged paw and seeing that it had been penetrated by the end of a knife blade that remained stuck there, she quickly withdrew the blade. The animal gasped in pain. Blood spurted from the wound, which the girl staunched with a bandage she made by ripping away part of her kimono. Quite soon, the animal became less tense, and he now simply stared, without any emotion, directly into her eyes.

Her work done, the girl continued on her way. For what seemed like ages, she wandered to no purpose. Thirsty and hungry, she was on the edge of despair. Her heart pounded loudly, but she did not think she could walk any further. She fell to the ground in the shadow of a large tree, intending to take a short rest. Suddenly, she looked up to see a woman dressed in a splendid kimono. With a broad smile on her face, the woman spoke: the girl should sleep and, when she awoke, her parents would be with her.

Taking comfort from the kind words of the stranger, the girl fell asleep. When she wakened, she beheld her parents looking down upon her. They too had been in considerable distress and had looked high and low for her to no avail until they happened to see a tiny fox in the distance. They knew that foxes often signify good luck, so they followed him and it was he who finally brought them to their daughter.

Many people fear and loathe foxes as wily and secretive, but, like women, Takao reminds Yoshiko, they are often more in need than men of disguising their true feelings. They are also known to have a special affinity with girls and women and, when they assume mortal form, they always dress as women of fashion.

When Hiroshi hears this story for the first time, he is enchanted with the magic world of the story, of the goodness of the little girl, of how the fox repaid a kindness.

CHAPTER EIGHT

1856

YOSHIKO'S FIRST TWO years in the Yoshiwara have passed unevent-
fully, although she remains caught in an emotional tug-of-war between
Harushiba and Takao, especially when one extols the utility of self-
enhancement and the other proclaims the virtue of selflessness.
She was never certain which system of belief to embrace, but,
chameleon-like, she soon learned, whenever alone with either, to be
exactly what was required.

If Harushiba complains about the horrible breath of a customer,
Yoshiko eggs her on and the two quickly are reduced to gales of
laughter, evaluating the atrocious clothing that customer possesses.
Should Takao, speaking of the same man, remark on his great
reputation as a scholar, Yoshiko says he is particularly well-spoken
and polite. When, in her presence, Harushiba and Takao almost
come to blows after Takao accuses the *oiran* of being disrespectful of
the same man, an important client, she remains silent, allowing her
eyes to wander back and forth following the various arguments
mounted by each.

Of one thing Yoshiko is no longer innocent. She has not yet
witnessed or participated in any sexual activity, yet she is aware that

this is the commodity marketed in the Yoshiwara. And she understands she is being trained to engage in the same pursuit. The truth dawns so gradually that it never assaults her. She recognizes that, without the protection of the Tamaya, she would be a penniless waif and must contribute to its well-being. In that regard, she does not become a disciple of Harushiba.

Takao insists Yoshiko learn all the duties of a *kamuro*. The very shy girl has to learn the identity of any client who does not give his true name or refuses to give any name at all. This happens all the time. She would wait for the unidentified man on the street and, when he appeared, rush over to him, cling to him and greet him by a made-up name. Caught off guard, he would correct her. Many a client, alone for a few moments with the *kamuro*, will quiz her as to her mistress's real sentiments about him. Yoshiko is instructed to make him believe that he is the only object of Harushiba's affection.

As Yoshiko matures, Takao notices an unusual thing about her disciple's face: one eye is flat-lidded, as it should be; the other is rounder and lidded like those in prints of the red-haired barbarians. The discrepancy should have disfigured the girl, but, strangely enough, it makes her even attractive, gives the impression she is even more unusual and, perhaps, enticing. Takao realizes that the girl's eye makes her look like a person who could be easily divided against herself — or perhaps torn apart.

Harushiba's contempt for the Yoshiwara accelerates during those two years. She never has a good word for Takao, the other three courtesans of the Tamaya, their sons, and the *wakai-mono*. When Harushiba is in a bad mood, even Yoshiko avoids her.

She frequently retreats to her room and is unbearably rude to everyone in the house forced to deal with her. Wisely, Yoshiko stays out of harm's way.

Everything Hiroshi hears about Harushiba makes him hate her. He would never put up with her nonsense.

Yoshiko tells her son how she became a mischief. He claps his hands in glee and is delighted to learn that she was capable, like himself, of being a troublemaker.

Without the knowledge of either Takao or Harushiba, Yoshiko had snuck into the rooms where visiting actors recreated scenes from kabuki to the delight of the courtesans. She chattered with the other *kamuro*, becoming a great gossip in the process. She lost at cards one day and, much to Takao's chagrin, allowed the winner to paint a black moustache on her.

Harushiba becomes furious when Yoshiko buys withered flowers from an unscrupulous vendor. When she misplaces a note from a patron, Takao gives her a whack; guilt-stricken, she hands Yoshiko a cookie ten minutes later.

Yoshiko learns to lie in order to elude the scrutiny of the two women who stand guard over her. If asked to make up her mind as to which of her foster-mothers was the greater impediment to her independence, she would not have known whom she would have chosen. Deprived of a mother's love, the child clings to the only two women who have ever cared for her. Even at the age of ten, she remains impossibly naïve, taking comfort in the fantasies concocted in the fairy tales she reads by the hour.

When telling Hiroshi of her youth, Yoshiko glides over the next ten years, implying that they were troubled ones containing events best unexamined lest they, like malignant ghosts, wreak havoc.

CHAPTER NINE

1858

UNDER THE TUTELAGE of Harushiba, Yoshiko becomes an excellent actress adept at reading the moods of her clients and playing the roles their needs demand. Since she can justifiably take most of the credit for her former *kamuro*'s transformation from apprentice to professional, Harushiba, in between bouts of bad temper, is lavish with her affection. Takao is delighted that she now has two *oiran* who are in frequent demand and command high prices.

The *yarite*'s joy is short-lived; Harushiba's rage-filled displays become more frequent. She drinks constantly and in drunken outbursts insults clients. The other three courtesans threaten to leave for another house and two of the *wakai-mono* vanish one day, obviously in pursuit of less troublesome work in Edo.

Then Harushiba begins to disappear, sometimes for two or three days at a time. When she returns, she takes to her room for a day or so, and although she goes back to work, she is unbearably sad and tear-filled. After about a week in this state, she starts again her sarcastic portrayal of the Yoshiwara as a flea-bitten place where no self-respecting woman could endure to live. Soon there are more drinking jags consisting of outbursts and recriminations hurled at anyone unfortunate enough to cross her path. Then suddenly she vanishes.

Yoshiko cannot understand where Harushiba possibly could go. Working women are forbidden to leave the Yoshiwara, although they can sometimes obtain day passes. If a parent or close relative has died, absences of longer duration are granted.

The next time Yoshiko sees Harushiba her corpse — together with that of her lover — is on display on Nihonbashi Bridge near the Yoshiwara's entranceway. As though she and her beloved are dogs, their hands and feet are bound together and their bodies wrapped in straw matting. Three days later, Yoshiko and Takao are the only persons in attendance at Harushiba's burial.

Chōemon, a wealthy rice merchant, first visited Harushiba in 1853, the year before Yoshiko settled there. Two years earlier, he had contracted a marriage of convenience to a woman of aristocratic connections. He was twenty-one when he met Harushiba, she was twenty-three. At first, he was simply one of Harushiba's many patrons.

Uncommonly handsome, he was a brilliant businessman but a fumbling lover until his passion for Harushiba took him over. Strangely enough, the courtesan, who had known every emotion except those associated with love, reciprocated his strong feelings. For about a year, Chōemon visited Harushiba once a week. In addition to their lovemaking, they shared a passion for poetry.

When the canny Harushiba finally knew the power of love, she did not wish to be destroyed by it. At first, she suggested she and Chōemon go their separate ways; he refused.

Hers was the fatal mistake. She uttered the lie of the courtesan, "I love you," but she meant what she said. His response was the standard lie of the client, "I will marry you." He was lying.

Harushiba did not necessarily wish to marry Chōemon, but she wanted to be with him all the time. The strength of her passion disturbed him because it threatened to unhinge the comfortable foundations he had established for himself. He told her he could not divorce his wife. He refused to make arrangements to purchase Harushiba's contract from the Tamaya and set up an establishment for her in Edo.

Harushiba's absence from the Yoshiwara when Yoshiko first arrived there had been contrived by Takao, who had taken the considerable risk of telling the *shirobei* that the courtesan's mother was dying. In reality, Harushiba had taken up residence with a friend, a former courtesan, in Edo. While there she stalked both Chōemon and his wife. This adventure lasted for five days until an irate Chōemon confronted her and threatened to break all ties with her unless she left the city immediately. Reluctantly, Harushiba followed her lover's instructions.

Over the next four years, Harushiba, in short visits away from the Yoshiwara, attempted to embarrass Chōemon. She confronted his wife; she humiliated him in front of his employees by making a surprise visit to his warehouse; she even screamed invectives at him in the street. In each instance, she reluctantly agreed to return home only after her lover pleaded with her to do so and agreed to visit her within the week.

Finally, Chōemon had had his fill. He did not keep his word. Having reached the breaking point, Harushiba journeyed once again to his warehouse, where she arrived after the close of business. He let her in; they argued violently; she began to throw huge canisters of rice to the ground; he lost control and stabbed her; realizing he had shamed himself beyond repair, he slashed his wrists.

Takao understands full well from the police report that Harushiba had been murdered, but she tells all those who will listen to her, including Yoshiko, that the lovers had committed *shinjū*, this being a much more acceptable explanation as far as she is concerned than the official report published in the newspapers. The two, in great contempt for society's standards, had killed themselves.

Such an account was in accordance with the romantic days of the old Yoshiwara, when great artists such as Utamaro had done woodcut after woodcut of *shinjū* lovers. Never a person to give a sinister twist to events, Yoshiko has become increasingly cunning: taking her cue from Harushiba, she dissembles when she tells Takao that she agrees with her that the *oiran* must have killed herself.

As far as young Hiroshi is concerned, Harushiba got what she deserved. For the first time he can recall, Hiroshi is furious with his mother. How could she have kowtowed to Takao in this matter?

CHAPTER TEN

1860

THE DEATH OF Harushiba leaves Yoshiko with a black mark on her soul. Years later, her son learns of the anguish that consumed his mother.

Yoshiko's mistress had disobeyed the fundamental laws of the Yoshiwara and had paid the price. At the age of fourteen Yoshiko knows she really has no choice: she must commit herself to the life chosen for her. If she does not do so, she will be ruined. She will also disgrace poor Takao and reduce her, as well as herself, to poverty. The two of them must cling together. Takao is not as clever as I am, Yoshiko tells herself, and I must now take the upper hand.

Takao follows where Yoshiko leads. Without thinking about it, Yoshiko has imbibed the *yarite*'s veneration for the past. She does not live in the Yoshiwara of 1860 but in that of 1760. Yoshiko does not see sex as the vital ingredient in a courtesan's career: she exists in a world of poetry, music, reading and letters. She is so extraordinarily beautiful and intelligent that her unwillingness to live in the sordidness of the present makes her an increasingly sought-after *oiran*; there are many clients who remain partial to the old ways.

Yoshiko is also resourceful and shrewd. One New Year, she and Takao have no funds to invest in new clothing or bedding, staples that are supposed to be renewed annually. A rival courtesan, the formidable Kayoiji, has wealthy patrons who provide her with a crimson kimono of heavy crêpe de chine on which she and her *kamuro* have basted numerous tobacco and pipe pouches. These pouches are made of the finest and most expensive multicoloured brocades and velvets; it is Kayoiji's idea that these be detachable New Year's gifts that can be pulled off her kimono as she parades to her *ageya*.

A distraught Yoshiko has nothing new to wear in the same procession, although a patron she has not seen in some time has belatedly sent her a gift of 200 gold *ryō*. For the procession, Yoshiko decides to make do with a plain white silk kimono and a black paper outer kimono with black satin reinforcements at the arms. She hopes that the starkness of her costume will stand in mark contrast to the gaudiness of her rival's.

When she departs her *ageya*, the layers of colourful hanging pouches make Kayoiji look like a giant bird. No sooner does she set out but a crowd of maids and *wakai-mono* are awaiting her. They swarm around her, shouting "Happy New Year!" and pull off the pouches. In a matter of moments, the courtesan is wearing a denuded plain-looking kimono. Startled and dismayed, she slips her outer kimono off, discards it on the street and retreats into her house.

Yoshiko does not parade. She leaves her house quietly, wearing her paper kimono and goes to a tea house near the Great Gate, where she has invited friends and servants to join her. After providing them with sumptuous food and the finest sake, she has Takao produce her patron's gift of 200 *ryō* wrapped in a purple silk cloth. Yoshiko, who does not deign to touch the money, asks the proprietor of the tea house to distribute the money as he sees fit.

The money vanishes within two minutes. The desired impression is created: Yoshiko is hailed as the embodiment of generosity. Kayoiji is now regarded as a bit of a fool. Although she gave generously to others, she will never escape the infamy of traipsing half-naked to the door of her own house. In the Yoshiwara, Yoshiko realizes, style, not prudence, counts most.

Yoshiko becomes even more devoted to the history of the Yoshiwara and the artists who had celebrated it. She loves the elegant *bijin-ga* of Eizan, where the beauty of the women and their tender feelings about the precariousness of life can be clearly seen.

Even at her tender age, Yoshiko is harsh in evaluating any departure from protocol. In one of his most celebrated triptychs from late in the eighteenth century, *The Taikō Hideyoshi and his Five Wives on an Excursion to Rakutō*, Utamaro had defied the shogunate by depicting historical figures and, in the process, making a direct — and unflattering — comment on the government of his own time. He had been sentenced to three days in jail and fifty days in handcuffs. Although she greatly admired the artist, Yoshiko despised him for flaunting the law. She thinks that his punishment was not severe enough.

For Yoshiko, the Yoshiwara and its customs should be venerated, never broken. At the back of her mind she knows that she would find it difficult to survive if she were forced to live in the present. She is happy to be a sentimentalist enamoured of the past. As he gets older, Hiroshi comes to intensely dislike the many ways in which his mother blinds herself to reality.

CHAPTER ELEVEN

———

1872

TWELVE SHORT HAPPY years. That is how Yoshiko sees the interval
since Harushiba's death. At the age of twenty-six, Yoshiko is one of
the most celebrated courtesans of the Yoshiwara. Six years earlier the
Tamaya closed down. The other three ladies of the establishment, now
in their mid-thirties, retired and, having paid off their obligations
to the owner who lived in faraway Kyoto, moved to Tokyo with their
now teenaged sons. Having worked to support their children, they
decided they would allow their sons to do the same for them.

The absentee owner, a former *yarite* who owned a bordello in
Kyoto, informed Takao that she intended to rent the Tamaya to
the neighbouring establishment. Yoshiko had been anticipating this
news and went the following day to the Ogi-ya, the celebrated House
of the Fan. The proposal she made to the owner, who had recently
lost his top *oiran* to another house, was impossible to resist. She was
willing to become a resident of his house, together with her *yarite*
who would now serve as both her maid and *kamuro*, if he would buy
out her contract, pay her one-half of the income she generated, buy
her clothing and bedding and allow her and Takao to live rent-free.

No proprietor in the Yoshiwara can survive unless his establishment possesses the aura of refinement and sophistication that only a courtesan of the first rank bestows, but if his house's reputation as a bastion of *fūryū*, style of the first magnitude, remains intact, he can tolerate some extravagance. He reluctantly accepted Yoshiko's offer, although it would stretch his resources considerably.

Takao's responsibilities do not change markedly. She remains in charge of Yoshiko's wardrobe, accompanies her to the tea houses, cleans her room and, in general, is a devoted and hard-working factotum. In her turn, Yoshiko is a dutiful friend who venerates the woman who has taken such good care of her since she was a mere child.

Yoshiko and Takao take great pleasure from the customs of their adopted home: the cherry-blossom festival on Nakanochō Boulevard in the third month, the lantern festival in the seventh, and the *niwaka* burlesque in the eighth. The beautiful, delicate scent of the cherry blossoms, when the air was heavy with perfume, thrills them both.

They are deeply touched by the lantern festival which is a memorial to Tamagiku of the Naka-Manjiya, a *tayu* who died at the age of twenty-five in 1726 from an overindulgence in sake. During those often raucous celebrations, they offer up special prayers for the soul of Harushiba, another courtesan with a fatal flaw.

If anyone had ever been presumptuous to ask Yoshiko if she was happy, she would not have known what to answer. All her physical needs are met; she only has to make herself available to generous, well-behaved clients — she is famed for often rejecting but never once offending; she has a remarkable assemblage of fine bedding and kimono; she has developed a passionate interest in the history of her adopted home. In particular, she knows the life histories of all the great *tayu* and *oiran* and the great images of them created by the likes of Haronobu, Koryūsai, Utamaro and Eizan. Of their tragedies in love she does not wish to know anything, so deeply upset does she remain about Harushiba's awful demise.

For Yoshiko, the end of the shogunate in 1868, the restoration of power to the Emperor, and the renaming of Edo as Tokyo are threatening simply because the old order has been toppled. She wants life in the Yoshiwara to continue at the same leisurely pace she has always known. Even at the age of seven, Hiroshi finds the Yoshiwara a place of complete boredom — a prison without bars.

Yoshiko has reasons to be unsettled. Like many denizens of the Yoshiwara, she notices with disdain the increasing number of pale faces that appear there. At first, the strangers are Dutch, whom she and her compatriots label red-haired monsters.

After the clumsily and cheaply built brothels in Yokohama's Gankirō district burn to the ground in 1866, Americans begin to make the long journey to Tokyo's northernmost section. They are easy to spot in their beards, long waistcoats with epaulettes, stovepipe hats and white trousers. Occasionally, they are clean-shaven and are garbed in dark-blue military uniforms.

Used to thinking that all Americans look like the photographs she has seen of Abraham Lincoln, Yoshiko is shocked when she hears that the Emperor Meiji often now dresses in such an outlandish way and that the Empress regularly appears at court in bonnets and crinoline hoop skirts.

Yoshiko often gives thanks that she has never had to deal with any of the barbarians. She particularly does not like the shiftless way they walk around, hands in their pockets. The breaths of the foreigners often reek of whisky rather than the sake she is now used to. All in all, she avoids them.

CHAPTER TWELVE

———

THAT OCTOBER, WHILE attending a celebration at the tea house next to the Ogi-ya, Yoshiko glimpses a barbarian from a distance. He is dressed in the American naval uniform to which she has become accustomed. His hair is a true black, unusual for an American. He is exceedingly tall, even for a foreigner, but the most striking aspects of his appearance are the porcelain whiteness of skin, the deep blue of his eyes, and the comeliness of his nose and chin. Seldom has Yoshiko been dazzled by a man's appearance. As she is leaving the tea house, she turns around to look at him once again and blushes when she catches his eye.

The next afternoon she receives a summons from the proprietor of a tea house to appear that evening so that she might consider the petition of a gentleman who claims to have fallen hopelessly in love with her. Used to such protestations and invitations, she thinks little of the matter before she and Takao arrive at half-past seven that evening, a half hour fashionably late. The man awaiting her, surrounded by two of his fellow officers, is Stephen Eliot.

That evening Yoshiko notices that one of the Lieutenant's eyes is made of glass. Although the fake eye matches the real one perfectly, the opening for the missing eye is smaller than that of the other.

Rather than thinking his face disfigured by this blemish, Yoshiko thinks the imperfection makes his other features all the more splendid.

Since a translator is required to handle the exchange of pleasantries between courtesan and client, everything that is said is completely conventional. He is madly in love with her, especially now that he beholds her again. As is the custom, she accepts these compliments, fishes for some more and arranges to meet in four days at the same time and place. If at all possible, Yoshiko does not accept a client after one petition.

When she returns home, Yoshiko knows there is something about Lieutenant Eliot that she cannot fathom. She does not understand why she finds him deeply attractive; she usually does not have such feelings for clients.

Takao dislikes this Barbarian immediately. She did not appreciate the way in which Eliot and his fellow officers had whispered back and forth to each other during the encounter: she considered them rude. Yoshiko forces her friend to admit she knows nothing of foreign customs and so is an unreliable judge of what she has witnessed. Takao fears Yoshiko is about to take leave of her senses.

At the next encounter, Eliot, accompanied only by a translator, makes polite inquiries about Takao, from whom he extracts two or three smiles. At the conclusion of that meeting, the now-smitten Yoshiko invites the naval officer to call on her at the Ogi-ya two evenings hence.

After that visit, Yoshiko is in thrall to Lieutenant Eliot. She wants to be careful to disguise the depths of her feelings, but she feigns no emotions during her time with him. Eliot, who experiences feelings he never knew he was capable of, is bitten by the passion that now overwhelms him. Without a quibble, he pays the proprietor of the tea shop Yoshiko's fees, the costs of the meals they take, and the huge list of extra fees associated with seeing an *oiran*. Within two weeks, the American becomes Yoshiko's only customer.

Realizing that he is paying an exorbitant amount of money each time he sees her, Eliot asks Yoshiko to marry him. This is a solution that has often presented itself in Yokohama. Military officers regularly undergo what they consider sham-marriages to Japanese courtesans. This arrangement lasts only while the man is stationed in Japan; at the end of his stint there he would divorce his Japanese wife so that she can freely resume her chosen way of life.

Takao considers such arrangements disgraceful. The usually wily Yoshiko, well aware that her friend is speaking the truth, is torn apart. Having never experienced love before, she wants to taste it like a traveller, long stranded in a desert, craves water. When Hiroshi hears this part of his mother's life, he finally begins to understand all too well the person she has become.

CHAPTER THIRTEEN

———

TWELVE LONG DREARY years. That is how Yoshiko now sees the interval since Harushiba's death. All of a sudden, she fully and painfully experiences the emotions that had overcome the woman who had been her *oiran*.

Yoshiko is filled with regret. She has for a long time, she tells herself, lived a completely uneventful, meaningless existence. Takao's words of caution might just as well be addressed to the wind.

Even if Yoshiko had been given proof that Lieutenant Eliot was a heartless scoundrel, she would not have believed it. The sad truth is that he is everything he seems not to be. Bestowed with spectacular good looks, he has been from early youth what can only be kindly called a scapegrace. When, at the age of fourteen, he was expelled from Phillips Exeter Academy because of his bullying of other boys, his father said to his mother: "Handsome is that handsome does." Eliot's mother, who had endured many cruelties of her own at the hands of her good-looking husband, simply shrugged her shoulders in response. She had a good idea of why her son had turned out to be reprehensible.

At Harvard, Eliot was a cheat. He never attended class, hired impoverished, scholarship students to write essays on his behalf and paid the same individuals to masquerade as him in the exam halls. In Cambridge, various unflattering appellations, such as whoremonger, drunkard and thief, were truthfully applied to him. Eliot lost his eye in a fight with a gambler to whom he owed money but refused to pay.

After his son's graduation, Stephen's father advanced him a considerable sum to purchase a partnership in a firm that imported and exported lumber. Stephen found his employment boring and never showed up for work. He only became sufficiently interested in his firm when he attempted to secure money by signing liens against it. When that ruse was discovered, Stephen's father, still of the persuasion that good-looking men have the natural right to act as they choose, had this matter covered up and purchased his son a commission in the American navy.

Although Takao understands not a word of English, she correctly guesses that Stephen and his friends spoke of Yoshiko in the most vulgar possible manner on the afternoon she and Yoshiko first encountered him. Takao is sufficiently versed in the perversity of certain kinds of men to discern subsequently that Eliot has indeed become besotted with Yoshiko; in her bones she also knows he will throw his new wife over whenever it suits him. The missing eye shows her the sinister aspect to Eliot's otherwise handsome face.

CHAPTER FOURTEEN

1873

TAKAO SHUDDERS WHEN she thinks of Yoshiko's wedding. She thought she had known every kind of unhappiness under the sun but nothing had prepared her for the assault the small wedding party had suffered at the hands of the bonze, Yoshiko's uncle. He had burst into the Christian chapel where the ceremony was taking place and denounced his niece as a disgrace to her people. He also called her a whore, a strange word since it was his brother who had sold his only child to Takao eighteen years before.

Yoshiko had been startled by her uncle's outrageous denunciation, but Takao and Lieutenant Eliot convinced her that he was simply a crank. Not since Yoshiko was a small child had Takao seen tears drop from her eyes. Even worse for Takao was her conversation with the American consul, who spoke passable Japanese. He translated the wedding toast by one of the Lieutenant's fellow officers, wherein he had, after saluting "America Forever," looked forward to the time when Eliot would partake in a real wedding to a white woman back in God's country.

Since the wedding five months ago, Takao has been living with the couple in a boarding house in the port city of Yokohama, near

Tokyo. She does not like to go outside, so different is this place from anything she is used to. Westerners are everywhere in this section of the city. Their houses and shops are filled with glass windows into which one is invited to vulgarly stare. Most of the pale faces have strange-looking *kume*, dogs which accompany them everywhere. And the rooms. That is the worst thing of all. The chambers of the foreigners are filled to bursting with large pieces of furniture on which they sit. The Japanese are content with hand-held mirrors but these invaders have mirrors as large as a person.

Now, things have gone from bad to worse. Ever since her failed suicide attempt so many years before, Takao does not believe in love. She does think that a semblance of decency is possible in affairs of the heart, but the recent behaviour of Lieutenant Eliot has disabused her of that notion. When out shopping, she has seen Yoshiko's husband following common women, waitresses and other such trash, that prey upon males in the streets. The Lieutenant is constantly drunk. Takao suspects that his money had been dissipated by gambling. The other day he borrowed money from her to pay the rent for the three small rooms he, Yoshiko and she share.

Years before Takao had pretended to Yoshiko — and anyone else who would listen — that Harushiba had committed suicide. That was a terrible mistake. She has helped educate Yoshiko in the subtle art of blinding oneself to reality. Although she has eyes in her head, Takao now laments, Yoshiko does not see what is before her. No man has ever been idealized quite as much as this American ignoramus! Hiroshi's blood boils when Takao tells him of these events. His father was obviously a consummate villain, his mother a willing victim.

To Takao's amazement, the Barbarian's behaviour changes overnight. Even Takao can see the Lieutenant is being excessively charming and courteous, just as he was when he courted Yoshiko. The bride thinks her groom has returned to his former ways, not that she has ever really noticed his departure from them.

The announcement does not surprise Takao. The Lieutenant will be returning to America within the week. Yoshiko is distraught. Her husband assures her he will return within a year. He is a man who takes his marriage vow of a thousand years seriously; he is not the kind of man, like some of his fellow countrymen, who dissolve their marriages when it suits them.

Yoshiko and Takao decide to return to the Yoshiwara, where Yoshiko will become a *yarite* and in that way support herself and her friend. Hiroshi is born at the House of the Chōjiya at the end of the year.

PART TWO

THE SWINDLER

CHAPTER FIFTEEN

1875

ALTHOUGH SHE WOULD never voice the thought, Yoshiko considers Hiroshi overly demanding of her time. He is a handsome, charming rascal brimming with mischievous ideas. Almost two-years-old, he is also precocious. He already speaks extremely well. Takao has begun to teach him to read. He asks countless questions and never seems satisfied with the answers provided. Of one thing Yoshiko is certain: her son must be treated as all male children. He is to have his own way, even if what he desires may interfere with what she and Takao consider best. Takao warns Yoshiko on countless occasions that this is no way to bring up a child: like everyone else, he should have rules, and he should be punished if he breaks them.

His arrival was not an easy one. For many hours, he refused to journey down the birth canal, despite the pleas of the midwife. In despair, she told Takao that a surgeon would have to cut him out. As if he heard and understood this threat, the baby immediately co-operated and was born twenty minutes later. Takao had never seen a Japanese baby of such prodigious size: he weighed almost ten pounds. He was lobster-red in colour and screamed mightily. I hope he does not intend to take after his awful father, Takao had reflected.

The boy has absolutely no difficulty in understanding what is asked of him. Compliance is where things take an unfortunate turn. Sometimes, he looks his mother directly in the eye and does the opposite of what she has requested. Yoshiko benignly throws her hands up in the air: what can one do when confronted with such a magnificent display of force? Takao, not Yoshiko, is the one who witnesses Hiroshi's face turn scarlet when he hurls himself to the floor in a temper tantrum after she denies a request he imperiously makes of her. He is often affectionate with his mother and Takao. Yet the child is a disappointment to Yoshiko.

Hiroshi is not like Lieutenant Eliot in appearance. Not a whit. His eyes, nose and mouth are his mother's. His mixed ancestry can be gleaned only by the colour of his skin, which is a creamy white. The cheeks of Japanese children do not blush as violently red as his do. Hiroshi is also extremely tall for a Japanese boy of two; he is more the size of a four-year-old. Since the boy does not resemble his father, he is not a keepsake of Lieutenant Eliot, from whom Yoshiko has not heard since he left Japan.

To Takao, Yoshiko is adamant that her husband will return any day now. It will be the most wonderful surprise. But before falling asleep at night, Yoshiko is overwhelmed by a sense of despair. She wants to believe that her beloved will return but, with every passing day, she thinks that this will never happen. If she were to admit this even to Takao, that would bring bad luck, ensuring a tragic outcome. Deliberately, Yoshiko blinds herself to reality and looks disdainfully at her foxy side, which she once cultivated.

So Yoshiko suffers in silence. Thank goodness, she guiltily reflects, Takao minds Hiroshi so well. The house that Yoshiko manages is a large one with twenty-seven courtesans. Her teeth fashionably blackened, her eyebrows shaved, and her hair arranged in a *marumage*, Yoshiko looks the role of proprietress to perfection. Unlike her previous residence, the Chōjiya has a cage on the first floor.

Some of the women are easy to deal with; others are troublemakers, who complain about everything: the food they are given, the bed-rooms they are assigned, the ungrateful clients, and the poor wages. If a woman is sick, Yoshiko must nurse her back to health. She must make certain that all the new health regulations — such as monthly checkups for venereal disease — are enforced. The maids need constant supervision in order to keep the premises clean and to attend the children when their courtesan-mothers are working.

Then there are the clients, many of whom are rowdy and noisy. Some, having used the services of a woman, refuse to pay up. With these men, Yoshiko must take a no-nonsense attitude and threaten them with beatings by the two heavily built *wakai-mono* hired for such occasions. The owner, who lives in Yokohama, is anxious that Yoshiko maximize his profits while minimizing all costs in running the establishment. And worst of all are the officials whose outstretched hands are rapacious in their demands for bribes. The Meiji regime has not been a kind one for the Yoshiwara: there are now all kinds of hidden costs in running a house.

The other *yarite* in the Yoshiwara are businesswomen, pure and simple. They admire Yoshiko's beauty, many of them having known her in her salad days as an *oiran*. She seems watchful enough in running her house, but she still speaks in the plaintive sing-song voice of the old days. She insists her girls wear their hair in ways that are now completely out of fashion. Yoshiko has even encouraged some of her ladies to write verse. The Chōjiya, clearly out of step with all the other establishments, remains popular with customers with a fondness for the past.

Until his fifth year, Hiroshi listened with rapt attention to his mother's stories about her early years. In those days he idealized her and did not mind that she spent so little time with him. Now he has lost interest in hearing the accounts he once found so fascinating. Nowadays they spend an hour or so together every week looking at the woodcuts. Yoshiko is delighted to educate the eye of her son in the subtle use of colours and on the fineness of line achieved only by the best carvers.

Hurt by her son's increasing independence, especially his indifference to her stories about her early life, Yoshiko is delighted that Takao is so attentive to his every need. In any event, Yoshiko has less and less time for Hiroshi.

Unflagging in her devotion to Yoshiko, the former *yarite* tries to blind herself to the fact that her former pupil is not a dutiful mother. How can she be? she asks herself. Yoshiko must manage for the three of us. Then her eyes fill with tears as she remembers the motherless little girl she encountered many years before.

Despite her fears, Takao soon grows to love the headstrong little boy, although his mother has spoiled him by never saying no to him. His propensity to disobey was well-developed and his stubborn streak did not endear him. But he also knew how to charm himself out of any predicament. When Takao chided him, he often gave her huge, wide-toothed smiles that caressed her heart. How could such a beautiful child do any wrong?

The boy was deeply intelligent and listened attentively when she told him stories. He especially liked the one about the wild child and his mother.

Once upon a time, a noble lady by the name of Yamauba fell in love with Sakata Kurando, a samurai who was a member of the Emperor's body-guard. A noble warrior and a loyal retainer, he was equally renowned for his gentleness. Another palace guard, jealous of the affection the Emperor bestowed on Kurando, accused him of removing a piece of netsuke from the Imperial bedchamber. This cunning person had removed this object himself and secreted it in the chamber in which Kurando slept. When his supposed knavery was discovered, the distraught Emperor refused to even look at Kurando ever again.

Disgraced, and without informing Yamauba, Kurando abandoned Kyoto and supported himself on the Tokaido highway by becoming a wandering tobacco merchant. The faithful Yamauba, not believing a word said against her beloved, set off in pursuit of him. She disguised herself as a maid who had been separated from her mistress, and with considerable hardship she pursued her lover for over six months before they happened to encounter each other at the same station. Kurando was delighted to see his lover, but he was a broken man, someone who could not be repaired even by love. Within two weeks of their encounter, he fled the place where he and Yamauba were staying. Distraught, she set off to find him again, only to encounter his corpse hanging from a tree.

Yamauba considered doing away with herself but she was pregnant and did not feel she could take her infant's life. She buried Kurando and set off for the Ashigara Mountain, where eight months later she gave birth to an enormous baby boy she called Kintarō. In their mountain retreat, mother and son lived by eating whatever berries and roots they could find. They were befriended by the animals with whom they lived.

From birth, Kintarō was an unusual looking child. He was not only large but was also extremely muscular and very strong. The most

unusual things about him were his colour, which was a bright crimson red, and his unusually thick flesh. Yamauba was not distressed by this since she was certain the gods had marked him as a special human creature who could live comfortably with the bears, deer, monkeys and rabbits that were their neighbours. She was not at all surprised when he spoke the languages of these creatures even before he learned to talk with her.

At one year of age, Yamauba gave Kintarō his father's axe, with which he felled trees. He was an ardent wrestler, finer than any sumo of the present day. He challenged bears to matches and easily defeated them. He captured giant carp, fought with boars and shook the wicked demons — the tengu — out of the trees and used them as kites. On one expedition he and his animal companions came upon a broad riverbank impossible to cross. The boy placed his huge arms around an enormous tree, wrenched it free from the earth, and threw it across the water, forming a bridge that allowed them to pass easily.

Despite her heartbreaking sorrow at the loss of Kurando, Yamauba was rewarded with the great closeness that developed between herself and her son, taking consolation in the warm embraces and kisses he passionately bestowed upon her. Enveloped in their love, they spent many happy years together.

The ending to the story of Kintarō mystifies Hiroshi since he now spent hardly any time at all with Yoshiko. On the other hand, he has become deeply fond of Aunt Takao, who gave him his favourite toy, a doll of Kintarō wearing a lacquered court-cap symbolizing his aristocratic birth.

From the time he is tiny, Hiroshi conceives himself as a hero, someone who can fly, leap mountains, and tame wild animals. At the age of seven, Hiroshi becomes fascinated with the identity of his father, the Kurando of Takao's story. When the boy asks his aunt about this, she brushes his question aside. But Yoshiko welcomes such inquiries.

He no longer wishes to hear about her early life, so she regales him with stories — carefully crafted fictions — about his father. His questions pour out. From her, the boy learns that Lieutenant Eliot lives far away beyond the sea in a strange place called America; in that place he is of the warrior class, a real samurai; he is a man who always overcomes any obstacle thrown in his path. Very soon, he will return to Japan, where he will sweep Yoshiko and Hiroshi into his strong arms and take them with him back to America.

That faraway country obsesses the child's imagination. His waking and sleeping hours become dominated by the fantasy of a frontier land peopled with wild animals and even wilder Indians. Like his father, Hiroshi will subjugate the wilderness, tame it and become its master.

The child prepares himself for his escape to the New World by becoming as much like his father as he can. In the process, he becomes bossy and stubborn. He is extraordinarily popular, however, because he can tell the most amazing stories, which he then inveigles the other children to enact. In the games, Hiroshi is always the hero. As far as he is concerned, since the games are his invention, he is deserving of the star roles.

CHAPTER SIXTEEN

———

1879

SOME DAYS EVEN the patient Takao finds Hiroshi a handful. It is still possible to entertain him with stories, but, in his sixth year, he pleads with her to tell him stories filled with brutality and violence. No others will do. The only tale in her repertoire that he now tolerates is the one about the subsequent adventures of Kintarō.

When he became an adult, Kintarō took leave of his mother, changed his name to Kintoki, and was soon one of the shogun's most trusted warriors. After outlaws dressed as goblins swept through Edo night after night causing wide-scale destruction, Kintoki volunteered to deal with the matter.

One evening, he disguised himself as a priest and entered the wilderness near the fortress where the outlaws lived. A god, disguised as a fox, told him what he had to do to survive: he would be invited to a lavish banquet where he would be offered wine which he must under no conditions drink.

When he reached the huge and impregnable-looking fortress, Kintoki was escorted by the outlaws into a splendid hall. At one end, on a low dais, sat a handsome young man who welcomed him graciously and ordered his servants to prepare a meal in his honour.

Kintoki was charmed. He had obviously made a mistake. No one so elegant and refined could have committed these crimes and although he was tempted to disobey the god's instruction, he heeded the warning. He pretended to empty his cup many times, but he allowed none of the liquid to even touch his lips. Kintoki and the young nobleman talked long into the night, much enjoying each other's company.

The night became darker. The torches were guttered. Soon after, Kintoki's host fell asleep. Curious about his gregarious and charming host but remembering that he had been forewarned, Kintoki approached him warily. Just as he reached the young patrician and was scanning his beautiful face, there was a horrendous sound. To Kintoki's amazement, the host transformed himself into a ferocious, gigantic and ugly monster. His head, now ten times its original size, was a deep magenta; enormous green blotches covered his countenance and arms; this creature looked at Kintoki with a huge, malicious grin.

Without hesitation, Kintoki attacked. Soon man and monster were locked in mortal combat. The monster would gain the advantage where-upon Kintoki would best him. The battle was long and bloody, but in the end Kintoki prevailed and slew the demon. Once he had done that, the outlaws reappeared and thanked Kintoki for saving them. They had been captured by the monster, who was named Shutendōji, and had been placed under his spell and forced to perform acts of brutality. In killing Shutendōji, Kintoki had released these vassals from servitude.

To have the cunning of a Kintoki became Hiroshi's ambition. Now the undisputed leader of the gang of boys who live in the Yoshiwara, he has become a ruthless tyrant whom no one dares to disobey. Even boys two and three years older than he bow to his authority.

In all the adventure games, Hiroshi takes the roles of Kintarō or Kintoki and, dependent on his whims, the other boys take turns being the bears and boars he subjugates. In order to keep his subjects happy, the little king is careful to circulate the highly coveted role of the giant carp that Kintoki pursues down a huge underwater chasm. In his daydreams, Hiroshi is a hero capable of subduing all

enemies by himself. His mother owns a print by Kuniyoshi in which the great archer Tametomo, his bow drawn back, stands poised at the end of a cliff. That fellow becomes the child's ideal best self. He wants to be as confident as that hero. On a daily basis, he teases Yoshiko to show him this print. Finally, she tells him he may keep it with his own belongings. This print becomes his most treasured possession.

Even heroes, Hiroshi discovers, need a rapt, adoring audience. His ability at *me kakushi* or "eye hiding" is a significant part of his apparatus of power. When he is Bluff the Blind Man, he has the unerring ability not only to catch the person closest to him but also to guess his name correctly. No one understands how he can be so infallible in determining his prey.

One day, a new boy, the same age as Hiroshi, calls him aside after the game has concluded. This fellow, recently settled in the Yoshiwara because his mother has taken over the management of one of the houses, is supposedly the son of the great kabuki actor, Ichikawa

Sōsaburō. Tedoya is at least four inches taller than Hiroshi and more muscular. Always dressed scruffily as if his mother paid no attention to his appearance, he carries himself with an enormous swagger, like someone already fully grown.

Looking Hiroshi directly in the eye, Tedoya congratulates him on his skill at *me kakushi*. Hiroshi accepts the compliment as his due and politely bows in his direction. When he was living in Tokyo, Tedoya continues, he was a member of a group of boys whose leader was also expert at this game. However, one day it was discovered that Iwai was so successful because he had cut a difficult-to-see slit in the cloth he used. Once that was discovered Iwai became an outcast.

Without further prodding, Hiroshi, realizing that his new acquaintance has excellent eyesight, offers to appoint him his co-adjutant in the running of the gang. The offer is immediately accepted, and the two become inseparable.

Previously, the private performances of kabuki that visiting actors performed for the courtesans had held little interest for Hiroshi but, under the tutelage of his new friend, he soon becomes enamoured of them. The two of them sneak into these performances and squirrel themselves in a dark spot in the back of the room where no one can see them.

The incessant family quarrels, the stirring battles and the love intrigues of kabuki hold the boys in thrall, as do the elaborate, brightly coloured costumes. A special favourite is the time one of the *sanbaso* dancers clad himself in crane feathers. Nor are Hiroshi and Tedoya immune to the moments of *nureba*, those instances of melo-dramatic sadness which force copious tears from most members of the audience. They thrill when an actor delivers a *mie*, ferocious glar-ing accompanied by crossed eyes.

Such eagerly anticipated moments are announced by the beating of a small clapper by one the actors. At this point the two boys are fully enraptured. In one scene, at the edge of the prow of a ship, the young hero, astride his elevated sandals, attacks the villain, whose face is painted pink and white to show what a dastardly character he is. Hiroshi is startled when Tedoya tells him that he wishes, just for once, that the villain could prevail over the hero. Tedoya is displeased when Hiroshi informs him that the older man, Benkei, having been conquered by the young Yoshitsune, becomes his vassal. Tedoya does not appreciate history lessons.

The friends become devoted to *aragoto*, the roughhousing in the comedies, and quickly import what they learn into their activities with the other boys. Many of the plays are about outlaws who steal from the rich to give to the poor. Quite soon, Hiroshi and Tedoya devise games wherein they right the wrongs of the peasants.

From references in some of the plays, Hiroshi and Tedoya acquire a great deal of second-hand information about the Tokyo underworld of gamblers, petty crooks, and prostitutes. The two become would-be merchants of the cutthroat variety. After buying up all the soap-berries, fruit of the *mokuran* tree, they sell the fruit, soaked in water for bubble blowing, at five times the usual price to the outraged mothers of young children.

Takao often shudders in Tedoya's presence. The other day, when the two boys were together, Hiroshi smirked when she asked him to do something; Tedoya's face remained blank, but she is sure Hiroshi is showing off for the benefit of his new friend. Perhaps, she wonders, this is the way Tedoya conducts himself at home?

Takao has heard that Tedoya's mother was a common-as-dirt Tokyo waitress who, having managed to sleep once with a very drunken Ichikawa Sōsaburō, claimed that her offspring, whose father could have been a hundred other men, was the son of the famous actor. Takao does not like the steely, intent look in Tedoya's eye: he is a boy who might grow up to become a thief — or even worse.

CHAPTER SEVENTEEN

1880

HIROSHI AND TEDOYA have become inseparable, so Yoshiko and Takao must put up with Tedoya. Yoshiko does not much care. She has so much on her mind that she is glad Hiroshi is constantly occupied. She has also begun to fear that her son has inherited her fox-like nature. At the age of seven, he is adept at showing whatever face his mother wants to behold. She does not like it when the table is turned on her.

In her more prosaic way, Takao fears that Tedoya is a bad influence on Hiroshi, although she has little evidence on which to base her feelings. In a nutshell, that is part of the problem. She is convinced that Tedoya has taught Hiroshi to be underhanded. Never for a moment does she consider the possibility that the relationship is two-sided and that Hiroshi may be corrupting his shadow, as she contemptuously labels Tedoya.

Hiroshi and Tedoya both despise their classroom, where the wind in winter whistles through the unheated room. They find the piles of tattered, mildewed books repulsive; they do not like sitting on stone floors; they mercilessly bait their teacher, a retired geisha, with sexual innuendoes. They bolt down their unappetizing lunches of cold rice balls and belch loudly. Generally speaking, the two youngsters are bored to distraction.

From Tedoya, Hiroshi learns about another kind of woodblock print called *shunga* — spring pictures. "If your mother has any of these, I'm sure she has never shown them to you!" Surprised, Hiroshi asks about those images. Grinning from ear to ear, Tedoya tells his friend in minute detail about the sex pictures in which huge penises are placed into the tiny holes of women. "You should ask your mother about all of that. Like all the women here, she's had sex with lots of men." Seven-year-old Hiroshi, who has already figured all this out for himself, does not enjoy being taunted by Tedoya. He decides to keep his mouth shut. In exchanges like this, Tedoya gains a glimpse of the softness in his friend's character. He files this observation away for later use.

Unbeknownst to Takao, it is Hiroshi who inveigles his friend to play hooky and teaches him just how easy it is to escape from the Yoshiwara for hours at a time. Although the *shirobei* and his assistants guard the portals with the delight that cruel wardens take in keeping their potentially wayward charges in check, it is easy for seven-year-olds to secret themselves under the canvas covers of the carts brought in and out of the Yoshiwara by rice or sake merchants. Waiting until a driver has walked a few yards away for a smoke or wandered behind a building to relieve himself, the two leap onto his cart and jump under the canvas. The boys have so perfected their art that they know they must wait ten minutes after departure from their home before jumping to the ground. Their way back is easily arranged. They hide behind the tall bamboo shoots by the side of the road and then jump aboard a cart for the return journey.

Once the boys have escaped the Yoshiwara, they do ordinary things, like capturing frogs, stealing birds' eggs, and staging mock battles. The real pleasure is in obtaining liberty, a much prized possession when denied.

On their fourth foray, the boys slipped away early in the morning, when they should have been at school. To freedom had been added the piquancy of truancy, and so the boys' enjoyment was doubled. At the juncture at which they usually met up with the wagons, when the ever-vigilant Hiroshi was about to set foot on the road to gain a vantage point, he saw in the distance a lone woman walking his way and cautioned Tedoya, who was ten steps behind him, to halt. The two crouched behind some bamboo, wondering who would be walking out of the compound in the general direction of Tokyo.

They do not have to wait long before Taye, a courtesan of the Miura, comes into view. Both the boys, who know her by sight, wonder to themselves why she would be out walking. Presumably she has obtained a one-day pass, now easily available, but she has, very unusually, requested her driver to put her down shortly after leaving the Yoshiwara. When courtesans visited Tokyo, they generally dressed in the Western costumes that were now so common in the big city. But Taye is clad in what is one of her best kimonos, a pale green one covered in pink and purple water lilies; a thick black ebo holds the entire ensemble together. The courtesan's beautiful thin face is covered in its usual thick white powder, but, as she passes them, the boys can see bright red seeping through. Biting her lips, she propels herself forward reluctantly, as if she has mixed feelings about her journey. A minute after she passes them but is still within their sight, the boys see a man approach her. It takes Hiroshi a moment or two to recognize Prince Saiko, whom he has previously seen on the streets of the Yoshiwara.

The man and woman retreat into the bushes and out of sight, but their screaming voices are easily heard, although the two children cannot make out what they are actually saying. After about five minutes, there is complete silence. Hiroshi and Tedoya look quizzically at each other, wait for a quarter of an hour, then decide to investigate.

Stealthily, the two walk in the direction where they had seen the couple leave the road. There is no sign of anyone. Both are now certain that the couple, having patched up their quarrel, are on their way to

Tokyo together. The boys begin a game of leapfrog, and then pretend to be sumo wrestlers. Tired of that, Hiroshi suggests a game of hide-and-seek and volunteers to be *it*. Tedoya goes over to the nearest tree to count to one hundred as his friend vanishes into the brush.

The always adept Hiroshi searches out a flat space where he can secrete himself. He remembers the perfect spot, one he has visited before by himself. He heads in that direction, pushing branches away rapidly. He breathes a sigh of relief when he realizes he is just about to reach that clearing. The soil here has been so invaded by the bog that it is now the consistency of mud. Even Tedoya will never find him here.

Victory, which Hiroshi can almost taste, is within his grasp when he stumbles upon the corpse of Taye. She lies cuddled in a heap as if sleeping, but the boy knows she is dead because she is covered in blood. He can smell it.

Horrified, Hiroshi calls out for Tedoya, who reaches him a minute or two later. The broad smile on Tedoya's face vanishes when he sees the body. The boys immediately abandon the murder scene. They decide to take the first cart they encounter back to the Yoshiwara. While waiting for their ride, the two swear a solemn compact to reveal nothing about what they have seen.

Two days later, a walker in the woods comes upon Taye's body. Her murder is soon the talk of the pleasure quarters. Known as a reserved young woman who saw only clients of the highest class, gossip suggests she must have encountered on her walk some low-life ruffian, who raped and then stabbed her. Four days later, Hiroshi overhears his mother telling Takao that Prince Saiko, once a customer at their house, committed *seppuku* the day before. Takao shakes her head in disbelief. What is the world coming to when such persons choose to abandon it?

Hiroshi and Tedoya, the only ones to know the relationship between both deaths, are certain Taye made demands upon the noble Prince, who refused to obey them. Maybe she wanted marriage? Or she wanted the Prince to arrange a marriage for her? Perhaps she threatened to tell the Prince's wife that he had fallen in love with her? The boys discuss the permutations endlessly, but they never talk about how frightened they had been. Hiroshi had soiled his kimono; Tedoya had briefly excused himself in order to empty the contents of his stomach.

CHAPTER EIGHTEEN

YOSHIKO NOTICES NOTHING different about Hiroshi. Takao is aware that the boy has been badly shaken, but she has no idea of what he has witnessed. Usually silent these days after Takao finishes telling him a tale, this one surprisingly provokes a reaction:

Oniwaka, or "Young Devil" as he was called, was born from a violent union between a beautiful young woman and the malicious abbot of the Kumano shrine. His father snatched the baby away from his mother and gave him to a wealthy relative. Disgusted with the youngster as he grew older, his foster mother sent Oniwaka to a temple where the monks, a dissolute group, taunted him.

Oniwaka was treated as a serving boy, the lowest of the low. Constantly humiliated, the youngster began to believe the very worst about himself. One day, he overheard one monk telling another that Oniwaka's mother had been killed when she accidentally fell into a pond and had been eaten by the giant fish who lived there.

Immediately upon hearing this story, Oniwaka ran to the pond, where he saw the enormous fish. He was so badly frightened that in his imagination the fish looked even bigger than it was. He looked down again and hesitated. Suddenly, overcome with rage, he plunged into the water and *jumped onto the back of the fish. Frightened, the fish carried Oniwaka down into the depths of the water, where the two engaged in a mighty battle.*

Although the combat was long and intense, Oniwaka prevailed. Once he had stabbed the fish to death, he swam triumphantly up to the surface of the water. That night he rested. In the morning, completely revitalized, he left the monastery.

Why, Hiroshi asked Takao, when life consisted of various kinds of carnage — fighting, murder, war — did she bother to tell him such stories? In them, the boy pointed out, the heroes always overcame huge obstacles. But, he had noticed, life was not really like that. For instance, he had never encountered anyone like Kintarō — and never expected he would. So weren't her stories a waste of his time and hers?

At first, Takao thought the boy was being surly. But, she was forced to ask herself, why did she bother with such meaningless accounts? She could have claimed that she was trying to teach Hiroshi about virtue, but she had to agree with him that all the myths she knew might be, in the light of her own experience of life, irrelevant.

CHAPTER NINETEEN

1889

TAKAO IS ANXIOUS. Yoshiko, often overwhelmed with the demands of running the House, is constantly distracted. Although she wants to linger in the museum of her mind, she cannot always do so.

Things have taken a turn for the worse in the entire Yoshiwara. The government interferes with every aspect of its running. There are taxes galore, and more officials than ever before to buy off or placate. The customers are not, by any stretch of the imagination, of the refined kind that used to frequent the place. Often, the customers are teenagers, young men who should be under their parents' roofs rather than seeking admission to the ones here. To make matters worse, pleasure quarters are now plentiful in Tokyo. Many business-men, too tired at the end of the day to make the journey to the Yoshiwara, settle for nearby conveniences.

The owner of the House sends frequent, nagging letters to Yoshiko: profits must be greater than they are. Yoshiko, always trying to cut costs, never succeeds in that endeavour and worries that she will be dismissed. Takao does her best to make helpful suggestions which, thank goodness, Yoshiko usually attends to. Despite her arthritis, Takao often assists the maids and servants in cleaning the rooms once the customers have taken their farewells.

When all is said and done, however, Hiroshi is Takao's greatest concern. Not that the young man *seems* to present a problem. Sixteen-years-old, he is no longer the churlish and difficult teenager who, a few years earlier, stayed out all hours of the night without explanation. He no longer screams insults at his mother. He has stopped ranting against the man who abandoned him and her. He no longer tells Yoshiko on a daily basis that her so-called husband made a fool of her. Long ago, he informs her, he gave up any dream he had of seeing his father and of being reunited with him in Japan or the New World.

At the age of nine, when Tedoya related to him in a matter-of-fact way the nature of the business conducted by his mother, Hiroshi was not shocked. He experienced only dismay. Later, he felt disgust at the way his mother so summarily removed herself from the real world. According to her, the courtesans depicted in her woodblock prints were women of education and refinement. When he realized that his mother had assembled a collection of advertisements for the services of women of pleasure, he was angry at her refusal to face reality.

Nowadays, Hiroshi has become quite the gentleman, one who is infinitely solicitous of his mother. At the end of the day, he often sits for hours on end chatting pleasantly with her. And he even has the time of day once more for Takao.

Perhaps the worst years of growing up have come and passed away, Takao tells herself. Since Tedoya returned to Tokyo with his mother two years ago, Takao can no longer place any blame on him. Unlike Yoshiko, she is suspicious that Hiroshi is gulling them into a false sense of security.

Although she would not breathe a word of her suspicions to Yoshiko, Takao, without a shred of evidence, wonders if Hiroshi is involved in the mysterious disappearances of huge quantities of rice and sake from the various houses. The police, incompetent as always, do not know how large amounts of goods can arrive in the Yoshiwara and then mysteriously vanish. It is as if an evil magician has enchanted the place.

Although Hiroshi castigates himself for having become a dissolute scoundrel, he has no intention of leaving aside his chosen profession of thief. Having devised an ingenious scheme to pilfer from the Yoshiwara, he and the other members of the gang have chosen to change their public profile. They no longer engage in pranks, get drunk in public or chase after the waitresses at the tea houses. Most of them have taken respectable jobs as *wakai-mono* and turn blind eyes when material arriving at one house is moved to another location to await its return to Tokyo, on a supposedly empty cart en route back to the metropolis. Hiroshi is the mastermind of this scheme. Through Tedoya, he has established contact with merchants willing to buy the contraband goods.

Boredom rather than material necessity has led Hiroshi to his devilish invention. He also enjoys playing the role in which he has cast himself as the helpful, genteel son. He has never had the ambition to act in kabuki, but he has mastered some of the tricks of that trade. He can imitate any emotion he chooses. He can be kindness itself to his mother, the embodiment of courtesy to his aunt.

The success of the highjacking ploy and his play-acting have come with a bitter price. Having re-established good relations with his mother and aunt, a small part of him would like to be what he appears to be. He has become a man firmly split in two.

CHAPTER TWENTY

THESE DAYS HIROSHI is haunted by one of the stories Takao told him as a boy.

Atsumori, the fifteen-year-old son of a general of the Taira clan, was renowned as a flautist. So beautiful was the music he made that even the enemy soldiers took pleasure in hearing his melodies drift to them through the pine trees.

Knowing that his young son was unskilled as a warrior, his father ordered him to stay behind in camp during the fierce battle which would be fought that day by their clan, the Taira, against the Minamoto. Atsumori agreed, but when the son rose and the soldiers marched off, he was so consumed with the desire to join them that he broke his promise. He borrowed a suit of armour, seized his bow and quiver and galloped onto the field of battle.

Filled with excitement, he knew this was the moment he had lived for his entire life. Finally, he was leaving boyhood behind. He was about to become a man.

As the sun rose higher, the fighting went against the Taira. They withdrew to their fleet of ships moored offshore. Atsumori joined the retreat but suddenly remembered he had left his flute back at camp. He could not leave without it. He broke rank, galloped back to the camp, retrieved his flute and then made for the water. He had nearly reached safety when a cry from shore made him turn back. An enemy warrior had challenged him. Atsumori galloped back to meet his opponent, Kumagai.

The enemy warrior had assumed he was challenging a mature soldier and was surprised that he felled his opponent so easily. When Kumagai tore Atsumori's helmet off, he gasped at how young his opponent was.

His own young son had died in battle the month before, and Kumagai decided to show mercy. What possible good could be served by killing such a youth? But at that moment, Kumagai's companions taunted him. Had he lost his nerve? His resolve to be compassionate dissolved and, with a prayer for forgiveness, he swung his sword down swiftly and killed Atsumori.

Atsumori was, according to Hiroshi's way of thinking, an idealistic fool, who, although he did manage to remain true to himself, paid dearly with his life. If he had been Kumagai, he would have killed Atsumori without giving a second thought. Yet, almost against his will, Hiroshi is moved by the spectacle of the young soldier-musician's idealism at the very same time that he castigates himself for entertaining such soft feelings.

CHAPTER TWENTY-ONE

1890

HIROSHI HAS BEEN in Tokyo for almost a month. His scam was too good to last, he tells himself. The gang was exposed when a Tokyo constable, one not connected to the investigation of the case, claimed he became intrigued by a supposedly empty cart returning to the city and demanded the driver show him its contents. Hiroshi is certain that someone tipped the policeman off.

Hiroshi was exceedingly lucky. Since it took the police a few days to establish the identity of the mastermind, he heeded a message from one of his co-conspirators to flee the Yoshiwara. The vastness of Tokyo made it the perfect place to escape to, although Hiroshi, for good measure, has changed his name to Saigo. He lives in fear that his milk-white skin will betray him as the *half-breed* — as the newspapers labelled him — responsible for the brothel robberies.

During his flight, secreted in the back of a wagon, Hiroshi had imagined how wonderful it would be to escape the clutches of his mother and aunt. The grim reality of day-to-day survival in the metropolis quickly modifies his optimism. Used to the confines of his birthplace, he soon discovers Tokyo to be vast and nightmarish.

Tokyo is a series of villages, with bits of green and open space interspersed between them, and the inland waterways, which fill the city, are the best means of transportation. However, the banks of the river are low and sedgy; at some points, they become a marsh. The loud, incessant cawing of the crows echoes everywhere. Hiroshi, used to the soft, mud-like paths on the edges of the Yoshiwara, and so familiar since childhood with the sounds of the birds that he pays them no heed, is not jarred by these aspects of city life. But some differences overwhelm him.

The constant rumbling of the trams is annoying as is the monotonous singsong of the street vendors beseeching passersby to buy things such as goldfish, tofu, and sweet potatoes. Tokyo has no drainage system and stinks. Hawkers sell plaster kittens, painted butterflies and puppet priests which, when you pull a string, clasp their hands in prayer. At night, the sewage collectors, accompanied by their carts, buckets and dippers, wail *"Owai! Owai!"* in hopes of buying human shit to use as fertilizer. Dust is everywhere, getting into Hiroshi's eyes and settling between his toes.

Many of the street names may be floral — Wild Cherry, Plum Orchard, Willow Branch, Flower River — but, after a rainstorm, the streets are filled with huge frogs and even bigger rats.

Despite the frequent visits of Westerners to the Yoshiwara, Hiroshi is amazed to discover that most of his fellow countrymen now dress in the same way as the foreigners. Only about half the women wear kimonos on the street. They too imitate foreign ways with dresses consisting of elaborate stays and petticoats. Some wear their hair in a pompadour called *eaves* because this style projects the hair outwards in layer upon layer like the eaves on a house. Some women have what is sarcastically called a *shampoo hairdo* because it looks as if they let their hair down to wash and then did nothing with it. Quite soon after his arrival, Hiroshi had his topknot removed and his hair is now in the *zangiri* style, the random, messy cropping favoured by Western men.

Although Hiroshi has never thought of himself as a country bumpkin, he finds his new home in the New Ginza, or the Brickworks, as it is usually called, too much of an urban jungle for his liking. The Yoshiwara was the first place in Japan to have gaslights, and so Hiroshi knows about this miraculous invention. But here in Tokyo, street after street is illuminated with an unnatural and ghastly yellow light which casts its pallor over everything. Walking on an evening through the orange-yellow air depresses him. Remembering the Yoshiwara, Hiroshi thinks that, like a waitress-whore who must wear the tawdriest, most outlandish-looking kimono to attract customers, Tokyo is determined to become the brightest city in the world.

Tokyo has always been a fire trap. In order to rid themselves of this threat, the city fathers decided all the houses and shops in the Ginza were to be made of brick. No more tinderboxes for them. As a result, dreary building after dreary building follow each other as far as the eye can see. Solid, unnerving monsters of red brick. They are damp, stuffy and mildew-ridden. This hodgepodge assortment of woodless buildings, large without a hint of majesty, are, the British architect boasts, models of convenience.

The temptation merchants — Hiroshi's term for the makers of coloured sugar candies — set up their wretched stalls and attempt to inveigle youngsters to win treats by aiming blowpipes at faraway, impossible-to-hit targets. Groups of street tumblers, usually boys of seven and eight years of age, make wheels of themselves with their arms and legs as spokes as soon as they spy a foreigner who might make a donation. Sellers of crystallized oranges, buckwheat cakes, noodles and roasted chestnuts crowd the streets.

At various public gardens, the foreigners have flower shows, botanical shows, even dog shows. They have set aside public space to play their games: croquet, bowls, quoits, even their own form of archery. Cups of tea, with or without milk and sugar, are sold. They eat a strange pastry called a donut. Hiroshi has even been told that the signs in English declare that NO FLIRTING IS ALLOWED.

In the Asakusa, where most of the beer halls are located, is the Twelve Stories, a huge, clumsy tower of red brick. It is visible everywhere. The elevator, the first in Japan, was used to take passengers, twenty at a time, to the eighth floor for a view of the city. Considered dangerous, it has long been closed down. Wares from all over the world are on sale in the shops. The Chinese shop even has goods supposedly from the Dowager Empress herself. Every square inch of space is filled with goods — this technique, Hiroshi is certain, his countrymen have appropriated from the barbarians. What foreign monstrosities will we not copy? Hiroshi wonders.

Unfortunately, I myself am half barbarian, he reminds himself. If he can avoid it, however, he does not like to think about his father who abandoned him. I am really Japanese, he unconvincingly tries to assure himself.

Places selling cow meat, pig meat and even Mountain Whale have proliferated, although until very recently the eating of such animals was, according to the government, dangerous; now, it is claimed, the flesh of these animals provides immunization against cholera, a disease from which the white devils seem immune.

Thank goodness, Hiroshi tells himself, he can go to the bay shore at Fukagawa and, standing by the shrine, look out to sea, where there is the contrast between sparkling blue water and inviting white sand, between waves and sailboats. To the south and east the jade-coloured Chuban mountains float upon the water. To the west can be glimpsed the white snows of Fuji. At low tide, young and old, man and woman, poor and rich, come out to test their skills at harvesting clams and seaweed.

Hiroshi frequents the filthy fish market near the Mitsukohi Bridge, only a few steps from the Mitsui Bank and the Bank of Japan. Fish guts are everywhere. The smells are preposterously awful. There is the obnoxious odour of the fish themselves but added to that is the rank perfume of urine and feces emanating from the two latrines at the eastern and western sides of the market. Only when he is in this much despised place, the only part of Tokyo which has refused to be made over, does Hiroshi feel completely at home.

The opening that spring of the Sumida festival and thus of Ryōgoku Bridge leaves him untouched. The wide river is full of boats and pleasure barges, hundreds of them of all sizes, undulating up and down, crowded together as darkness approaches. Millions of lanterns make the sedate Sumida into a sea of sparkling light. Then the fireworks cascade down, showering the spectators in bright colours. Hiroshi's heart is so filled with bitterness that the light and noise only irritate him.

Although he would not admit it even to himself, Hiroshi is lonely. There is scarcely room for him to stand in his room at the boarding house. Soon after arriving in Tokyo, Hiroshi searched for Tedoya. First, he looked in the beer halls, coffee houses and cafés, where most young men congregate in the evening. No one had heard of him or his mother.

Knowing that his friend liked to be in the vanguard of fashion, Hiroshi decided one evening to seek him out at the Rokumeikan in Hibiya Park. This recent building was another shameless capitulation to the West. Although brick, it has mercifully been made to look like a Florentine villa rather than like an American monstrosity.

One moonlit evening Hiroshi makes his way to the Rokumeikan and wanders through its ballroom, music room, billiard room, and reading room. At the bar, English cigarettes, German beer and American cocktails are on offer. He looks askance at the heavy, overstuffed furniture into which someone could sink and perhaps disappear. In a moralistic mood, Hiroshi decides that sofas embody

Western decadence. These people are sybarites, he tells himself.

Tedoya is nowhere to be found. In fact, there are few Japanese enjoying this pleasure palace. Hiroshi decides to abandon his search and is heading for the front door when he is accosted by a tuxedo-clad man of his own age.

"Are you Suzuki-san? I have been waiting a long time for you!"

Hiroshi shakes his head no, but the man, who tells him his name is Gotō, does not believe him.

"I hope you're not trying to shake me off, just because you don't want to bother to show me around."

Politely, Hiroshi tells him he has him confused with someone else. Mollified, Gotō asks for a cigarette. Hiroshi hands him one and then produces a match.

Gotō inhales and then confesses that he has no wish to be at the Rokumeikan with all the white devils. However, his cousin Mitsuko, having heard him express a vague wish to see the Club, arranged for her friend Suzuki, a member, to show him around. Gotō had wanted to see one of the legendary suites in which there are alabaster bathtubs, six feet long and three feet wide. From solid-gold faucets, he had been told, water thunders most magnificently into the huge containers, filling them instantly.

Apparently Gotō has forgotten his desire to see this marvel of Western ingenuity and suggests he and Hiroshi stroll down to Asakusa. When asked his name, Hiroshi splutters and stumbles before saying Saigo and receives a worried look from his companion, who is obviously wondering if his new acquaintance is insane or has something to hide.

The two young men, one in a tuxedo and the other in a kimono, wander from one drinking place to another. Only when they are thoroughly drunk does Saigo ask Gotō for advice. He says he arrived in Tokyo three weeks before and is quickly running out of funds; he asks about finding work, any work. That is easy, Gotō assures him. His father owns the largest sake brewery in Tokyo and has been on the lookout for a driver who can deliver his wares to the Shinto shrines. The gods of those places, who like to be happy all the time, are in constant need of liquid refreshment. And that is how Saigo obtains his very first legitimate employment.

In the evenings, Saigo is often in the company of Gotō and his friends. The newcomer is slightly out of place among these wealthy young men, who do not have to work. Yet Saigo's intelligence and wit allow him to fit in, although he remains perched on the edge of the group.

He becomes fond of good-natured, generous Gotō, but this does not prevent Saigo from delivering less than the assigned number of casks on an increasingly regular basis. Some old monks, at the edge of senility, take the delivery man's assurances that he has delivered twenty casks whereas he has only given them eighteen; some monks are simply too lazy to count what is being donated to them. There are also the casks that supposedly fall to the ground and crash into the proverbial million pieces. So Saigo lives on one source of income and puts money aside with the other.

Unfortunately for him, Hiroshi-Saigo is a thief with the remnants of a conscience. True, he can easily rationalize his bad behaviour: I am poor and have to survive; if I don't make extra money, I must stay home at night with nothing to do. He is also sufficiently self-aware to know that he enjoys gulling others. And yet this young man, possessed of a morally delicate side, begins to suffer pangs of guilt at the very same time he takes enormous pleasure in his criminal exploits.

After six months in the service of the brewery, the worst possible thing that could befall Hiroshi happens: he becomes inordinately bored with his job. One night when they are out carousing, Gotō, grabbing Hiroshi by the shoulder, asks him if he knows the identity of the drunken old man who stumbles out into the street, having been turned out of the house of pleasure at the corner. Looking intently, Hiroshi sees the remnants of a human being, a leftover person whose soul has long walked away after the body has suffered carnage on a daily basis.

"Grandfather has seen many better days," Hiroshi tells his friend.

"I agree," Gotō assures him. "But you are looking at what remains of Master Yoshitoshi, Japan's greatest artist."

Since early childhood, Hiroshi has loved this artist's prints: seldom have brave warriors been so movingly portrayed. And then there are his beguiling *bijin*. If someone had asked him about Yoshitoshi a few years before, he would have told them that as a lover of violence he had never seen any artist who could render it more vividly. Heads severed from corpses; rooms filled with blood and body parts after a villain has murdered a family: these were once The Master's stock-in-trade. Nowadays, Hiroshi feels he has left such childish interests behind.

"The Master has made himself into a laughing stock," Gotō observes. "In fact, he is having trouble at the moment getting anyone to work with him, so disagreeable is his behaviour."

Surprised, Hiroshi asks if The Master is indeed looking for an apprentice and is assured that he is very much in need of one. "As if anyone could bear to be around him!" exclaims Gotō.

Perhaps, Hiroshi wonders, employment with an idiot-genius will suit me more than my present occupation.

CHAPTER TWENTY-TWO

IN BROAD DAYLIGHT The Master is even more of a wreck. Once upon a time he must have been a handsome man. His eyebrows still arch delicately, his lips are full, and his eyes have a commanding presence. Now, there is only a semblance of bygone days. The wrinkles on his face are so deep that they look etched; his teeth are bright orange. Not only is his kimono stained with food but he stinks. The Master's excessive drinking is commemorated in the excessive red colouring of his cheeks. His doctor, who informs him that he has *nōjūketsu*, brain congestion, cannot suggest any remedy. In addition, the artist is so malnourished that he has contracted beriberi.

His most recent troubles began a few years back, when, informed by a necromancer that his lodging was inauspiciously located, he built a new house in Nihonbashi in downtown Tokyo and moved all his possessions there before it was ready. That night, thieves robbed him of everything he owned while he snored away, exhausted after designing a costume for a kabuki actor.

Inordinately suspicious in response to the robbery, Yoshitoshi is now fearful of everyone he meets: shopkeepers, publishers, and other artists. To add to all his troubles, The Master, who was forced a few years back to act as guarantor of a large loan, is convinced the debtor will renege and leave him responsible and, thus, destitute.

If they are going to work together, The Master expects complete loyalty from Hiroshi and extracts an oath from him promising unswerving devotion. Even after having done that, Yoshitoshi still looks askance at Hiroshi.

Yoshitoshi is especially suspicious of women. From Gotō, Hiroshi learns that Yoshitoshi has been notoriously unlucky in love. After separating from his first wife, he married the daughter of a ballad master and then took up almost at once with Okiku, a waitress at the Suzukiya tea house. Distraught at their poverty, his second wife returned to her family home and, soon after, sold herself into prostitution. Then, Yoshitoshi took up with Oraku, a geisha, who left him after two years of constant bickering. He seduced his neighbour's young niece, then became infatuated with a renowned courtesan so mysterious that she was known to him only as Maboroshidayū, The Phantom Lady. This woman claimed she modelled herself after a fifteenth-century courtesan, The Lady from Hell.

Lowering his voice, Gotō continues his narration. Evidently, the artist wanted The Phantom Lady to perform unspeakable, degenerate sex acts. She agreed but later sent him a bill for one hundred yen, a month's salary for him and a lot of money for an evening of sado-masochism, no matter how uninhibited. After the quick breakup of his relationship with this woman, the artist married Tai, his neighbour's niece. That lady is nowhere in evidence when Hiroshi arrives at The Master's home.

Hiroshi has trouble moving around in the cramped quarters, so clogged are they with discarded paints, rags, papers, pieces of wood and other refuse. Despite his employer's protests, Hiroshi cleans up the mess and establishes a semblance of tidiness. Then he prepares green tea and rice which he and the old man share.

In between bouts of coughing and uprisings of phlegm which discharge themselves from both his mouth and nose, Yoshitoshi offers to train Hiroshi as a woodblock artist, just as Master Kuniyoshi taught him many years before. Although flattered, Hiroshi knows that Yoshitoshi has had many apprentices, all of whom he has fallen out with. Nevertheless, the young man is of a mind to take a serious turn with his life.

Yoshitoshi may be Japan's greatest artist, but he lives in rank poverty. That is the first unappetizing fact of an artist's life which Hiroshi discovers. In the next two months, the young man learns a great deal about the harrowing complexities of making woodblock prints. Only the finest white mountain cherrywood can be employed for the blocks themselves. Sometimes there are as many as ten used for one print. The key block, usually printed in black, contains the transcription by the carver of the artist's drawing. This is printed and then the artist decides what colours go where and hands that back to the printer. Each colour, which requires its own block, must be printed in its turn onto the paper on which the impression from the key block has been affixed. In order to keep the colours lined up properly every time the sheet of paper is moved to a new block, the corner of each piece of paper is fitted into a L-shaped *kento* on each block. Light colours are applied first, then the darker ones. The pigments are ground by hand.

Like Yoshiko, The Master has a large collection of prints. When he is in the mood for conversation, he invites his disciple to look at them with him. The "big head" portraits of *oiran* — even the now celebrated ones by Utamaro — seem too remote and reserved to Hiroshi, but The Master shares Yoshiko's taste for them. The older man points out how the inner world of the courtesans' existences is displayed by Utamaro. Yoshitoshi loves the subtle blues, purples and pinks — the fugitive colors — that are lost when a print is exposed to too much sunlight. For the first time, Hiroshi grasps what his mother loves about these old prints. He comes to see these images through her eyes.

The Master is surprised how quickly and well Hiroshi performs each task he assigns him. Very soon, Hiroshi, who has a good understanding of all the steps in making a print, acts as his Master's ambassador to the outside world. Basically, the young man's job is to negotiate on Yoshitoshi's behalf with the various carvers, printers and publishers who are in contact with the artist on a daily basis. If the printer has not produced a good key block, Hiroshi breaks the bad news and offers suggestions on how the problem can be rectified. If the colours are not right, he must inform the person responsible and get him to mix the pigments to obtain the exact shade required. Yoshitoshi is inordinately fussy and frequently does not like how the carvers render his lines onto the woodblock. Hiroshi must deal with outraged master-carvers and tell them how to draw correctly. The publishers are a greedy lot, and it is Hiroshi's job to extract the best possible prices from them. When turning his hand to this task, Hiroshi is more aggressive and sharp-tongued than he would be if he were negotiating on his own behalf.

When he has a few moments to spare, Hiroshi spends the time drawing. At first The Master has no interest in such scribblings. Then one day he asks to see what his young assistant is up to. He grunts and then dismisses the young man from his sight.

Three days later, while drinking the tea prepared for him by his assistant, The Master laboriously clears his throat. He informs Hiroshi that he has a little bit of talent, which he might consider cultivating. "As you know, although I draw and draw, I make no money. The life of the artist is the life of a poor dunce, but you might consider it if nothing better presents itself." Wide-eyed, Hiroshi looks at the

Master, who promptly turns his head away and begins talking about that afternoon's work schedule.

Why, Hiroshi asks himself, would I want to become an artist? The Master holds nothing but contempt for all artists, including himself. He has spent, he claims, his entire life lazily, as if in a daze. He wonders why he ever bothered to take up such a profession. Then he answers his own question: "All artists are misfits, people who do not fit into society. We are the dregs, the lowest of the low." He has many other moments of self-deprecation: "Artists are people who cannot get on with the business of living. They can only observe."

Despite the Master's words of self-loathing, Hiroshi notices the two early prints he keeps by his working table. They illustrate a story told to Hiroshi long ago by Takao.

The tenth-century poet Fujiwara no Yasumasa was a dreamy sort of man. If his wife did not prod him, he sometimes forgot to eat. Early in life, looking for a way to survive, he became a court official and, later, the governor of Tango province, near Kyoto. Of course, he was a complete incompetent in this position of authority, preferring as he did to spend his time playing the flute and writing poetry. His friends gossiped endlessly about Yasumasa: how could such a complete nincompoop manage to survive? True, he was a charming man, but he paid absolutely no heed to the necessities of daily existence. Behind his back, they shook their heads dismissively. Music and poetry were all very well, but they were not essential.

One night, Yasumasa was home alone when a group of wandering thieves chanced upon his house and decided to break in. Overhearing their plans, Yasumasa, hid beneath the floorboards while the ruffians took all his possessions, except his hichiriki. As soon as the miscreants had left, he came out from his hiding place, found that flute and began playing a melody which resounded through the streets. When the thieves heard the music, they were so touched that, repenting their crime, they returned all of their victim's possessions.

A bit later, one moonlit night, as Yasumasa was strolling along the highway on the lonely moor of Ichiharano, the bandit Hakamadare Yasusuke saw him from a distance. Being a fierce, blood-hungry villain, the destitute outlaw determined to kill the poet-politician so that he might steal his clothes and discard the rags in which he was clad. Crouching in the underbrush, Yasusuke waited for his intended victim to make his way to him. A man of low cunning, the bandit imagined the pleasure he would take in ridding the world of yet another being, this one being a particularly useless specimen of humanity. He could almost taste the blood of Yasumasa in his mouth.

As usual, Yasumasa, lost in thought, approached his would-be assailant, he took up his flute and began playing the most intoxicating tune imaginable. The sound so enchanted the villain that he followed close behind in order to hear every note.

Only when he reached his home did Yasumasa emerge from his daze; he was, after all, a man who spent his time daydreaming. When he finally noticed Hakamadare Yasusuke and the rags in which he was clothed, he politely excused himself and, soon afterwards, returned with a magnificent kimono which he presented to the bandit. From that day onwards, so legend states, the criminal abandoned his way of life and became a Buddhist monk.

The absent-minded Yasumasa, Hiroshi is sure, was a fool, someone who did not have to worry about surviving on a daily basis. Even now, Hiroshi can hear the earnestness in his aunt's voice; he remembers fondly the gentle cadences in which she framed this narrative. And yet the man who has brought this sentimental story to life in his art is not only poor but filled with self-loathing. What a strange way, Hiroshi reflects, some people lead their lives.

CHAPTER TWENTY-THREE

1892

ALTHOUGH THE MASTER would never wish anyone to accuse him of being kind-hearted, such an adjective is the best one to use in describing his behaviour towards Hiroshi. True, most days he is laconic, grunting in response to his disciple's queries. Some of the words that escape his lips are acidic, especially when he feels his pupil is not doing his best. But behind the harshness is the expectation that Hiroshi has the makings of a genuine artist. If Hiroshi had been dumb, loyal and untalented, The Master would have treated him kindly. As if looking at his younger self in the mirror, Yoshitoshi bestows upon his disciple all the harsh words that he feels should have been directed his way fifty years before. This young man, Yoshitoshi tells himself, is very much like myself at his age: although he seems tough and uncaring, he is too gentle for his own good.

Being a quick study in reading personalities as well as in print-making, and although his feelings are often hurt, Hiroshi understands the method in his Master's madness. One thing is never spoken of: the fast approaching death of Yoshitoshi, who now coughs blood daily. Knowing that he will soon be extinct, he drinks himself to sleep every night. Hiroshi knows the old man wants to forget, but he also knows the sake is being used as a very necessary painkiller.

Then The Master begins to spend more and more time sleeping, not even bothering to rise from his tatami mat. On those days he drifts in and out of consciousness. Some days he laments his loss at an early age of his mother. On others he remembers arriving, as an eleven-year-old child, at his master Kuniyoshi's studio. That recollection fills him with intense pleasure, leading to exclamations of reverence for his dear, long dead teacher.

The various characters Yoshitoshi has immortalized have become real to him, ghosts with whom he can converse. He speaks to  the handsome young samurai who had willingly given their lives for their lords. One of those prints, pinned to the wall, reminds The Master of Hiroshi. Hiroshi blushes when the old man points this out to him. He can see the resemblance, but he does not like the idealistic demeanour in the face of the young warrior. In his mouth, Masatsura holds a *saihai* — a baton for commanding his soldiers. Fantasies about warriors are fantasies for weaklings. Hiroshi's ambitions must be part of the real world.

There are the women, from both Tokyo and the Yoshiwara, that Yoshitoshi had made even more beautiful than they had been in real life. Then there are the murderers and evil *daimo* he had skewered with his pen. Filled with rage at their defilement, they threaten to exact their revenge upon him once he joins them in their domain. Haunted by both heroes and villains, Yoshitoshi is torn asunder in his final days.

Against his will, Hiroshi has developed tender feelings for The Master. He wants to assist Yoshitoshi to obtain a semblance of peace before he dies, but that seems an impossible goal. When he has some time to spare, Hiroshi searches in the apothecary shops for the best salves to relieve The Master's pain. He prepares and serves the older man steaming broths made from the finest fish he can afford. Most days he simply sits beside Yoshitoshi, listening to the often crazed words that escape the dying man's lips. Hiroshi holds the skin and bones that remain of the artist's hands. In the final days, Hiroshi spends many sleepless nights tending The Master.

During his last three days of existence, Yoshitoshi sleeps soundly and then dies without regaining consciousness. To his own amazement, Hiroshi, alone with the body when it is cremated in Kameido, a northern suburb of Tokyo, on June 9, breaks down in tears. The taste of the salt in his mouth surprises Hiroshi, who has not experienced grief.

Two days later, many friends and acquaintances attend the service at Senpukuji temple in western Tokyo, where The Master's publisher, Akiyama Takeemon, offers employment to Hiroshi, which he gratefully accepts.

1893–1894

The next two years go by in an alcoholic blur. A ruthless businessman but a good employer, Takeemon expects a great deal of Hiroshi, who now negotiates with artists for the sale of their work. He does his job well: he exacts the lowest possible prices from them in order to maximize Takeemon's profits. Disgusted with himself for taking advantage of men at the edge of poverty, Hiroshi's own ambition to become an artist wanes.

Without doubt, Takeemon has the soul of a miser, even though his heart occasionally takes him in other directions. He is a wizened man with delicate, slightly distorted features. His blind left eyeball is an unsightly mess and renders his eyesight poor. His hair is grey, but his entire body seems that colour, possibly because he smokes constantly. His body appears warped to most people he encounters: in order to use his good eye, he always turns sharply to the right in conversation. What always comes as a surprise is his beautiful voice — sweet, vibrant, alluring.

Takeemon's rapacity does not extend to Hiroshi, whom he soon reckons as the son he never had. Despite the unsought fatherly affection bestowed upon him, Hiroshi remains contemptuous of Takeemon. Hiroshi continues drinking to excess every night. Often, when he goes drinking with Gotō, his friend has to drag him home, help him undress, and then sit by him for an hour to ensure that he will not get up again in search of more sake.

After about six months, Takeemon's patience begins to wear thin. He wants his protégé to reform himself, but Hiroshi assures him this is an impossible task. Despite the alcoholic and emotional haze in which he exists, Hiroshi remains an excellent businessman. He tells Takeemon that he has no real cause for complaint.

In addition to feelings of despondency, Hiroshi is once again bored. He needs some sort of challenge, but he is unsure in which direction to head.

Although committed to screwing out the lowest wages from the many artists who work for him, Takeemon is an ardent collector of ukiyoe, particularly the early work of Harunobu, Hokusai, Hiroshige, Toyokuni I and Utamaro. Although he may love these prints, he is a shrewd judge of market value. Once upon a time, woodblocks by those masters were used to wrap pieces of porcelain and pottery being exported to Europe and the United States. Then artists there began looking at those pieces of scrap paper and discovered that their Japanese counterparts had created a whole new way of seeing the world. Now those once worthless pieces of paper are being increasingly sought after by millionaire collectors.

Takeemon finds this reversal of artistic fortune amusing and ironic: "They are, after all, merely pictures of actors and courtesans. Not the nicest sort of people. The landscapes mainly depict commonplace sites along the Tokaido." Yet they offer him the potential to augment his income substantially. "We must always be on the lookout for good pieces at give-away prices," he commands Hiroshi.

The young man keeps his eyes open for opportunities to fleece those who might not know the value of what they possess. Such chances do not present themselves very often. However, he remembers the huge cache of prints owned by his mother, whose assemblage had begun with a large collection left behind by some courtesan who was murdered years before he was born. As a child, Hiroshi recalls seeing his mother leaf through the myriad prints that reminded her of the glory days of the Yoshiwara.

The prints would be easy enough to pilfer. He could return home and whisk them away before Yoshiko and Takao were aware what had transpired. For a week or two, he gives serious thought to this possibility but then discards it: they would know very well who committed the deed and would silently endure one more dastardly act from an ungrateful scapegrace.

Gradually, another, more complicated scheme asserts itself. What if he returned to the Yoshiwara, made his way to his mother and aunt, and then asked to borrow the collection on the pretext that it would assist him in his ambition to become an artist? He would tell them he wanted to study the work of the masters in detail in preparation for becoming a woodblock artist.

If this ploy is successful, he would use his hard-won skills to make copies of them that could be passed off as originals. Such a scenario would allow him an entertaining challenge. If it worked, that would be wonderful. If it failed, he would have at least occupied his time in an amusing way. In any event, he would return the prints to his mother.

Hiroshi muses on his plan for about a month, then decides to act. He proposes to Gotō that he and their friends visit the Yoshiwara the following week. There are so many beautiful geisha and courtesans in Tokyo that Gotō, who knows nothing of his friend's background, is hesitant. Hiroshi responds by rhapsodizing about the place that contains the most famous bordellos in all of Japan. He mounts further arguments. Their journey will take just over an hour. A visit to the Yoshiwara will be a wonderful novelty. Finally, Gotō's curiosity gets the better of him and so Hiroshi will return to his birthplace the following week.

CHAPTER TWENTY-FOUR

1894–1895

HIROSHI DOUBTS ANY of the guards at the entrance to the Yoshiwara will remember him. Not only is he older, but he dresses and wears his hair in the Western fashion. Just to make sure, the normally exuberant young man makes himself as inconspicuous as possible by walking with his head down, sandwiching himself between two of his companions at the rear of the small procession headed by Gotō. As they walk down the main street that Hiroshi sometimes crossed a dozen times in a single day, they are overcome by the scent of the cherry blossoms, which are now in full bloom this spring evening.

An exultant Gotō, who has already caught glimpses of dozens of entrancing, readily available young women, congratulates Hiroshi on his wonderful proposal that they spend a night here. True to the plan he has concocted, Hiroshi, a few minutes later, calls Gotō aside. Not only have the last few nights caught up with him, he explains, but he can feel a fever taking him over. In the light of that, he is going to return to Tokyo immediately. Unfailingly polite as always, Gotō, in between feasting his eyes on the courtesans, offers to accompany him. No need, Hiroshi assures him. The trip back will be relatively short, and he is going to take to his bed. Gotō nods reluctantly in agreement as Hiroshi quickly takes his leave.

For a minute Hiroshi walks back in the direction of the entrance-way and then turns to make sure that his friends are proceeding without him. Once he sees them laughing and joking outside one of the cages, he doubles back and heads in the direction of the Chōjiya, his mother's house.

If she is surprised to see Hiroshi, Yoshiko does not show it. She embraces him warmly and comments on how wonderfully he has grown into his good looks. "You are more handsome than ever!" Takao is not restrained. She bursts into tears while exclaiming how happy she is that he is safe and sound. In between her words of joy, she exclaims again and again her relief that he is well.

As is her custom, Yoshiko asks no questions. Takao has many queries. Where does Hiroshi live? What does he do for a living? What can she and Yoshiko do for him?

Hiroshi provides both women with a sanitized version of his life during the past seven years: in order to escape being imprisoned for his small part in the pilfering of goods from the Yoshiwara, he took off for Tokyo, where he lived a largely hand-to-mouth existence until he became the apprentice and factotum of the great artist, Yoshitoshi. After his death, he has had the great pleasure of working for Akiyama Takeemon. He has changed his name to Saigo.

Well aware of both Yoshitoshi and Takeemon, Yoshiko looks at Takao. Her face beams, as if to say, "I told you so." Although pleased with this turn of events, Aunt asks a lot of questions, all of which Hiroshi has anticipated and to which he has rehearsed answers. Takao is of a skeptical but tender habit of mind, and it is soon obvious that he has satisfied any doubts on her part.

Hiroshi looks around and notices that the Tamaya has fallen into serious disrepair. Some of the mats are badly torn, the corners of doors need to be reinforced or replaced by stronger wood. When he was a child, Yoshiko was particular about such matters. Hiroshi also perceives that his mother is frayed at the edges. She stoops slightly when she walks, her hair has greyed. Before, Takao always looked much older than Yoshiko. That is no longer the case. Aunt still carries herself well, as if she were an aristocrat.

When Hiroshi proposes to stay with them for a day or two, the two women are delighted. Takao rushes off to prepare a room for him. Only when he plies her with questions does Yoshiko admit that she and Takao are having a difficult time surviving. Men do not turn up in the large numbers they once did. The Yoshiwara is now a place that tourists from the provinces, staying in Tokyo, venture out to see. The place has become little more than a museum.

An upset Hiroshi then poses a difficult question. What about Lieutenant Eliot? Has she thought of getting in touch with him for assistance?

No, his mother replies. Tears gather in her eyes as she continues: he died five years ago. Mrs. Eliot, obviously a woman of good manners, wrote to tell her of his passing.

Takao's return silences Yoshiko. Hiroshi moves the conversation in the direction of his mother's prints. Would it be possible for him to take a look at them in the morning? Ever since he began working for Master Yoshitoshi, he has become fascinated by such woodcuts. Yoshiko is delighted. Yes, they will go through them together in the morning. If she is at all suspicious, Takao does not show it.

After Hiroshi had tired of hearing the stories about her life, Yoshiko's substitute for that activity had been to show him the prints. At those times, Hiroshi had been bored, especially when what he really wanted was for Takao to tell him a story.

Remembering the past, Yoshiko is surprised at how slowly Hiroshi and she now go through the woodcuts. He takes delight in the monumental, carefully posed actor prints by the first Toyokuni; he is knowledgeable about the often fugitive colours that are preserved in most of the prints she owns; he is moved by the lives of the women captured in the *bijin-ga* of Utamaro and Eizan: Yoshiko is amazed at her son's ability to speak with great assurance about the gentle sweetness in the faces of the great courtesans immortalized by these two men, her favorite artists. She is touched that her son takes such obvious delight in these objects that have given her so much pleasure.

Carefully holding them at their edges, Hiroshi lifts many of the woodcuts to the light so that he can see them better. He comments with assurance about such things as the carver's skill in rendering the lines of faces, the gauffrage or blind printing that gives texture to the *washi*, and particularly beautiful alignments of colours. My son has become quite a connoisseur after my own heart, the proud mother tells herself.

Hiroshi cannot help but admire the masterpieces in his mother's collection; at the same time he reflects that her taste is decidedly old-fashioned. She has no landscapes or warriors, genres that became popular in the 1830s, well before his mother was even born. Mother is, Hiroshi reminds himself, a traditionalist in every aspect of her existence.

Not wishing to arouse suspicion, Hiroshi waits two days before asking Yoshiko if he can borrow about forty of her masterworks. He would like to study them at leisure since the only way to learn about fine prints is to handle them on a daily basis. If she would consider this request, he would return them all to her within six months.

Takao is a bit suspicious, suspecting that Hiroshi might intend to sell them. "Those prints are the only things of value that your poor mother owns. They will go to you when she dies, but there is the possibility that she may have to sell a few in the next little while."

Hiroshi bows his head in complete agreement. He will compile a register of those items he has borrowed and will be certain to return them within the specified time. Not completely taken in by Hiroshi's assurances, Takao would have refused his request. The ever naïve Yoshiko, flattered that she has at long last found common ground with her son, urges him to take whatever he wants. During their polite exchanges, Hiroshi understands that his mother's frame of mind has become even more rigid than before. She dwells completely in the past.

Upon his return to Tokyo, Hiroshi decides on his first course of action. He will make a copy of one of his mother's finest prints: an Eizan. His first task is to search out a cache of *washi*, the old mulberry paper, of which the prints are made. This is a fairly easy thing to do. Then he buys some woodblocks of the finest cherrywood. His next job is to make the dyes. He cannot use any modern chemistry, such as the aniline ones now in widespread use. The duplication of colours almost a hundred years old proves his biggest stumbling block, but there are guidebooks that provide accurate recipes.

Finally, he is ready. First, he sketches all the lines of the Eizan and compares his work to the original. His work disgusts him. I don't know the first thing about drawing, he chides himself. For the next three weeks, he makes copy after copy until he is satisfied that he has penetrated the mind of the artist. Then, he transfers his best drawing to a woodblock. Once again, he is dissatisfied. Only on his fourth attempt does he make a decent key block. After that he makes rapid progress completing the rest of the blocks. His first prints do not look right, but his fifth attempt pleases him. If he places the genuine Eizan next to his own, he cannot see much difference.

If he is going to be successful, Hiroshi will have to fool a lot of people. Will his forgery be good enough to fox Takeemon?

CHAPTER TWENTY-FIVE

1896–1903

TAKEEMON IS LOOKING particularly wizened this morning. He has not slept well. His gout is acting up and no amount of medicine will ease the pain in his big toe. He hobbles badly before sitting down on the floor. He confesses to Hiroshi that he would not have consented to see him but for the fact that he claims to have found a genuine masterpiece.

Hiroshi explains that he came upon the stand of an *ehon* seller the day before yesterday. Since the illustrated books on display were of good quality, he asked the old man if he had any prints. Not really, the old gentleman replied, but he pointed to a stack of old newspapers and miscellaneous junk that had just been delivered to him. He told Hiroshi that he might have the pleasure of being the first person to sift through the material. Taking advantage of the offer, Hiroshi spent several hours probing this motley assemblage, mainly of trash, before coming upon a superb Eizan nestled among some humdrum prints. Keeping the Eizan from sight, he asked the cost of the lot and soon agreed to a price with the vendor.

Takeemon is in too much pain to question the accuracy of Hiroshi's story. In fact, he wants to be rid of his young assistant. He demands to see the print. With considerable flourish, Hiroshi removes it from his satchel and places it before his employer. The portrait of the courtesan is breathtaking. Of a sudden, the colour leaves Takeemon's face. This is exactly the kind of woodblock the foreigners in Switzerland and Germany are looking for, he exclaims. Then the old man recovers himself. He instructs Hiroshi to leave the print with him. There will be a special bonus, he proclaims, for this discovery. Takeemon has no intention of sharing any money with Hiroshi, who is very well aware of this fact. He leaves rejoicing. If he can fool Takeemon, he should be able to scam almost anyone.

Hiroshi the forger advances his new-found career slowly. His next project is a particularly rare Toyokuni of a kabuki actor dressed as a wood sprite. When he is ready to offer this print for sale, he chooses one of the Barbarians as his victim.

The Scotsman Graham Bruce has lived in Tokyo for almost thirty years and speaks Japanese without the trace of an accent. A small, delicate, bewhiskered man, who lives in a house on the edge of Ueno Park, he makes his living by collecting Japanese antiquities in order to sell them in Europe. Takeemon loves to joke about his old friend Bruce, particularly his clothing. This afternoon, Hiroshi understands why. First of all, food stains adorn the Scotsman's kimono. Second, he mixes Japanese and Western clothing indiscriminately. Over his kimono he wears a Harris tweed jacket; the crown of his head is adorned by the kind of headband usually worn only by samurai; thick black leather boots cover his feet.

If his clothing is a mishmash not so is Bruce's mind. He examines the print carefully for several minutes before uttering a word. He begins by saying that it looks completely genuine, but he has never heard of such a late-eighteenth-century Toyokuni. He is a bit suspicious of its authenticity because its colouring is so perfect. On the other hand, he knows of many early prints that have survived intact with the fugitive colours such as blue and purple as pristine as on the day they were printed. On reflection, he would like to buy the piece and offers a sum way beyond Hiroshi's wildest expectations. He is so dumfounded that he cannot speak, causing the Scotsman to add a third to his original offer. Having gained control of himself, Hiroshi nods assent.

During the next seven years Hiroshi becomes a wealthy man. After two further years in Takeemon's employ, he sets up in business by himself. As a dealer he now travels all over Japan in pursuit of lost ukiyoe and becomes famous for uncovering the most fabulous pieces. Hiroshi does buy a great many authentic pieces, which he is able to resell at high prices because of his consummate reputation. Having exhausted his need for his mother's prints, he has returned them to her.

Hiroshi's stock now consists of two kinds of ware: genuine ukiyoe and then his own versions of prints. Rather than the mere copying with which he began this undertaking, Hiroshi now invents Utamaros, Hokusais, and Hiroshiges. So perfect is his understanding of those masters that he is given great credit for unearthing long-lost masterpieces. A wise forger, he knows that the best way to hide one's duplicity is to have a stock salted with genuine articles. He cannot be held responsible if his customers think his own productions are superior to the real ones.

Of his faking, Hiroshi experiences neither guilt nor shame. He has become a master craftsman reproducing works of great beauty which give his customers great pleasure. What could be wrong with such a scheme? His renditions of the masterworks of others look so undeniably authentic because somehow he is able to penetrate to the core of the souls of the original creators. What does it matter that he reinvents the past so creatively? What wrong is he doing?

Hiroshi is soon hated by the other print dealers, who are convinced he is underhanded. How does he obtain such fabulous prints? When they inquire, he smiles shrewdly, his lips firmly sealed. A good professional, he implies, never reveals his sources.

Sometimes, Hiroshi's would-be villainy is arrested in its tracks. Once, visiting a collector living in Arashiyama, an hour outside Kyoto, he allowed himself, against his will, to be overwhelmed by a glimpse of the Japan of old and the Japan coming into being. There, the long wooden bridge reminded him of old Japan whereas the nearby railway station told him he could be back in the centre of Kyoto in less than an hour. From the bank of the Oi-gawa, he saw in the immediate distance the mountainside thickly covered with cherries and pine. The pines dropped steeply, allowing an excellent view at dusk and early evening of the local fishermen, firelights in hand and trained cormorants at their beck and call.

The village itself was a combination of old-fashioned and new-fangled modern buildings. Although the doctor's office remained a simple wooden stuccoed building, it had an elaborate arched entrance and doorway which, the architect had insisted, combined the best of Japanese and Western design. The Telephone Exchange, which housed all the other utilities, was completely made of white stone quarried in Jozankei. Yet this building had what Hiroshi knew was a

European look — consoles over the entrance doorway and upper-storey windows, arched windows below, and a patterned frieze running along the middle like a ribbon — in keeping with the aspirations of its French-trained architect. The tea house, the brewery, the butcher shop, and the market stall had been there for at least two hundred years. They were unimproved.

At the Tenryu-ji temple, in the centre of the village, he realized that, befitting its shape taken from the Chinese character *kokoro*, the pond was a place for the enlightened heart — or for anyone who seeks a state of bliss. At its edges, surrounded by small dark-red maples, nosy, bad-mannered carp stuck their heads out of the water. He was enveloped in an affectionate embrace by the smell of the plum trees that graced his path to the home of Suzuki-san.

The collector's house, surrounded by maple trees, was a simple enough but large two-storey affair. The two formal rooms were fourteen and twelve tatami mats apiece; tatami surrounded the irori hearth.

Hiroshi showed his host two genuine Utamaros. The old man liked both prints, but, he remonstrated, he had expected to be shown some Harunobu and Koryūsai. Apologetically, Hiroshi explained that he had sold those the day before. In reality, the young man, his mind whirling in response to all the beauty he has witnessed that day, did not have the heart to offer a fraudulent print to the trusting old gentleman, who settled for the two prints on offer.

Hiroshi took his time returning to Kyoto. He visited Mount Atago, the home of the fire god. He also stopped at Adashino Nenbutsu-ji, the desolate space where unclaimed corpses were deposited. He gasped aloud when he beheld the grave markers, rocks on which likenesses of the Buddha had been carved. The sight of row after row of these stone figures desolated him.

Great beauty and deep sadness, Hiroshi realized, had invaded him these two days outside Kyoto. He did not wish to resist the beauty, but the sadness was overwhelming. It is perfectly possible to have one without the other, he assured himself. He did not like the compassion for the old man that had asserted itself. That was bad for business. He resolved to turn his back on sorrow.

CHAPTER TWENTY-SIX

1903

A MAKER AND a faker. Hiroshi's considerable success renders him deeply vulnerable. Like all thieves, he is afraid that someone will unmask him. One night the twenty-nine-year-old has an unsettling dream in which both Takao's story of Kiyotsune and Yoshitoshi's woodcut portrait of the same young lord of the Taira clan are enacted. Hiroshi can hear his aunt's melodious voice at the very same time as the high stern of the warship of the doomed young man makes its way towards him.

Kiyotsune, very much a warrior-artist in the mould of Atsumori, was a gentle young man, very much like his own father Shigemori, a member of the Taira. His grandfather Kiyomori, the ruthless head of the clan, had great contempt for the mildness and restraint practised both by his son and grandson. In fact, Kiyomori's violence had often to be restrained by his son,

so bent on the violent spilling of blood was the old man in his bitter rivalry
with the Minamoto clan. Because of Shigemori, far fewer women of both
clans were savaged and raped; many innocent children from both sides were
wantonly murdered.

More of a poet than a fighter, Kiyotsune nevertheless left his wife at
home and joined the Taira forces on their westward voyage along the coast
of the Inland Sea. At Usa an oracle told him that all his efforts would prove
to be of no avail because the Minamoto finally would crush the Taira at the
naval battle of Dannoura.

A man not really made for living in this world, Kiyotsune was filled with
a paralyzing sense of despair. A few days afterwards, he took himself to the
top of the ship, where in the distance he could see fires alight on the other
ships of the Taira. He knew both his father and grandfather were dead.

Although gentle, the young lord was not cowardly. He knew his end
would soon be at hand, and he was not afraid to die. But he did not wish his
life to be extinguished in battle. And, as the last of his clan, he wanted
his death to be a memorial to a family that prized art as well as war.

Looking down from his perch, Kiyotsune took his flute and played a
haunting dirge that moved all the sailors and warriors aboard his ship to
tears. When he finished, the nobleman, drawing himself to full height,
plunged to his death in the water far below.

Kiyotsune may have been a good man, but his virtue was of little
avail to him. He may have had an honourable death, but he wasted
his life. These are Hiroshi's defiant thoughts when he awakens in the
middle of the night, his forehead beaded with sweat. In the dream,
the stern moved relentlessly towards him until he was about to be
impaled on it.

Despite his increasingly guilty conscience and nighttime tremors,
in daylight Hiroshi continues to meet greater and greater success in

his profession of dealer. Now he is a very fit companion for Gotō and the other wealthy young men. Like them, he dresses in the finest kimono. One or two of his new friends have even borrowed money from him. Drinking, whoring and more drinking: that is Hiroshi's nighttime existence. He has even moved to a small house of his own in the Ginza.

One night as he is about to enter a beer parlour not far from his home, Hiroshi catches sight a few doors down of a face illuminated in the yellow light of a street lamp. What captures Hiroshi's attention is the almost obscene sneer on the face of this person. Hiroshi continues on his way but then turns back as this man walks out of the shadows towards him, his hand extended. Only then does Hiroshi recognize Tedoya, whom he has not seen in more than a decade.

As they near each other, Hiroshi can see that his old friend is a bit taller than he and that his badly fitted clothes are frayed at the edges. He is probably down on his luck and anxious to borrow money, Hiroshi decides. Otherwise Tedoya would have contacted him earlier.

As before, Tedoya speaks with a silver tongue. He has been on the lookout for Hiroshi for many years but has never found him. "You have not come upon me because my name is now Saigo," Hiroshi informs him. Why is that? Tedoya wants to know.

Icily, Hiroshi tells him: "I would think you would have known that someone fingered me for our highjacking of sake and rice from the Yoshiwara."

An extremely solicitous Tedoya proclaims complete lack of knowledge of that event. Around that time long ago, his mother became extremely ill and in order to save on expenses, he and she moved a short distance away to Yokohama, where he lost contact with all his Tokyo friends. His mother died soon after the move, leaving him, a mere teenager, destitute. In the following years, he took whatever jobs came his way. He worked aboard a ship carrying food supplies up and down both coasts of Japan; then he took a turn at trying to become a blacksmith. Nothing suited him until he returned to Tokyo three years ago, where he now works as a lowly bookkeeper for an importer of foodstuffs. Such has been the ignominious way he has had to lead his life.

How does Hiroshi make his living? Tedoya then asks, obviously noting the fine garment in which his friend is clad. Omitting all incriminating details, Hiroshi tells him how he began working for Yoshitoshi and then Takeemon before setting up in business for himself. Rather impolitely, Tedoya asks how profitable his line of work is. Hiroshi brushes him off by replying that he is on the edge of becoming comfortable. In the darkness, Hiroshi can discern a hint of a snicker remaining on his old companion's face. He is also aware of Tedoya's eyes searching his face hungrily, as if hoping to find there the key to making his own fortune. He is wondering, the guilt-ridden Hiroshi tells himself, if I am up to no good. If I am, he wants to join me in the enterprise.

As they part, Tedoya asks Hiroshi if he might call on him: "Since we have so much in common, we should keep in touch." Hiroshi has no choice but to give him his address.

CHAPTER TWENTY-SEVEN

1903–1904

TEDOYA HAS TAKEN to turning up unexpectedly at Hiroshi's house. At first he arrives at supper time in hopes of cadging a meal. In the past month he has twice arrived in the middle of the day, usually when Hiroshi is busy manufacturing an eighteenth-century woodcut. Carefully locking the door to his workshop, Hiroshi answers the front door and invites Tedoya in.

Always Tedoya offers the same excuse. He has finished work early and is stopping off on his way home. His firm is just three streets away, and he is eager to re-establish their former intimacy. One day he confesses that he still has nightmares about seeing the blood-strewn corpse of Taye. Often he sees the Prince murdering his inamorata by stabbing her repeatedly and violently. In other nightmares, the angry lover strangles her; in others he drowns her by walking her to a pond, throwing her to the ground and then holding her head down in the water until she is dead. Sometimes, he simply sees the bloated corpse of Taye floating in blood-filled water.

Did that event change Hiroshi's life? he wants to know. His reaction, Hiroshi replies in a general way, has been a slow time in coming, although he is certain he has suffered in similar ways. What he does not know is that the long-ago murder of Taye has burrowed deep into his psyche, making it difficult for him to place trust in any human relationship. What Hiroshi is conscious of, however, is of wanting to rid himself of Tedoya. He would feel better if his childhood companion did not insist on renewing old ties.

In February 1904 Hiroshi has a strange encounter with Graham Bruce to whom he offers a very early Toyokuni I, a real one. A month before, while in Mashiko in northern Honshu, Hiroshi had, in that long stretch of a town filled with pottery shops, come across a dealer in antiquities who had two prints for sale, one was a badly discoloured and worm-eaten early Hokusai, the other an exquisite Toyokuni in pristine condition, all the fugitive colours intact. In this kabuki print, the villain hovers menacingly behind the heroine. Since the scraggly old vendor had only the vaguest notion of the value of this masterpiece, Hiroshi soon negotiated a very low price. This print he offered to Mr. Bruce.

Although reticent in the past, Mr. Bruce is positively garrulous today. He has always wanted to own one of Toyokuni's early and much-prized actor prints. The customer asks in considerable detail about the vendor and the town where the print was discovered. He also inspects the print with more care than normal, taking the unusual step of looking at every portion of it with a magnifying glass. "It is perfect, perhaps too perfect!" he finally exclaims. Not having yet given his client his price, Hiroshi waits for Mr. Bruce to ask.

Finally, the client broaches that delicate topic. Hiroshi asks for twenty times the amount he paid and is stunned when Mr. Bruce, who usually bargains him down, chooses not to haggle.

A few days later Hiroshi receives a puzzling note from Takao, addressed to him under his assumed name of Saigo: she and Yoshiko urgently need to see him. Can he visit with them on the following day?

Although he is preoccupied with putting the finishing touches to his latest masterwork, Hiroshi leaves for the Yoshiwara early on the following morning. When he arrives at the Chōjiya, the maid shows him into the largest reception room, where Yoshiko, Takao, a Western woman and a man with a mane of pale yellow hair are seated.

A deeply blushing Yoshiko rises and goes over to her son, whom she strikes in the face. Takao rushes to her side, motioning her to resume her seat. Attempting to restore a tone of civility, Takao informs Hiroshi that the lady is Mrs. Eliot, his father's widow. The gentleman seated by her side is her translator, Mr. Wiley. As soon as these introductory words are spoken, Kate Eliot rises and tells Hiroshi to be seated.

Still smarting from his mother's unprovoked attack, a perplexed Hiroshi is happy to sit down. Even for a Barbarian female, Mrs. Eliot is exceptionally tall, perhaps six feet. She is dressed in a bright-green plaid dress, a brown jacket with collar, lapels and sleeves of the same material as the dress and a brown straw bonnet on which sit, a bit uneasily, four peach-coloured roses. This ensemble had been the vogue in Boston a decade ago. In Japan her garment is in the vanguard of fashion. Particularly impressive is the enormous bustle that makes it precarious for her to sit on the floor.

Looking in the direction of Yoshiko, Mrs. Eliot begins to speak. She paces herself: one minute for herself, one for the translator.

Mr. Wiley listens attentively, takes in what she says, and then, after a few moments digesting it, renders it into fluent Japanese. This cumbersome process results in the widow Eliot taking a long time to tell her story.

When Lieutenant Eliot died, she wrote to his other wife to inform her of the sad event. That letter began a correspondence which has been going on for about fourteen years. As a widow, Mrs. Eliot had little to occupy herself since her late husband, her chief cause for existence, was no longer with her. Therefore, she was grateful when Yoshiko and Takao invited her to visit with them in Japan. She stops. She was delighted to undertake this journey even though she was fully aware of the nature of the City of Night, as she prefers to call the Yoshiwara.

Thinking that she may have given offense with that remark, she continues as if she had not made it. When she arrived in Tokyo, Mrs. Eliot was immediately in touch with all the American diplomatic and consular officials, many of whom hail from Boston. At a supper party three days after she arrived, she overheard the wife of the Ambassador telling a friend that a most intriguing mystery was under investigation. It seemed that a young man of doubtful family — she interrupts herself to apologize: that is exactly what was said — was being investigated by the Japanese police for selling exorbitantly expensive woodcut forgeries to Americans and other foreign nationals. Knowing full well from what Yoshiko had told her that Hiroshi was a dealer in such material, her ears pricked up. Although the Ambassador's wife did not know the man's name ("All their names are so strange and unpronounceable, dear," this woman had told her listener), she was certain it began with the letter H.

Her curiosity now thoroughly aroused, Mrs. Eliot called on the Ambassador the following afternoon. That gentleman, reluctant to divulge information confidential in nature, attempted to put her off. "Everything will be known in good time, Madam." At that point, the widow mentioned that she had heard a great deal the previous night from the lips of his wife. The Ambassador blushed, but he was not going to budge. Finally, she played her trump card. Was he aware that her brother was Secretary of State? She intended to telegraph him in Washington that afternoon. All of a sudden, the demeanour of the interview changed, as if a thick morning mist had arisen in a split second.

The young man was, the Ambassador assured her, of marginal interest, although he was a half-caste with American blood. Indeed, his father had once been a member of their proud nation's navy. The fellow in question was called Hiroshi, and he had been unmasked by a man called Tedoya, a member of the secret police. This scoundrel Hiroshi had just the day before brazenly sold a terrible fake to Mr. Bruce, the renowned collector. Within the next day or two, he would be arrested and that would be the end of this trivial matter. He smiled and then drew a deep puff from his cigar.

Hiroshi's face has turned deep scarlet as he nervously snatches glances at his mother's tear-streaked face and the mask-like countenance that Takao assumes when she is trying to pretend she is not upset.

Mrs. Eliot continues. She at once explained to the Ambassador the full identity of the half-caste, whom she takes the liberty of calling her foster son. Finally understanding the real nature of his visitor's request for information and mindful of the identity of her brother, the Ambassador offers his assistance in any way he can. Thinking quickly, Mrs. Eliot tells him a lie: she has long been considering adopting her late husband's offspring; in fact, she has come to Japan for the sole purpose of removing him from what his mother has informed her is an increasingly degenerate way of life. Could the Ambassador — despite some minor infractions — allow her plan to proceed apace? A man who relishes the opportunity to display power, the Ambassador promises to erase all her foster son's misdeeds, provided she takes him immediately to the New World. He will gild the lily with the Japanese authorities by informing them that Hiroshi is an American citizen.

Mrs. Eliot now looks directly into the eyes of the miscreant and informs him that Yoshiko, Takao and she have devised a scheme, one they have no intention of negotiating. In two days, he will be leaving Japan with his mother and herself — Takao will be left in charge of the Chōjiya. From the port of Yokohama, they will sail to Southampton. The three of them will remain in England for six months or so, ample time for Hiroshi to learn English.

After that, Yoshiko will return to Japan whereas she and Hiroshi will continue on to Boston, where she intends to find work for him at the Museum of Fine Arts. She is an acquaintance of the senior Japanese curator, Okakura Kakuzō, who is in desperate need of someone to authenticate the legions of Japanese prints in their collection. Perhaps, she looks at him a bit spitefully, he will enjoy cataloguing that collection and, in the process, weeding out the fake from the real? For the first time since he set out on his life as an imposter, Hiroshi fully experiences the unsettling twin feelings of guilt and shame. He is not really sorry for what he has done, but he has been publicly humiliated. His face blushes a deep red.

PART III

THE AUTHENTICATOR

CHAPTER TWENTY-EIGHT

1904–1905

ALTHOUGH THE SHIP encountered bad weather for a few days out of Yokohama, the sea now restricts itself to the gentlest of tilts and the sun is resplendent. Life aboard HMS *Trafalgar* is idyllic. Hiroshi can see that his mother's normally good-natured, pacific demeanour has been restored. Mrs. Eliot nods and smiles in his direction whenever they encounter each other. The sea breezes have refreshed Hiroshi considerably, although he worries about what life in England and then the United States will be like.

A consummate organizer, Mrs. Eliot has instructed Mr. Wiley to give Hiroshi English lessons for two hours each morning in hopes that the six-week sea voyage will prove profitable in an educational way. Poor Mr. Wiley is extremely busy because he must translate for Yoshiko and Mrs. Eliot who take all their meals, including tea, together.

Tall and fair-haired, Mr. Wiley often looks harassed. Once a scholarship student at Harvard where he specialized in the languages of the Far East, he was delighted when, at almost a moment's notice, Mrs. Eliot summoned him to accompany her to Japan. As a poor student he had been the recipient of her largesse; she had paid his living expenses in Cambridge. He was anxious not only to be of service to her but also to fulfil his ambition of seeing Japan. What he did not reckon with was his employer's energy. Since every moment of her day has to be crammed full of good works, so of necessity are his. On the voyage out, he had given her Japanese lessons, acted as her amanuensis, and, in general, been her factotum. If her morning tea was too pale, he had to negotiate a solution with the kitchen crew. If her stateroom was cold, he had to ensure it soon became warmer.

Wiley does not like translating the confidences exchanged between Yoshiko and Mrs. Eliot. Sometimes, despite his best efforts, his face is flushed when he listens to what those women tell each other. His awareness of Hiroshi's career in crime embarrasses him. A secretive man of an elevated turn of mind, he would rather not know of the misdemeanours of others. Scholarly matters are one thing, personal exchanges another.

Hiroshi, Wiley soon discovers, is a brilliant linguist. He has no trouble retaining the increasingly large vocabulary lists his teacher assigns him each day. He seldom confuses tenses. He is masterful at absorbing idioms and putting them to use. He begins to read some of the books in the ship's library, including an awful potboiler called *Broken Blossoms*.

When he looks at Wiley's bespectacled face, Hiroshi cannot discern much of a personality in any of the four ice-blue eyes. His teacher is so blond that he might as well be an albino; he is so tall that he reminds Hiroshi of one of his new words — giraffe.

Many afternoons the two young men take tea together. At that time of day, Hiroshi answers Wiley's questions about Japan. He also quizzes his teacher about Mrs. Eliot. She is from one of the finest families of Boston. For some reason, these people are called Brahmins, a term Hiroshi thought referred to a class of high-born Indians. Although the widow Eliot spends her days in doing all manner of charitable deeds, her chief interest is in helping Italian and Jewish immigrant girls in obtaining an education and, in general, bettering themselves.

At the outset of the voyage, Hiroshi, seated across from her and his mother in the ship's lounge, saw many amiable pleasantries pass between the two women. A week later one afternoon, his mother broke down, tears assailing her pretty face. Hiroshi rose to comfort her, but Yoshiko got to her feet quickly and left the room. During the following week, the two women seemed at odds with each other, as if quarrelling. Mr. Wiley's face darkened considerably during these interviews. Then, a week later, the two women seemed closer than ever. They now walk everywhere hand in hand.

Knowing that Mr. Wiley is sworn to reveal nothing, Hiroshi does not ask anything about that matter. Instead, he asks the tutor about how Japan is seen in the West. He is assured, in the most general terms, that Japan is the "rage" in England and the United States. This vogue had crystallized twenty years before in *The Mikado* of Mr. Gilbert and Mr. Sullivan. This comic opera, of which Hiroshi has never heard, may have been a bit on the silly side, highly inaccurate as it was on Japanese life and customs, but it had called attention to kimono, cherry blossoms, and low wooden houses. Rather than quoting from the libretto (which he knows very well), Wiley limits himself to general observations. As a result of this operetta ("Not at the same level as grand opera") and the writings of the designer Dr. Christopher Dresser, he assures Hiroshi, anyone with a modicum of education is fascinated by Japonisme: the flat surfaces, the lack of perspective, the unusual colour combinations. Remembering his pupil's criminal past, the fastidious Mr. Wiley does not mention Manet, Gauguin, Toulouse-Lautrec and Van Gogh's "borrowing" of Japanese woodblocks in some of their most celebrated paintings.

Sheer relief. That is how Hiroshi describes his feelings to himself in some of his first words in English. He has escaped. Like some miraculous goddess in one of Takao's stories, Mrs. Eliot has rescued him. He vows never to allow himself to be entrapped ever again by his own greed — and cleverness.

The six weeks aboard ship pass swiftly. Hiroshi, now equipped to order meals in restaurants and ask directions from Hampstead to John O'Groat, disembarks with his mother and Mrs. Eliot at Southampton, where they say goodbye to Wiley, who is sailing to Boston in a few days.

The train taking Hiroshi and the ladies from Southampton to London is much more modern than any he has seen in Tokyo. From his window seat, he is amazed at the strange-looking houses and buildings in which these people live and conduct business. Equally outlandish are the pastures filled with sheep, the barges floating on the rivers and the canals, and the smoke billowing from the factories. As the train reaches the city, it passes through a neighbourhood obviously reserved for the poor: jagged walls, battered roofs, crowded gables, broken windows. Although he is used to many Western innovations, Hiroshi has only seen them piecemeal; now, surrounded by them, he is overwhelmed and appalled. Is he looking at the future of Japan?

Hiroshi's single room at the Savoy, next door to the suite shared by the two ladies, is enormous. He does not know what to do with so much space. On board the ship he was able to sleep in the small cramped bed in his stateroom; in his bed at the hotel his mattress is so soft and feathery that it makes his back ache. He takes to sleeping on the floor, leaving the bed, to the consternation of the maid, undisturbed.

Walking down the Strand near the Savoy is nightmarish. Even in Bricktown, the brick buildings did not tower over him to this extent. He is disgusted at the way shopkeepers attempt to entice passersby to look into their windows in order to be ensnared by the wares on display. He does not like descending by elevators and stairs deep into the earth in order to take the Underground. The streets themselves are crowded with horse-drawn carts. Unlike Tokyo, there are beggars, particularly children, everywhere. The air is smoke- and smog-filled. To him, London is a place of deformity of brick and mortar, deformity of mind and body.

Hiroshi is surprised not to find many remnants of home, although he has been led to believe he will. Many things might be said to be Japanese-style, he decides, but few are Japanese in feeling. For one thing, the fabrics of women's clothes have the look of kimono, but the lines of the dresses and coats are severe, clipped and pinched. They do not fall gracefully to the ground. Occasionally Hiroshi comes across a bright pink or a strong purple in a painting or an etching, but the overall effect is sombre. These barbarians create from darkness rather than light. For him this is the basic difference between West and East.

A visit to Oxford and nearby Kelmscott Manor depresses Hiroshi. The university town seems trapped in the past whereas Morris's home is filled with trinkets — painted metal caskets, four-poster beds with medieval Latin mottoes on the top panels, rush-seated armchairs, a reclining chair upholstered in chintz fabric with a strange yellow flower called a daffodil — that are said to be quintessentially Japanese in feeling but fail to remind him of home.

Despite her best attempts to hide behind a mask of uprightness, Hiroshi's charm quickly exposes that side of Mrs. Eliot's personality as a sham. And Hiroshi is relieved that he does not have to pretend to like her. He is beginning to fall under her gentle sway. Mrs. Eliot even reminds Hiroshi of Takao. Like her, she is a shrewd but sympathetic observer of the lives of others. To her son, Yoshiko remains a cipher. Her old affectionate ways have returned, but she remains distant, as if unconnected to him.

Hiroshi's conversational skills in English have reached the point where he can replace Mr. Wiley as the translator for the two women. So much of his time every day is spent with the two ladies, who, in his presence, exchange pleasantries. In the mornings, Hiroshi and Mrs. Eliot chat in English to the extent that he has acquired some of the harsh nasal tones of her Boston accent. Except for his slanted eyes, he has become the perfect American expatriate in London. He even has a new name. Henceforth, he will be known as Hiroshi Eliot, although the young man is not sure he wants his father's name to be affixed to his own.

CHAPTER TWENTY-NINE

1905

HIROSHI PERSPIRES FREELY during the performance of *Madama Butterfly*. In the end he sees little resemblance between his mother and Butterfly. The woman in the opera is filled to bursting with strong feelings about her family, the man who abandoned her and her child. She is a woman caught in the grip of her emotions. Although still very beautiful like the soprano on stage, Yoshiko has always concealed herself from him — and, he suspects, from everyone else. He has never really known the strange woman who gave him life.

I am very much my mother's son, Hiroshi reluctantly tells himself. I do not wish to be betrayed by the likes of my father. I do not wish to be butchered like Taye. I have always chosen to go my own way lest others trap me in their webs.

As he looks at Mrs. Eliot's face this evening, the worries that beset her are apparent. Once or twice, her face blushes red. Kate Eliot often tries very hard to pretend she is indifferent to vexing circumstances, but Hiroshi knows her well enough now to know that she is a bad actress.

And what about the mysterious Mr. Eliot? When did he die? What did he die of? No one has bothered to inform Hiroshi, although he has been careful not to inquire. For him his father is a permanent absence, someone who disappeared before he was born. How can he care for such a person? Why should he have any feelings — love or hate — for such a scoundrel? If they arise, Hiroshi promptly smothers them.

Yoshiko is tearful as she takes leave of her son and her friend. When Hiroshi kisses his mother, his thoughts are really of Takao in far away Japan. Kate Eliot embraces Yoshiko passionately, sadly aware that they will probably never meet again. "I shall take excellent care of Hiroshi," are her last words as she and Hiroshi walk up the gang-plank of the *Abraham Lincoln*, which will take them on their ten-day journey to Boston.

Hiroshi and Kate have become quite accustomed to each other, but they do not know each other well. "These few days at sea will allow us to talk freely," she tells him, almost as if issuing an order. Hiroshi is afraid that he will now be given all kinds of information he does not wish to know about his late father. Or, worse, Kate will confess all kinds of secrets about herself to which he will be ashamed to share. As it turns out, the lady has no intention of revealing any intimate details about her own existence. She makes only passing references to Mr. Eliot's career as a merchant banker, his membership in the best Boston clubs, and his untimely death at the age of forty-four. Only once does she allow a cutting remark to escape her lips: "He often wrestled with his conscience, and he always won."

No, Kate speaks at great length only of the good causes to which she devotes her life. Her absence from Boston means that she has lost contact with the women she helps and her fellow coadjutors in administering that charity.

"With great wealth comes great responsibility." That is Kate's favourite saying. In his mind Hiroshi rephrases that dictum: "With great wealth comes enormous guilt." Kate's chief interest is in assisting those unfortunate Italian and Russian Jewish women whose families are packed together in Boston's North End. The Irish, who make up the largest part of the population there, hate and taunt the newer immigrants. "Their lives are a constant battle," she tells Hiroshi. "The buildings there lack sanitary conditions — disease is rampant. I know of six families who live together in four crowded rooms with beds in every room, a small toilet in the cellar and plenty of bugs and enormous rats for company." Sometimes, supposedly kind gentlemen offer to assist these girls and, "of course, they lead them into lives of horrible sin."

Realizing she has inadvertently wandered into terrain that might embarrass her listener, Kate shifts directions. She has a number of projects dear to her heart: a "Little Housekeepers' Club" for twelve-year-olds; a "Current Events Club" for teenagers, a "Lily of the Arno Club" for Italian girls. One of her groups is devoted to avid readers who study books like *The Prince and the Pauper* and *Pinocchio*. "America is a country of great opportunities, and I wish to make these young women aware that their horizons, although clouded by poverty, can be made bright. By becoming interested in civic and economic affairs, they will naturally wish to become educated. If they are well-educated, they will eventually obtain material prosperity."

Although Kate does not like to talk about herself, she is obviously fascinated by her travelling companion and questions him about Tokyo. "In many ways it is much more modern than dear old-fashioned Boston. Once upon a time, my native city was the Athens of America." A smile crosses her face, she sniggers: "It is now called the Ass-end of America!" Taken by surprise by the witticism, Hiroshi laughs loudly. Kate follows his lead and, of a sudden, a new plateau in their friendship is reached.

Many of Kate's friends have moved to New York City to follow their husbands, all great captains of industry. She explains to Hiroshi that Boston's fall from grace followed in the wake of the Civil War, which ended forty years before. "Boston is a place of ancient money, merchant greed and impoverished workers." Lest she leave Hiroshi with too negative an impression, she assures him that the cultural life of Boston is still the finest in the New World. He will meet many people who share his interest in art.

Hiroshi is uncertain how prepared he is to confront yet another new culture. In the past eight months he has given thought to that curious, abstract English word, "redemption." That is what he needs to achieve. He must live in a new way, throw over the past and become a better person. Kate is trying to teach him by example, but he cannot follow in her footsteps. If he redeems himself, Hiroshi dares to hope, perhaps his guardian will allow him to return to Japan.

Although many of Kate's neighbours decamped a decade ago to Back Bay to build splendid houses on land reclaimed from the sea, she has remained constant to Beacon Hill, where she was born. As a child, she fondly remembers being the apple of the eye of the writer Louisa May Alcott, who lived only a block away. As the only child of her parents, the wealthy Fordyces, to remain in New England, she has retained possession of the family mansion on Louisburg Square.

The drawing room is ostentatiously beautiful. The white sofas are from the Federalist period, when Kate's forefathers became wealthy merchants, then vehement protesters against high taxes and, finally, Founding Fathers and patriots. Hiroshi admires the beautiful dark woods of which the mantelpiece, the side tables and chairs are made. In this room, Kate breathes easily, almost regally. Foster mother and adopted son spend most of the following three days together in this room. Their talk is of the Republic and how it was threatened by the Confederate States. With considerable sorrow in her voice, Kate tells how the valiant patriarchy of the North subdued the rebellious temptress that was the South. The Civil War may have ended forty years ago, Kate reminds Hiroshi, but its scars remain fresh.

Hiroshi stays with Kate for a week before moving to rooms around the corner on Pinckney Street, a much less elevated address. Kate, who is well aware that the young man will probably not tolerate direct supervision, has made this arrangement. She jokes with him: "I have arranged for you to be perched on the outer rim of the hub of decency."

Although Hiroshi misses Kate, he is delighted to shed the immediate trappings of wealth and takes to his fifth-floor garret room that is tactfully furnished only with tatami mats; he is glad, however, that there is a closet where he can store his clothes and luggage. This room — the most civilized habitation he has seen since leaving Tokyo — consoles him at the same time that it renders him homesick.

Unlike both Tokyo and London, Hiroshi finds Boston a compact city where he can roam freely. Wood, as in Japan, is much in evidence in the construction of the older buildings here — much more so than in London — and that comforts him. On Chestnut Street, he likes the simple modesty of the three houses that the enterprising and far-sighted Hepzibah Swan built decades before for each of her daughters. This mother was so solicitous about her offspring, he is told, that she restricted the sizes of the stables at the rear so that her daughters' views at the back of their properties would remain unimpeded. Hiroshi admires the statue of Christopher Columbus that dominates the tiny patch of greenery at the centre of Louisburg Square opposite Kate's house. Once or twice he wanders among the gravestones at the Old Granary Burying Ground. The Boston Common reminds him of the lost pleasure of promenades in the parkland around Ueno in the north part of Tokyo.

He especially enjoys taking the crowded tram from Beacon Hill to Cambridge, even though he has to stand up all the way. He overhears the most interesting snatches of conversation because most people assume the almond-eyed young man does not understand a word of English. Sometimes other immigrants — an Irish labourer or a Scottish housemaid — stare at him until he catches their eye, at which point they look away. Shopkeepers are jolted when Hiroshi speaks to them in perfect English, their faces criss-crossed with incomprehension: what sort of strange fellow is this?

If the people he passes on his walks are startled by his exotic appearance, they never show it. No one insults him or walks away from him, but he notices that blacks are referred to, sometimes politely, as "coloured," or "negroes"; more often they are called "niggers." Even well-dressed, respectable people use this derogative term; they also refer to Jews as "kikes". Bostonians are not tolerant of a Southern accent. Hiroshi discerns for himself that the Civil War has settled very few differences between North and South.

A Japanese gentleman, especially attired in the latest modern fashion, is such a small minority that he often evades close scrutiny and, thus, open contempt. The servants of the wealthy are the one group openly affronted by Hiroshi. They show their disdain by being more polite to him than they would be to a visiting Rockefeller or Carnegie.

Lest Hiroshi be tempted to take up with any riff-raff or to make bad use of his time, Kate has arranged for Mr. Wiley, as she puts it, to "show you the ropes." This idiom puzzles Hiroshi, though he knows exactly what she means.

In his home environment, Wiley, who is a year or two younger than Hiroshi, is even more a model of old-world propriety than he was on board the ship from Tokyo to London. Kate considers him a bit of a "stuffed shirt" (another idiom that gives Hiroshi trouble), but he has a "good heart" (by now, Hiroshi knows the considerable stock English speakers put in referring to that organ of the body).

As if doing his Japanese charge a great favour, Wiley tells him he may, if he wishes, call him by his Christian name, Harold. Not accustomed to intimacy of any sort, Wiley believes he is being generous to the pagan youth. The truth is that Wiley spends almost all his time in his room at Cambridge memorizing grammars of various Oriental languages. For the past month, Assyrian has claimed his undivided attention. Looking after Hiroshi is a necessary distraction if he wishes to retain the good opinion, and financial backing, of his patroness.

Unaccustomed to the company of others, Wiley is not certain where to take his former pupil. In daylight hours, there is Harvard College and its libraries and the various museums in Boston. The night hours are more difficult. He has heard some of his students talk of Billy Park's pub, where members of that elite group of aesthetes calling themselves "The Pewter Mug" congregate, and he decides to take Hiroshi there.

Park's is dark, crowded and filthy. Hiroshi is polite about the malt liquor he feels compelled to down as if he enjoyed it, but he is somewhat astonished at the Elizabethan twang his now sharply tuned ear can discern in the voices of the men there. (He realizes that the Shakespeare-sounding language is affected, but he does not yet completely understand how it is so different from the language he has been trying to master for almost a year).

At pains to find something to speak to Hiroshi about, the pedantic Wiley discourses on his own devotion to White Rose Day, as the feast day of King Charles the Martyr is called in the Book of Common Prayer. The celebrated Mrs. Gardner, whose museum-home, Fenway Court, opened a few years before, commemorates this event with an anniversary supper at her establishment. On such occasions, she is costumed as Mary, Queen of Scots. Last year, when he had the privilege of an invitation, Wiley had appeared, to his hostess's delight, as Sir Walter Raleigh.

When Hiroshi loses track of a conversation, he takes pains to conceal his bewilderment by lapsing into uneasy silence. He has no comprehension of the strange religious rites that are being praised. He has become very drunk, and maudlin feelings take him over. He simply nods and shakes hands with the few men to whom Harold introduces him.

He is rattled by the hostile stare given him by one of these persons — a tall, dark-haired, black-eyed man by the name of Peter Wyman, a former student of Wiley's. If a smile can ever be said to be malevolent, that would be the correct word to describe that look.

CHAPTER THIRTY

KATE ELIOT HAS become positively kittenish in Hiroshi's presence. She and her foster son laugh and joke freely before the fire in her sitting room two or three nights a week. She has also become very catty. In talking of Isabella Stewart Gardner, she says: "She is a source of great vexation." Immediately, she adds by way of explanation: "She was, you know, born in New York City!" When a very amused Hiroshi informs her that she is speaking nonsense, she concedes he has made a good point.

There is no doubt that Mrs. Gardner remains a conundrum to Kate — and to many other members of her class. At one event the previous year at which she was present, Kate tells Hiroshi: "Isabella was costumed as Cleopatra, tightly swathed round and round with layers of gauze, gold-embroidered. Around her neck was a diamond and ruby necklace; ropes of pearls adorned her neck. But it was her head that caused all of us great concern. *Everything* was covered but her eyes. She was enwrapped in soft mull as tight as a bandage! Two huge diamonds, held by strings of jewels with a pendant in the centre, hung just above her nose!"

The lady's streak of exhibitionism irks the deep Puritan streak in Kate, who adds: "Her motto is 'C'est Mon Plaisir.' One does not advertise oneself that way in Boston." Torn between contempt and affection for another society woman, she feels compelled to tell Hiroshi: "Isabella has done a great deal to keep the culture of this city intact. I do not know how to read her. I suspect you will have many opportunities of forming your own opinion from first-hand observation."

On the following day, Hiroshi is to report to Okakura Kakuzō at the Boston Museum of Fine Art on Copley Square. Kate reminds him that his countryman and Mrs. Gardner are close friends, although she has no idea why they should be attached to each other. "Did you ever meet Okakura in Japan?" she asks him.

Hiroshi, who is ten years younger than his new boss, has heard a great deal about him but has never encountered him. "I am not a serious person, and he is reckoned a formidable intellect." A wry smile crosses Kate's face; she obviously disagrees with this self-analysis.

Hiroshi feels like adding that Okakura, like himself, has been forced into exile. If he were to state this fact, he would have to add that his countryman is not, like himself, a thief. No, Okakura no longer lives in his native land because he is a great patriot who insists that Japan — and other Asian countries — create their own art out of their individual cultures rather than slavishly imitating American and European art. The government in Tokyo is so hostile to such nationalistic sentiments that, ironically, Okakura has had to emigrate to the United States to further his mission by writing and speaking in flawless English on the controversial topic of Pan-Asian art. In fact, Okakura has landed in Boston because the previous — but still influential — curator of East Asian art, Ernest Fenollosa, insisted he be hired as the principal cataloguer of the museum's Japanese and Chinese collection.

Okakura has a purpose to his life, Hiroshi believes. Will he catch the fire of patriotism from his fellow exile? Hiroshi doubts this will happen: he has, after all, never been able to think beyond his own selfish needs.

On his walk through the Common on the way to Copley Square on this bright June morning, Hiroshi remembers hearing that Okakura is so committed to his ideals that he has no time for pleasantries. A stickler for detail, he is an insatiable, tetchy master. His time at the Museum will be a trial, Hiroshi is certain, but he resolves to do his best in a difficult situation.

Upon his arrival at the Museum, Hiroshi is directed by one of the guards to the offices on the top floor. As he walks up the grand set of stairs, he is appalled to be stared down at by Gilbert Stuart's high-minded portraits of the great American leaders. The staunch, no-nonsense countenances of presidents and merchant princes warn him that no infractions of responsibility will be tolerated, for even a single moment.

The door to which Hiroshi has been directed is open and so he wanders in. The room itself is enormously long, more like a corridor than a work space. He has arrived so early that empty desk after empty desk greets him. He decides to walk to the end of the room, where he views the assortment of Japanese brush-paintings on the wall. He becomes completely absorbed by these until he notices the reflection in the glass of someone standing behind him.

Unless he knew it for a fact, he would never have believed that the man before him is only a decade older than himself. At the age of thirty-two, Hiroshi looks like he could be in his early twenties. The man he is now inspecting looks old enough to be his father. It must be the pouches under his eyes that make Okakura-sensei look so old. Like Hiroshi, Okakura is slim and his hair, jet black, is parted neatly down the middle in the Western style. No, it is not the bags under his eyes, Hiroshi of a sudden realizes — it is the sorrow that infiltrates every aspect of his countenance.

One of the crucial differences between the two men this morning has little to do with age. As is his custom, Hiroshi is dressed in a Saville Row suit of the finest wool. Although he has allowed himself to be corrupted in the way he wears his hair, Okakura always wears a kimono. Hiroshi wonders if his master will censure him for having abandoned the traditional style of dress.

Having evaluated Hiroshi for a moment or two with his habitual look of melancholy, a huge smile now crosses Okakura's face as he bows to his fellow countryman. He then opens his arms and embraces Hiroshi in a bear hug. Startled, Hiroshi almost attempts to struggle free before surrendering to this American display of affection.

Okakura, it turns out, has been eagerly awaiting Hiroshi's arrival. There are thousands of Japanese prints that require cataloging and this is a subject about which Okakura knows almost nothing. He is deeply grateful that Hiroshi "has chosen" to assist him. Without seeming to allude to the route by which his new coadjutor has reached Boston, he lowers his voice slightly to confide that he suspects the Museum has many fakes on its hands. It will be a part of Hiroshi's job to separate the goats from the sheep.

For a long time, the prints have been weighing on Okakura's conscience. Not only is he delighted to be rid of that burden, he is also happy to have a fellow countryman with whom he can speak Japanese. The great joy for Okakura is that he will have more time to accept speaking engagements in which he educates his American listeners on contemporary Japanese art, on how it must be allowed breathing room. He will also have more time to write; he is now completing the sequel to *The Ideals of the East*.

Without the slightest hint of condescension, he tells Hiroshi he is happy to place the eighteenth- and nineteenth-century Japanese ukiyoe in Hiroshi's "very capable" hands while he devotes himself to the cares of the present century. Correctly, Hiroshi understands that the world of the woodblock prints — filled as it is with pictures of actors and courtesans — has no part in Okakura's "ideal" Japan. For him, these pictures are about servitude, corruption and the evils of the past.

Hiroshi had suspected Okakura would place him on probation, watch over him carefully. This is not the case. Hiroshi has his own job to do and must accomplish it as he sees fit. The Master will be happy to assist in any way he can, but, as far as he is concerned, Hiroshi is his own boss.

Okakura issues one injunction. Within the next few weeks, he wishes Hiroshi to call upon Mrs. Gardner at Fenway Court. Okakura has mentioned him to her, and she would be delighted to receive him. Perhaps he should write to make an appointment? That lady, a great connoisseur of Western art, has the capacity to make him aware of an immense repository of culture of which he might otherwise remain ignorant.

Later that morning, Hiroshi begins to inspect one of the many large morocco leather-bound containers filled with ukiyoe. The prints have been gathered from many sources, although many of them were hand-picked by Ernest Fenollosa a decade earlier. Some are recent acquisitions, including a horizontal *ōban* of his mother by Kiyomine. As he inspects masterpiece after masterpiece that first morning, Hiroshi comes across a Hiroshige of his own devising. Punctured by this reminder of a past he is anxious to erase, he places that print in a folder he labels "FAKES".

CHAPTER THIRTY-ONE

———

1908

IF HIROSHI'S DAYS are often boring, the same cannot be said for his nights. The dreams begin simply enough. In one he is sleeping on his mat when he awakens to see a huge gleaming white skeleton, as large as fifteen men, leaning over him. He struggles to find a sword, but the monster rushes forward with his two bony hands to restrain him. As he stares at the creature, its eyes begin to pulsate menacingly. Hiroshi tries to wrestle himself free but is powerless against the monster. His struggle with the creature goes on for a long time but finally comes to a conclusion when Hiroshi manages to pull himself to consciousness.

That one is almost comical in comparison to those that follow. In one, he is alone with his mother, who looks very much like her ordinary self. Suddenly her appearance changes. She is almost completely bald. Then, her right eye looks up while the other, much larger than the other, is swollen shut. Even in his dream Hiroshi remembers the plot of *Yotsuya kaidan*, one of the kabuki plays that frightened him as a child.

There are other nightmares. He is in a small village somewhere in Japan. The sky, the earth, the trees, the shops and the inhabitants are the brightest colours imaginable: deep blues and oranges, translucent greens, garish pinks. Hiroshi is delighted to be in such a wonderful place. He then wanders up a set of stairs and into someone's chamber. Wandering over to the bed, he looks down at the blood-smattered corpse of his father. One of his eyes is missing. Blood from the empty socket oozes freely.

When daylight comes, Hiroshi tries to push the dreams away by not thinking about them. My fiendish parents wish to avenge themselves on me, he tells himself. I shall not give them that satisfaction. They have no right to haunt me. If anyone has the right to harbour rage-filled thoughts, it is me.

The nightmares make it difficult for Hiroshi to rest soundly. Tired and disgruntled during the day, he cannot look forward to the solace of sleep.

After careful deliberation, Hiroshi resolves to make peace with his parents. Now, when he sees Yoshiko in a dream, he does not try to resist her. Instead, seeing paper and pen set out before him and exercising control over the pen, he creates an image of his mother as she actually looked the last time he saw her.

With his father, the process is impossible. With considerable difficulty, Hiroshi finally draws the face of a handsome Westerner, in appearance like the portraits by Winslow Homer he had seen in Boston. Just as this drawing is completed, it disintegrates, whereupon a distraught Hiroshi awakens. No matter what I do, Hiroshi wonders, will I ever make peace with Lieutenant Eliot?

When he inspects himself in a mirror, Hiroshi sees an ordinary man looking back at him. He has been told countless times that he is handsome, but he does not believe this to be true. I wonder if I cannot look at myself properly because my father never taught me how to do so? He scoffs at this interpretation as ridiculous.

Sometimes, however, when looking at his own reflection, Hiroshi can feel a presence behind him. He speculates that this might be the ghost of his father, but he also brushes this thought aside.

CHAPTER THIRTY-TWO

1909

ONCE HIS TIME is no longer eaten up supervising the move of all the prints — and many other Far Eastern treasures — from Copley Square to the Museum's new home on the Fens, Hiroshi has more time to devote to a crucial responsibility: the cultivation of wealthy collectors of Japanese prints so that their holdings eventually find their way into a permanent home at the Museum.

The Spaulding brothers — William Stuart and John Taylor — have been collecting for less than a year and have over a thousand prints! These merchant princes, who do not do anything in a small or unostentatious way, finally — after intricate negotiations — invite the new curator to visit them. "We are sure you are anxious to examine our holdings, and we are eager to inspect you."

When he arrives at the Spaulding mansion on Beacon Street, Hiroshi is shown by the butler to a large sitting room-cum-office, where the two brothers sit across from each other. Their desks are identical, as are the tickertape machines on each, and the light grey suit-coats and dark-blue cravats in which each man is attired. Forty-four-year-old William is five years older than John, but the two look like identical twins. The faces of both men appear completely drained of blood; their noses are like owl beaks; their small blue eyes are recessed, shrewd and anxious.

They speak slowly and deliberately to the young Japanese man until they realize his English is perfect. Then they mercilessly quiz him on his knowledge of Edo publishers and on the various signatures found in the work of the first Toyokuni. Satisfied that they are dealing with a genuine expert, they ring a bell, a signal for four hefty footmen to enter the room, each carrying a huge wooden box.

"We are delighted to show you our treasures," John declares. William adds: "Only a rare few are allowed to view our plunder." The two men laugh as if a particular witty *bon mot* had been uttered. Then, exchanging glances with each other, they realize that such a remark might not be best uttered to someone from Japan.

Putting aside such doubts, they command the manservants to deposit the contents of all four boxes in four neat piles, two to each desk. After their helpers have left the room, John asks Hiroshi to go through the first pile with him. Since he allows only a second or two for each print, Hiroshi cannot really get a good measure of what he is seeing, although he glances approvingly at many beautiful prints.

Neither brother spends any time with individual prints except to remark on colour and impression. "Here the colour is as fresh as on the day of publication," William points out. "In this Harunobu, the key block and every one of the six colour blocks touched the paper in exactly the right way," observes John. The subject matter of the prints is of no interest.

Hiroshi interrupts the progress of the two brothers through the third pile by asking to examine two remarkable kabuki *chūbans* by Shunshō — a distraught husband about to confront his adulterous wife, a woman about to commit murder. The brothers look on impatiently as Hiroshi lingers on the pair; as far as they are concerned, he is delaying progress and thus wasting their precious time. For these two men the prints are units of measure — bars of gold — in which rarity and money are the only important things. The materialism of the Spauldings appalls Hiroshi. These are the kinds of persons he once did not mind cheating.

Okakura-sensei has asked Hiroshi to open negotiations with Miss Smith for the acquisition of her collection, which the lady has hinted she intends to will to the museum. His superior promises Hiroshi that Miss Smith is very different from all the other great Boston collectors. For one thing, her collection is limited to Sharaku. For another, although she is a recluse, she runs a huge business empire from a small office on the ground floor of her home. "She is a strange woman but one of indomitable spirit," Okakura observes in his enigmatic way. He then adds cryptically: "She has had great need of courage in the face of the adversity life has thrown at her." Hiroshi is not certain how such a successful and wealthy person has confronted major obstacles in her path through life.

Yoshiko possessed only a few examples of Sharaku because, even as a young girl, she found his work repulsive. She has never liked life as it really is whereas Sharaku was overly concerned with truthfulness. This particular artist was the only major ukiyoe artist Hiroshi had never dared to forge.

If he thinks in terms of the English literature of which he is now an avid reader, Sharaku, in Hiroshi's imagination, occupies a position above the murdered Christopher Marlowe but slightly below that of Shakespeare. The identity and daily life of Sharaku are even more shadowy than that of Shakespeare. From May 1794 until early January 1795, he was enormously productive: 145 known individual woodcuts and eighteen drawings. According to one source his real name was Saitō Jūrōbei and he lived in the Hachōbori section of Edo while he was a Nō actor in the troupe of the Lord of Awa.

Since Sharaku's style bears a close resemblance to that of the Osaka master Ryūkōsai than to any Edo printmaker, he has been said to have been born in Osaka. Also, many of Sharaku's prints are of Osaka actors who performed in Edo. These men may have been his friends. There is another intriguing piece of evidence. The Lord of Awa arrived in Edo in April 1793, left the following April and then returned a year later. If, as is likely, Sharaku did not have to travel with his master, he would have been free to explore his talent for printmaking.

Many scholarly busybodies have denied the Lord Awa connection and suggested that Sharaku was, among others, the artist Hokusai, the artist Toyokuni I, the artist Kiyomasa, the artist Utamaro, the publisher Tsutaya Jūzaburō, and the haiku poet Sharaku of Nara.

The next mystery is why Sharaku's career as an artist was so brief. Did he have to leave Edo in the Lord of Awa's troupe? Were his prints unpopular with the public? Did he fail to depict actors as they wanted to be seen — and as the audience wanted to see them? Other theories are rife. He was really an *onmitsu* — a spy — and his talent during his brief career can be explained by his training to look at other people realistically and thus without the smallest tinge of sympathy. Others believe he was murdered, either by a group of kabuki actors or by their managers. By showing the actors as they really were, he was robbing them of the allure and glamour so necessary to that profession. Something had to be done to stop him. Perhaps Miss Smith has opinions on these complex matters? After they have exchanged letters twice, Hiroshi is invited by her to visit her collection at her home on Beacon Street, three doors away from the Spauldings. The collector phrases her missive as to suggest that she herself is of incidental importance; she would in no way wish to intrude herself between Hiroshi and the masterpieces that interest him.

The Smith home is constructed in the manner of a Florentine-style palazzo, a suitable home for someone of ducal status. The enormous downstairs public rooms and long gallery are crammed with eighteenth-century English and French furniture — mainly made of mahogany, large Chinese porcelain fish-bowls, and armour from East and West. Miss Smith, who is about Kate's age Hiroshi guesses, is nondescript: she is tiny, pasty-faced, and wizened. Her chartreuse frock, although it is of the finest silk, is slightly frayed. No prints are on display; indeed, no work of art of any kind graces the small reception room to which the manservant shows him.

After Miss Smith and Hiroshi have exchanged pleasantries, the manservant returns with a substantial, *ōban*-size collector's box. Would Hiroshi like to look at the pictures by himself? She will be happy to retire to the next room. When Hiroshi asks her to stay, Miss Smith seems surprised but nods her head in agreement.

The prints are arranged — the only complete set in existence — in what the owner considers the correct chronological sequence. Since Yoshiko had owned only four Sharaku and the others he had seen were reproductions, Hiroshi works his way slowly through the collection. Sharaku was, Hiroshi can see, an excellent observer of surface detail, the eyes, eyebrows and mouths of his actors are rendered in bold, thick lines whereas thin, delicate ones are used to portray other facial features. Unlike an artist such as Toyokuni, Sharaku had comparatively little interest in costume; his colours are earthy: browns, blacks, dull reds.

Sharaku's actors are show-offs who call attention to themselves; some by a particularly outrageous *mie*, their eyes cross-eyed ostentatiously; some use their large lips to arouse interest in an audience; some know that a slight flicker of an eyelid is a sure way to rivet attention; some realize that exaggeration of a nostril or an eyebrow is the actor's only real route to worldly success. All exhibitionists, each of them discovering his own way to perform his job splendidly.

Incised into each countenance is a deep and haunting loneliness; they have done everything within their power to achieve worldly success, but each of these faces is filled with desolation. Behind the surface Sharaku's actors are world-weary and sad. The pursuit of the limelight has been a tedious process; the search for fame has been merely a path to disillusionment and dismay.

Patiently and timidly, Miss Smith studies every face with Hiroshi, almost as if she is beholding the images for the first time. Often, she smiles benignly, soothed by the presence of great art.

Hiroshi is anxious to quiz his host on the enormous questions that confront all students of Sharaku. Why did he make prints for only ten months? Was he murdered? Did he move away from Edo? Did his talent dry up? Was he discouraged because no one would purchase his work?

Miss Smith is used to such questions, having been asked them many times before. "No one believes me," she hesitates, almost wearily. Then an air of confidence enters her voice, "but I think he did all he wished — or was capable of — and then stopped. That's why I think there are so few Sharaku."

"So there is not really that much of a Sharaku mystery?"

"Exactly. So stunning and mysterious is the accomplishment of a Shakespeare or a Sharaku that we lesser mortals are inclined to search out clues that will help us comprehend them. In the process, we create many Shakespeares and many Sharakus."

Miss Smith pauses. "I think that both these men may have lived ordinary lives devoid of glamour. That is why so little evidence survives about them. If I am right, all their creative juices are simply in their works. The truth lives there. The men themselves simply disappeared."

She pauses for dramatic effect: "I myself have been guilty of a horrible misconception. Until very recently I have not understood how all great artists are majestic liars and cheats."

Hiroshi is astounded. "How can they be liars and cheats?"

The lady shrugs her shoulders. "From the matter-of-fact world of ordinary life they create works of elaborate beauty that make us believe our existences mean something."

"And don't they mean something?"

Looking around her, Miss Smith smiles slyly. "Perhaps, but it is the artists who make us aware of such possibilities." She halts, as if unsure of exactly what she wishes to say. "If artists did not produce dream worlds, we would not have places to live with any semblance of comfort."

Having completed their examination of the prints, Miss Smith suggests they might take tea in her sitting room.

In that room, Miss Smith becomes a different person. For one thing, she must deal with pressing business concerns. Four young men — secretaries — arrive together, all with urgent questions. Although she is the greatest importer and distributor of coffee beans in the world, she has never set foot in her firm's warehouses. In fact, she has never tasted a drop of coffee in her entire life. She learned her father's business at his feet and, after his death, simply continued managing the company from home. Calmly, she tells one young man to refuse an offer from Brazil — the price is simply too high and, in a day or two, she is certain the price will be lowered. Perfunctorily, she issues similar commands.

When her assistants withdraw, the lady proposes that she and Hiroshi drink green tea, a proposal to which the young man responds eagerly. After a servant pours out their beverages, Miss Smith asks her guest if he has settled into life in Boston. "With considerable difficulty," he says. She nods her head sympathetically. "I once spent ten months in Japan, and the memory of your homeland's beauty has never erased itself from my heart. In fact, I should like to have remained there." She adds: "In permanent exile."

Without skipping a beat, she observes, as if taking the conversation in a logical direction: "I was a great disappointment to my parents. I was a girl when a boy was wished for. I paid heavily for my inadequacy. I was named Magdalene. What a name to give a young girl — the name of the woman of easy virtue whose pitiable life was transformed by the Saviour! As a youngster, I was teased mercilessly."

As if she had against her own will transgressed her own privacy, she quickly moves the subject away from herself. "Which of the ukiyoe artists do you most admire?" On reflection, Hiroshi informs her, that artist is Utamaro. She frowns. He has answered incorrectly.

Only when he is walking back to Pinckney Street does Hiroshi understand that Magdalene Smith must be M. Smith, the author of *Bitter Blossoms*, the sentimental novel about the daughter of Utamaro. That book — he remembers its lavender-coloured spine on board the ship's library from Yokohama to London — was innocuous enough. The story line — completely made-up — concerned Sachie, an illegitimate offspring of the great artist. The novel would have passed into justified oblivion had M. Smith found a publisher in America. Unable to do so, she posted the manuscript to Macmillan in London, where the book was taken up with great aplomb. Less than a year after submission, the book was published to dismal reviews. To add insult to injury, the publishers lost the manuscript. When they wrote to apologize, the author — distraught at the way she had been mauled by the critics — cared not a whit.

There the matter rested for two years until a sensational murder took place in Kyoto. A Parisian print dealer shot dead a competitor from Amsterdam. Under investigation, it turned out that the Dutchman had journeyed to Japan in pursuit of some hitherto-unknown Utamaro portraits of courtesans, a whole series of twenty splendid *ōbans* previously unknown but secreted in the ancient capital city. Having heard of his rival's activities, the Frenchman had followed him there and, in a moment of rage when his rival refused to tell him what he had discovered, shot him dead.

The list of the missing Utamaros was found on the corpse of the murder victim, who had not located the prints. As it turned out, there were no prints to find. Somehow or other, a page of M. Smith's manuscript — separated from all the other pages — had found its way into the hands of a London printseller, who had contacted the Parisian. That sheet of paper listed — in minute but completely fictional detail — the series of twenty prints, paying especial attention to the name of each courtesan and her house of assignation.

Without the consolation of even the merest hint of literary success, Miss Smith had inspired a murder. Any desire she had entertained of returning to Japan was quashed. In fact, her sense of shame was so enormous that the lady never again left her Beacon Street home.

"Magdalene's life has been cursed. There is no other way to put it." This is Kate's assessment of her childhood friend's existence. "As a girl, she was strong and impulsive but very loving. She tried to dote on those miserable parents of hers, but they would have none of it. Her mother was what the doctors called 'anemic.' She was bone thin, never smiled and seemed to inhabit a permanent state of gloom. Her husband worried about her. I am sure that Mr. Smith blamed Magdalene for the bad health his wife endured, from pregnancy until her death when Magdalene was but a child of sixteen.

"As a teenager Magdalene spent her every waking moment at her father's side. His huge mutton-chop whiskers made him look like a disgruntled walrus. All of Magdalene's friends, including myself, were terrified of his snarling temper."

Colonel Smith — he liked to be called such from his days spent fighting in the Union cause — was determined that his daughter fulfil his dead wife's responsibilities as a hostess. He also demanded that she learn everything there was to know about his business affairs. Magdalene accompanied Colonel Smith to Japan because he decided he must absent himself from Boston to rid his mind of his dead wife. He was of the opinion that removing his daughter from all her friends would be some sort of well-merited punishment.

"If that was Colonel Smith's plan, it backfired," Kate continues. "Magdalene loved Japan. She adored the winters and even cherished the sweltering hot days of July and August, when she and her father took refuge in the Japanese Alps.

"She blossomed in Tokyo. She became fascinated with that strange genius, Sharaku. She had been from childhood an avid reader, and she had long cherished the idea of writing a novel; given the conditions of her sequestered existence, she wrote *Bitter Blossoms* by candlelight during the only hours her father left her in peace.

"Colonel Smith died unexpectedly while father and daughter were on a train taking them from Kyoto to Tokyo. After having made arrangements for the body of her father to accompany her on the next available crossing from Yokohama to Boston, she took leave of your native land. She vowed, she told me, to return within two or three years. You have figured out what happened next."

"Her life was one of broken dreams as well as bitter blossoms?"

"That is an apt way of putting it," Kate tells Hiroshi. "Life may have offered Magdalene great wealth, but it gave her nothing more. From birth she was an outcast."

CHAPTER THIRTY-THREE

1911

FINALLY, GATHERING UP the courage to face yet another Boston collector, Hiroshi, after putting the matter off many times (in spite of the clearly-expressed wish of Okakura-san), writes to Isabella Stewart Gardner, whose home is very close to the Museum of Fine Arts. By return of post comes a reply from Fenway Court inviting him to take tea a week hence. In her missive Mrs. Gardner suggests he may wish to arrive an hour or two before their appointment in order to wander at his leisure "through my little assemblage."

Taking the lady at her word, Hiroshi arrives just after noon on the appointed day. The door is opened to him by the butler, the thickly moustachioed Theobaldo Travi, known as Bolgi, dressed in a full-length camel hair greatcoat. On his head is a magnificent, deep blue Napoleonic-looking cap with Mrs. Gardner's coat-of-arms emblazoned in gold thread. At the great man's feet are three tiny fawn-coloured dogs that Hiroshi remembers are called pugs.

After giving a brief description of the layout of Fenway Court, Bolgi leads him into the courtyard, which takes the newcomer's breath away so overcome is he by the flowers, palms, fountains and statuary that fill it. The butler has witnessed this response many times before; he winks at Hiroshi and takes his leave.

Hiroshi is aware of the history of Fenway Court, of how the Gardners deliberately chose a location reclaimed as a massive draining project in the Fens. He has been told how the building had been constructed by turning the façades of a Venetian palazzo inward on each other; he knows that substantial portions of the building were transported from Italy. But nothing really prepares him for how light streams through the skylight bathing everything in its path.

He admires the man-eating lion stylobates in the North Cloister; he is entranced by the passive muscularity of Piero della Francesca's *Hercules* in the room set aside for the early Italians; the enchanting delicacy of Vermeer's *Concert* touches him; Botticelli's *Madonna of the Eucharist* brings tears to his eyes: the beauty and loneliness of the lady reminds him, briefly, of his mother.

Much as he is taken with individual works, many of whom demand his attention, the rooms gradually take him over. There is a wonderful artistry at work in putting all these pieces together. Paintings, sculptures, pottery, tapestries, tables, chairs and mirrors may be crowded together, but they live and breathe side by side. He is not looking at Mrs. Gardner's collection — he is gazing into her soul. He has entered an enchanted garden.

Hiroshi has been at Fenway Court for just over two hours when a maid approaches him with a message from Mrs. Gardner, who has just telephoned from Brookline. She has been delayed by a flat tire but hopes he can stay until her return. When Hiroshi tells the maid he is free to do so, she suggests he wait upstairs in her mistress's sitting room. She leads the way, and Hiroshi makes himself comfortable on the small sofa on the far side of that room.

A few minutes later, the same maid shows in two gentlemen. The older of the two, by name of Elias Stuyvesant, is a large, cumbersome-looking man attired in a pale grey silk suit. Most of his hair is gone, his skin is pinkish in hue, his nose resembles a snout, his eyes are recessed and his lips are much too large for his face. His companion Hiroshi recognizes immediately as Peter Wyman, he of the sneering countenance. In the full light of day, Wyman, who looks to be in his late twenties, is a handsome man, Hiroshi decides. However, his appearance becomes monstrous the moment he uses his eyes to focus on another person. The intensity of emotion generated betrays contempt for his fellow human beings and, in the process, ruins what could be a noble face.

Hiroshi rises and bows deeply in the direction of the two strangers. They nod curtly to him and then take possession of the large settee opposite Hiroshi thirty feet away. Wyman is anxious to talk with his companion, but Stuyvesant shushes him:

"You cannot be too careful, my dear chap."

With contempt and disdain for Stuyvesant and Hiroshi tangible in his voice, Wyman replies: "I know this fellow. He was introduced to me at Billy Park's by the insufferable Wiley. He does not know a word of English. He is a lackey acquired by the Boston Museum to catalogue its Japanese prints. We have nothing to fear."

Mr. Stuyvesant looks over in Hiroshi's direction, obviously hoping to see if even the most primitive comprehension of what they are saying is registering. Hiroshi stares blankly ahead.

"He must know some English if the Museum hired him."

"The Jap may know how to read and write in English, but he does not understand anything when you speak to him."

Stuyvesant is a bit doubtful, but he agrees with Wyman. "I suppose you're correct. As I was saying, our approach must be two-pronged. Your job is to talk about Van Gogh's pathetic existence in the most affecting possible way. The years of struggle. His cutting off of his ear. The sad circumstances of his passing."

"I must make her fall in love with the Fallen Romantic Artist!"

"Exactly. You're very good at that sort of thing. The dear lady in conversation with me will mention how limited her resources are, how she cannot contemplate spending money in acquiring a picture that does not really fit into the scheme of Fenway Court. I shall tell her how Van Gogh is the rage in Europe, how all the great collectors are acquiring him. She has the opportunity to possess the first Van Gogh in the New World. In this instance, she would be ahead of the Metropolitan."

Wyman becomes mirthful. "You've learned your lessons well at the hands of the Master!"

Stuyvesant smiles. "Berenson claims that all collectors are the same. They always want to get a leg up on each other. For them" — he sweeps his arms around the room — "these things are conquests! If we wish to extend Berenson's analogy, Isabella Stewart Gardner is a modern-day Catherine the Great!" He laughs at his own joke and then stops — another sales point having come to him: "There is something else. The presence of this chap here reminds me. Not only was Van Gogh inspired by the flatness of Japanese prints, his colours are Oriental. A whole new palette never seen before in Western Art. Mention that to her."

Wyman sniggers.

So pleased are they with themselves that the two men are startled when the maid opens the door to tell them Mrs. Gardner is awaiting them. Unfortunately, her mistress can only spare them a quarter of an hour this afternoon. When they rise, the two men do not even bother to look in Hiroshi's direction.

The conversation deeply disturbs the listener, catching as he can a glimpse of his own attempts at salesmanship when he was, it now seems such a long time ago, a "dealer" in Japanese prints.

Mrs. Gardner is a minute creature. This woman he has heard so much about is so small that she sinks into the Empire settee on which she has asked him to sit beside her. Her pale-lavender dress is elaborate in a way that recalls some portraits he has seen of the

Empress Josephine; the rubies and diamonds around her neck out-sparkle her large, sapphire-blue eyes; she wears her hair up, a fashion very much in vogue. Nothing conceals her blotchy, grey-tinted skin or her bright red hands, which she constantly moves up and down and side to side.

Not having spoken with a New Yorker before, he is surprised how unrefined her accent is in comparison to the Boston ladies he has encountered. Perhaps aware of Hiroshi's thoughts, she comments on his amazing command of English. "If I were to close my eyes, I would swear I was speaking with a Yankee peddler from Salem, Massachusetts!" She stops and looks the young man directly in the eye: "You obviously are a perfect mimic! You do not have even the slightest foreign accent! What a remarkable young man you must be!"

Fearing that Mrs. Gardner is merely offering empty flattery, Hiroshi intends to pay no heed to such compliments. And yet he notices that her gaze is unflinching. The lady has a regal bearing, and he heard her issue peremptory orders to her maid. But he wonders if he is gazing into the eyes of a naturally reclusive person whose circumstances of life have never allowed her to be anything but a public person.

This afternoon Mrs. Gardner wishes to talk about Japan, which she visited twenty years ago for almost ten weeks. Her inventory of places she has been — Tokyo, Kamakura, Kanazawa, Kōbe, Osaka, Kyoto, Uji and Nara — encompasses many locales Hiroshi has never seen. She assures him that much of what she saw has retained a firm and loving possession of her memory. She spent an entire day at the Shintomizda kabuki and had tiffin there. At Nikkō, she visited the mortuary shrines of the first and third Tokugawa shoguns. She purchased photographs of the most celebrated *sumo* wrestlers of the time; she even had some of rickshaw men, kabuki actors, and "ladies of the night." Hiroshi has heard that Mrs. Gardner is a great fan of all sports. In fact, she has even allowed boxing matches to take place at

Fenway Court. In a somewhat unseemly manner for a Boston lady in conversation with a young gentleman from Japan, she tells him about one particular sumo match: "I was particularly amused by the man in the box next to us — his beautiful clothes were carefully put aside on account of the heat and there he sat, smoking a most elegant pipe with nothing on but a waist cloth and a European straw hat!"

Mrs. Gardner, having embarrassed herself and turned red in the face, decides to move the conversation in a more elevated direction. Upon returning to the Boston area, she tells Hiroshi, she planted irises and installed stone lanterns in a Japanese-inspired garden at her country home in Brookline. At the moment, she regrets not owning much Oriental art and wonders if Hiroshi can assist Okakura in making recommendations?

Hiroshi assures her he would be delighted to do so. She thanks him profusely for his kindness, but then, perhaps in response to her recently concluded conversation with Stuyvesant and Wyman, she observes that many pictures press their claims on her. "So many paintings, so little money," she laments. And then, with a hint of comic malice in her voice, she adds: "These days, many pictures are called, very few are purchased!"

When the conversation turns to her own collection and Hiroshi confesses his admiration for the Botticelli, Mrs. Gardner reflects: "Maternal love. The deepest and for me most transient of all feelings." Knowing that the lady's only child — a son named Jacky — did not live even two years, Hiroshi realizes how much the painting must mean to her.

In an attempt to change a painful subject and yet still caught within the melancholic haze that has overcome her, Mrs. Gardner tells Hiroshi how fortunate he is to work with Okakura on a daily basis: "If I had not known him I would have gone to my grave with a hard heart. Although he is infinitely polite, from him I learnt the lesson of seeking to love instead of seeking to be loved."

At that moment, when the maid enters the room with the cart containing tea, Mrs. Gardner becomes busy. She gives detailed instructions to Millicent about pouring the tea and asks Hiroshi if he can possibly assist her in a small matter. There is a young designer, about his own age, with the improbable, cumbersome name of Addison Brayton Le Boutillier. This fellow, always in search of inspiration, is preparing some tiles for Fenway Court. Could Hiroshi make some suggestions to him about Japanese subject matter? When they take their leave of each other an hour later, although Mrs. Gardner has restored herself to the post of chatelaine of a magnificent latter-day palazzo, she presses Hiroshi's hand warmly and asks him to return to Fenway Court.

CHAPTER THIRTY-FOUR

"EVERYONE CALLS ME LeB. Please do the same. It simplifies every-thing." Addison Le Boutillier had made this suggestion the day before yesterday, when he called upon Hiroshi in Copley Square. Today the two are on the South Shore train to the town of Egypt, where a horse and cart will take them to the village of Scituate, where the Dreamwold estate was finally completed two years ago.

An architect turned designer, pasty-faced and slightly portly, LeB is the same age as his new acquaintance. Not given to revealing too much about himself, LeB admits to Hiroshi he acquired his strange name from his Huguenot ancestors, although his family emigrated to the States from the Isle of Jersey, off the coast of England, in the 1850s. A "doodler" from the age of two, LeB persuaded his minister father to allow him to leave school at sixteen in order to pursue his ambition to become an artist. At first, he was successful but after a few years, when he lost his job in Boston, he cast a wide net and began taking any commissions he could get. In the past five years he has designed jewellery, silver, clocks and advertisements. Two years ago he became the designer for William Grueby's pottery, which manufactures vases, bowls and tiles. In order to provide Grueby with the best designs, LeB spends much of his time at the Boston Museum getting ideas from the paintings and sculptures there. He also spends hours at the Harvard library pouring through histories of ornament.

Hiroshi and LeB are journeying to Dreamwold because some of the designer's finest work is on display there. If Mrs. Gardner wishes to commission him to do Japanese-inspired tiles for Fenway Court, LeB thinks his consultant should see what he has accomplished there.

As they chat, Hiroshi pronounces the estate's name as *Dreamworld* until LeB corrects him. "You must drop the r from the estate's name. A wold is a tract of high, open and usually uncultivated land. I think that Mr. Lawson chose wold because it is an Anglo-Saxon word and sounds more romantic than world." Being a person of a gentle — some would say repressed — frame of mind, he does not bother to offer the opinion that *wold* is more pretentious than *world*.

Mr. Lawson, LeB continues, is a rags-to-riches millionaire who, although he was born in Massachusetts, made his money on the stock market on Wall Street in New York by the time he was thirty-five. The boy wonder was transformed into the Copper King when he, with one of the Rockefellers, organized the Amalgamated Copper Company and offered shares to the public. Lawson has written a controversial best-seller — *Frenzied Finance* — exposing the chicaneries practised by stock manipulators. He knows all about such scams from his own experience as a con artist.

As soon as their driver turns into the main gate at Dreamwold, they pass a wide assortment of stables, including the nine-hundred foot long show stable on the right. Then comes the riding academy, its tanbark ring being second only in size to the one at Madison Square Gardens in Manhattan; and, after that, the stallion stable built in the form of an arc with small high windows to prevent the confined males from seeing each other. At this point the driveway divides. On the right are the kennels, where English bulldogs and King Charles spaniels are bred; beyond them are the dairy barns and silos, the home of the imported Jerseys, including the celebrated Flying Fox, Mr. Lawson's fifty-thousand-dollar Jersey bull. On the left-hand side fork in the driveway is the half-mile race course with judges' stands and a dovecote. Other buildings can be seen in the distance: a sewage plant, a firehouse, a savings bank, a water tower — reputedly the largest in the world — and a Dutch-style windmill. Hiroshi now understands why it took more than a thousand workmen to build Dreamwold.

Directly ahead of them Hiroshi and LeB can now see the Hall. Built in an antiquated colonial style, it consists of a main building with two wings joined at either side by passages. As they enter the enormous entrance hall, they see the doors at each end leading to the dining room and the living room. LeB informs Hiroshi that connected to the dining room is a butler's pantry, which, contrary to its given name, is a long room lined with cupboards housing priceless china and crystal. The pantry terminates in the kitchen and servants' quarters. The living room is connected to a conservatory, a library and a billiard room.

The downstairs woodwork has been chemically treated to its owner's taste. The entrance hall is almost black; the dining room is russet and is accompanied by a huge Tiffany candelabra lamp in the shape of a pumpkin; pale fawn prevails in the living room, where a great deal of space is taken up by a pipe organ.

On the train, LeB has told Hiroshi that there is the slight possibility that Mr. Lawson might be home today; the rest of the family is in Europe on holiday. A few minutes after the butler has shown them into the hallway and told them they might roam at their leisure, an agitated, fiercely barking Smike, Mr. Lawson's bulldog, confronts them as they are leaving the living room. Right behind the dog approaches his owner dressed in an immaculate white linen suit. He puts his cigar down in order to take LeB's outstretched hand in his two bear-sized paws. He is delighted to meet Hiroshi and "tickled pink" that Mrs. Gardner has sent him to look at his tiles, "the very best that money can buy." When Hiroshi shows an interest in the now calm Smike, Mr. Lawson tells him: "Picking a bulldog is the same as picking a wife. It's a case of eyes — just eyes. If it's a pal for a dance or a romp in the woods, form and front may be taken into the reckoning, but when it comes to palling with a girl for a lifetime, then the picking must be done through the eyes."

Since Hiroshi is from the East, Lawson is certain that he must be interested in elephants, although he knows that those mammals are native to India, not Japan. Lawson insists that his two guests return with him to the living room so that he can lecture them about his famous collection of elephants made of ivory, gold and silver. "I'm not sure LeB has the good sense to be interested in these creatures, but I can see you're the kind of fellow who would enjoy meeting them."

After his two guests have exclaimed over this collection for almost an hour, Lawson decides to show them his gems, each jewel meticulously wrapped in masses of white tissue paper. He laboriously turns back the layers of paper concealing each and reveals diamonds, rubies, sapphires and emeralds, all of them of grandiose size.

Mr. Lawson says he would like to accompany his pals — as he now calls the two young men — in looking at the tiles, but he has some pressing business to attend to. "Without further ado I must return to my tickertape."

Left to themselves, LeB and Hiroshi wander from bathroom to bathroom where they inspect the various tile installations depicting pond lilies, turtles, tulips and processions of horses. The subjects are commonplace, but LeB's genius for rendering objects simply and then placing them against dark green and pale blue is nothing short of amazing to his Japanese friend. LeB is the first artist he has encountered in the New World who has an innate sense of Japanese design.

LeB is quietly pleased by Hiroshi's kind words. Since darkness is now approaching, he suggests that they ask their driver to get the cart ready for their return to Egypt. They are about to take their leave when a thickly bearded beanpole of a fellow about their own age walks out of the dining room.

The normally phlegmatic LeB shouts at him: "Russell, I had no idea you were to be here today!"

The man confesses that he also is surprised to see LeB.

Turning to Hiroshi, LeB announces: "Hiroshi, here is the strange and uniquely gifted Russell Crook, the premier arts and crafts artisan of all New England!"

With considerable flourish, Crook accepts the compliment and offers his hand to both men. He is delighted to learn that they are returning to Boston this evening and asks to join them, although he knows it will be a tight squeeze in the small cart. "Nonsense," LeB assures him. "We have plenty of room."

Crook, who has just completed two days working at Dreamwold, has been repairing the pumpkin tiles in the dining room that Grueby manufactured, supposedly, to his design and specifications. Unfortunately, the frieze-effect so craved by Lawson required extra-thick tiles that come easily out of place. Crook thinks that Mr. Grueby should have stood up to Lawson's bullying and said no. However, he did not do so, and Crook has to make frequent adjustments to the tiles lest they crash to the ground and break.

The trio reaches Egypt just in time to catch the seven o'clock train back into the city. In the darkness, light from the various buildings they pass momentarily disrupts the darkness. The train carriage is badly lit, but the light in Crook's eyes is bright. Unlike LeB, he is outspoken in his beliefs. How can he and LeB not die of despair when they have to serve people such as Lawson? As he speaks, the glint in Crook's eyes becomes dangerous. He is so consumed with rage that he needs to voice it, even though he has just met Hiroshi.

According to Crook, Lawson is Mammon. The equation is pure and simple. For Crook, art and life are interchangeable terms. He is forced to cater to the wealthy, the only ones who can afford to buy objects that will allow him to buy his daily bread. In order to survive, he creates bright orange pumpkins for Dreamwold and, in so doing, he comes to hate himself. "Lawson and his kind are, if they but knew, the enemies of art. So that I do not starve, I must serve them. I am allowing myself to be corrupted by vermin."

LeB keeps his mouth shut, but Hiroshi knows that he feels the same way as Crook. A sad thought crosses Hiroshi's mind: if the artist is true to himself, there is the grim possibility that no one will be interested in his work and, reduced to despair, he might feel compelled to take his own life. Since he has been merely the imitator of the work of others, Hiroshi has never encountered this predicament before.

CHAPTER THIRTY-FIVE

KATE IS ASTOUNDED by Hiroshi's accounts of Fenway Court and Dreamwold. She and Hiroshi are drinking port after a leisurely supper in her morning room, where she takes her meals when she is alone or has only one or two others with her. The dining table is mahogany, the chairs in the Gothic style, the side table gilded, and the walls crammed with paintings, mostly of her ancestors. The room is, according to Kate's way of thinking, simple and plain.

During his brief stay in Boston, Hiroshi has become sufficiently educated to know that the tapering turned legs of the table terminating in ball and claw feet indicate that this piece was made during the reign of George II. The side table is from the early years of the reign of George I. Most of the paintings are by artists trained in England. All are what is now being designated by a recently coined expression: museum-quality. When Hiroshi mentions this, Kate scoffs. "I have no idea what these things are worth. I do remember the story of how my great-grandfather, at the outset of the Revolution, considered throwing out everything that was made in England. His wife informed him that the conflict with England would not be resolved if they had nowhere to sit, no plates to eat on, and no silver with which to carve their food! He kept his mouth shut but, a few weeks later, he commissioned from the patriotic Mr. Revere the large silver bowl that now lives on the mantelpiece."

The acquisitiveness of Mrs. Gardner and Mr. Lawson amazes Kate. How can they spend their lives buying up everything that takes their fancy? Although mildly amused by her slightly holier-than-thou attitude, Hiroshi realizes that Kate herself has never acquired anything of value. She is the inheritor of her family's wealth and possessions, but she would never think of adding to those treasures. Of course, she would never part with them either, even if their sale might assist the immigrant girls to whom she is so attached. When Hiroshi mentions that he recently met two artisans, men of his own age, who were designing pottery vases and bowls of exceptional merit, she shows no interest.

Despite her stay in Japan and her innumerable conversations with his mother, Kate has no real understanding of the Yoshiwara and the ukiyoe that depicts that precariously floating world. She may be aware that Yoshiko and Takao were once courtesans, and that Yoshiko is the *yarite* in a now increasingly run-down bordello. She knows and yet does not know. For her the facts are meaningless because she has never experienced them. She can stand apart, perhaps elevate herself, from the force of circumstances that have governed the lives of her Japanese friends.

Hiroshi may be correct in his estimate of this side of Kate, but he underestimates how shrewd a judge of character she is. Before her, she sees a very handsome, well-built young man who, although he is modest in the Japanese way, shows great self-assurance in telling her about Mrs. Gardner, Mr. Lawson and the two young potters. Hiroshi does not realize she is perfectly well aware of her young charge's many insecurities: his inability to chart a steady course for himself, his uncertainty about his future, his pain at being a half-breed caught between two very different cultures.

Tonight Kate expresses relief that she has heard from Yoshiko again. Both his mother and aunt sorely miss Hiroshi and have been delighted to learn he is settling in nicely to his new responsibilities. Takao's health is excellent; she has managed their business affairs so well that the Chōjiya has shown a considerable profit, the first one in a long time. Takao will continue to look after the Chōjiya while his mother recedes more and more from life.

For Hiroshi, the sentiments in the letter are woodenly expressed. Once upon a time his mother could force herself to infuse a semblance of animation into ordinary tasks. That has vanished. She is — Hiroshi thinks of an English expression — like a bee fixed in amber.

At the Museum, Okakura-sensei leaves Hiroshi to his own devices, although he is always willing to lend an ear when his subordinate has a problem or a concern. Knowing how much Hiroshi must miss traditional Japanese food, he invites him to dinner at his Newbury Street flat. Somewhat embarrassed, Okakura confesses he has done his very best with the resources available in Boston. The *kamaboko*, cakes of boiled fish paste, have proved to be a source of vexation: "I couldn't find the right fish, but I persevered and improvised with codfish; I dissolved the *gofun* and mashed it very fine with flour to make it look right. As you know, American flour is very white and much too fine. So our cakes are burned black." The *sushi* with sour plum in the centre of each turns out perfectly, and, as far as both men are concerned, the meal is a great success, reminding each of their homeland.

Like Russell Crook, Okakura-sensei has very decided opinions, which he does not mind sharing when he is away from the Museum. He hates what he calls the Japanese pursuit of the pseudo-classic and the pseudo-European, art which merely imitates remnants of the past and in the process copies that of the West. "Art must be national in attempting to understand its own past and then creating new vital work from that understanding." Japan, he warns Hiroshi, will be a lost civilization if it becomes merely a pale imitation of work done in Europe and America.

His exile from Japan has made Okakura deeply unhappy, but this separation from his homeland has made him appreciate even more what is in danger of being destroyed. Moreover, Americans have no concept of the Japanese character. He reminds Hiroshi of Lafcadio Hearn's eyewitness account of the moment a captured thief confronts the young son of the police officer he had murdered. "I went with a great throng of people to witness the arrival at the rail station at Kumamoto. I expected to hear and see anger; I even feared the possibility of violence. The murdered man had been much liked." Hearn was wrong. When the criminal was brought before the little boy, the officer somewhat laconically informed him: "Little one, this is the man who killed your father." The child sobbed, whereupon the murderer also burst into tears himself and threw himself at the child's feet, imploring his forgiveness. "Americans have no conception of the meaning of that incident, of how the thief repents his crime."

Emboldened by Okakura's candour, Hiroshi interrogates him about the essence of the art he is trying to save. Okakura smiles, knowing how difficult it is to answer such an abstract question. Far too clever to speak directly, he begins with an anecdote about the Buddhist and the Taoist: "One day a monk of each persuasion stands before a jar of vinegar — the emblem of life. The Buddhist dips his finger in the brew and finds it sour and bitter; the Taoist pronounces it sweet."

"I think you are telling me that you refuse to define the nature of Japanese art because every man must find his own way."

Okakura replies deftly by observing that he has always been more of a Taoist than a Buddhist. He offers an aphorism: "The greatest pleasure of which we are capable is doing good deeds secretly." Then he delivers a paradox: "True art consists of hiding beauty in order to discover it."

"You are saying each man must be open to the world as he experiences it?" Okakura, refusing to be drawn further, offers his guest some sake.

As he walks back to Pinckney Street later that night, Hiroshi recalls a Chinese legend Takao told him, much to his delight, when he was a boy of eight or nine:

> *Once in the desolate ravine at Lungmen stood a magnificent Kiri tree, the king of its forest. It reared its head to talk to the stars; its roots reached so deep into the earth that they mingled with the coils of the dragon that slept beneath.*
>
> *One day a mighty wizard ripped the tree from the ground and constructed from it a wondrous harp, whose spirit could be tamed only by the greatest of musicians.*
>
> *For generations the harp was treasured by the Emperor of China but vain were the efforts of all the musicians who tried to draw music from its strings. All that came out were harsh notes of disdain and discord.*
>
> *At last, Peiwoh, the prince of harpists, asked for a turn. With a tender hand he caressed the harp as one might soothe an unruly horse. He sang of nature, of the seasons, of high mountains, and flowing waters. The tree's memory was awoken. Once more the sweet breath of spring played amongst its branches. The wail of the cuckoo, the roar of the tiger, and the pattering of rain: all these sounds were captured in Peiwoh's playing.*
>
> *Astounded, the celestial monarch asked Peiwoh why he had succeeded when all others had failed. "Sire," the musician responded, "the others failed because they sang of themselves. I allowed the harp to choose its own themes and did not know whether I was the harp or the harp was me."*

Would that I had a theme according to which I could lead my dissolute existence. That is Hiroshi's sad thought this dark moonless night. These days he experiences sorrow for all the missteps he has taken in his young life. Sorting sheep from goats is a job that gives him a limited amount of satisfaction, but he has come to despise those who deliberately confuse the real with the fake. Now that he is an advocate for truth, he is forced to despise the person he once was.

CHAPTER THIRTY-SIX

THE TRIP TO South Lincoln to visit Russell Crook requires many transfers: a tram, a train, and, finally, a horse and cart. LeB has volunteered to make the trip because it is vital that Hiroshi have the opportunity to see Crook's vases. Intrigued by the claims that the quiet but fiercely single-minded LeB has made for his friend's art, Hiroshi has insisted on making the cumbersome journey.

"He is an artist. I am merely a designer," LeB asserts.

Hiroshi, who has a high opinion of LeB's talent, is loath to agree with him. "Your work may be different. That does not mean that Russell's is better."

"You don't understand! He lives and breathes his art. I am an ordinary man incapable of great passions. I also lack the vital ingredient of genius."

Hiroshi decides not to respond. He knows that LeB, a married man with small children to support, will not listen to him if he tells him each man must live according to his individual capacity. Coming from Okakura, those might be words of wisdom, Hiroshi reflects, but they are hollow sentiments, he decides, when mouthed by someone who has no claim to be called an artist.

Russell's home is a small two-room cottage on the outskirts of South Lincoln. The kerosene-lit main room, which serves as a living room, a dining room, a work space and a kitchen, is dark even in the early afternoon. Since his two friends are running late, Russell suggests they take their meal immediately, a simple ploughman's lunch — bread, cheese, and chutney.

On his own home ground, Russell is more relaxed, but just as fervent in espousing his belief that Americans must create an authentic American art instead of imitating Europe or the Far East. He is of the decided opinion that although someone like himself can glean much from the flat planes of Japanese art, he must be sure he makes any such borrowing his own. "Mere copying is the anathema of art," he roars. Hiroshi wonders what Crook would think of him if he knew how he once made a comfortable living.

Crook also lambastes the factories that are taking over America. Quite soon, no handmade goods will be available because no one will be able to afford to create them. "The factory worker is little more than a dumb animal doing endless, repetitive tasks — that is exactly what people like Lawson want him to be so that they can fully exploit him. Lawson can only build his castle on the backs of the poor and downtrodden."

After supper, Russell places six large vases on the dining table for Hiroshi to inspect and becomes much calmer. All the pieces are large — approximately ten inches in height — and all have black as their ground colour. On each is a different animal — a deer, a moose, a fish, an elephant, a deer, an antelope — rendered in a white mixed with black. The effect is strange and haunting because the animals look like ghosts momentarily straying into view. Hiroshi has the strange sensation of not really being sure the rendition of the animal is physically present. Perhaps it is only the soul of the creature that has been captured? This man may be slightly mad, but he is a genius. This is the only conclusion to which Hiroshi can come.

Touched by Hiroshi's fervent admiration, Russell mentions that since he learned a great deal from the woodcuts of Hokusai and Hiroshige about the rendering of line, he is deeply pleased that their fellow countryman understands what he is doing. Changing the subject slightly, Russell asks if he is interested in Van Gogh, whose work was heavily influenced by many of the great masters of ukiyoe?

Hiroshi says he has heard the name only once.

As it turns out, Russell has a scrapbook devoted to the Dutch artist. Would he like to leaf through it? Hiroshi says that he would be most interested. For the next hour, the three men pour over the reproductions, many of them in full colour. Within a matter of minutes, Hiroshi comes face to face with an artist who looked closely with his heart and soul at the great Japanese masters and then used their work to suit his own purpose. Vincent learned from the Japanese — he did not steal from them.

On their return journey to Boston, LeB, as is his wont, lavishes praise on Crook and diminishes the quality of his own work. Hiroshi nods politely in agreement followed by disagreement because, his mind distracted by the ghost of Vincent Van Gogh, he yearns to see the painting on offer to Mrs. Gardner.

That night, back in his room on Pinckney Street, Hiroshi feels overwhelmed. The joy that he takes in the Dutch artist is accompanied by a crushing sadness. Those dreadful twin emotions of guilt and shame invade him. For the first time he fully understands what a horrible crime it is to counterfeit any work of art. He had been robbing the souls of other men.

CHAPTER THIRTY-SEVEN

NORMALLY ALERT TO his surroundings, Hiroshi is in a daze; he is running late and breaks into a trot as he makes his way out of a meeting at the Parker House. He does not notice the pale-gray Daimler that pulls up next to him and the man who emerges from it. He is startled when his name is called out. When he turns around, he is shocked to behold Tedoya, who holds his right arm out, Western-style, to shake his hand.

Today, Tedoya is dressed, very much like Hiroshi, in a black business suit. Tedoya's hair glistens with brilliantine, and there are hints of gray at the sides. The silk fabric of his suit is finer than Hiroshi's Boston-made counterpart. The gleam in Tedoya's eyes is so intense that it looks menacing. When Tedoya learns that Hiroshi is en route back to the Museum, he insists on giving him a ride.

Hiroshi agrees, and Tedoya informs the manservant accompanying him that he and his childhood friend were so close in appearance as boys that they were often reckoned to be brothers by those who did not know they came from two different families. Even today, Hiroshi reflects, we look very much alike. He is a bit taller than I, but our facial features are mirrors of each other. Grey, however, has not yet touched me, Hiroshi comfortingly assures himself.

When they are settled in their places, Tedoya immediately quizzes Hiroshi about his life in the past ten years. Hiroshi tells of his sojourn in Boston but does not confide any information about the circumstances surrounding his departure.

Tedoya, who needs no prodding, is delighted to tell Hiroshi that the past decade has been very kind to him. "As you know, I worked briefly for the police as an undercover investigator." No further reference is made to his betrayal of Hiroshi. "Soon tiring of a profession that did not exact my full capabilities, I went to work for Nikkei, the munitions manufacturer. I began in a lowly clerical position, but the tremendous effort I put into every task assigned to me led to one promotion after another. I am now Managing Director. I am an example of what the Americans call a Horatio Alger. I have gone from rags to riches beyond even my wildest dreams."

Ever since Japan decided to take its position seriously as a modern nation, Tedoya proudly declares, Nikkei's fortunes have risen steadily.

Tedoya invites his old friend to join Nikkei, perhaps as his personal assistant. Not bothering to turn Tedoya down, Hiroshi changes the subject and shakes hands formally with his old friend as he steps out of the car.

So hurried was Hiroshi's departure from Japan that he had not had the time to say goodbye to his old drinking companion, Gotō. Quite often in the following years, Hiroshi has wondered what happened to his friend. Did he become, like his father, an industrialist? Or was he still a bit of a reprobate, a remittance man living off his family's wealth and good name?

Three months following his encounter with Tedoya, Hiroshi receives a letter from Gotō, who had attended a meeting at Nikkei and learnt Hiroshi's whereabouts. After many years of evading his father's net, Gotō tells Hiroshi, he reluctantly joined the firm. The truth is, sadly, that he is not really cut out for the cutthroat world of high finance. He is tolerated at Takada Building Supplies because he is the owner's son. Otherwise, he would long ago have been fired.

Gotō has written to ask a favour. He has to be in Boston for two weeks or so and would like his friend's assistance in conducting some business. Although Gotō has been taking English lessons for over a year, he is woefully inadequate in speaking it. If need be, can he rely on Hiroshi for help?

Hiroshi replies at once and offers to do everything in his power to assist Gotō. When he does not receive an answer, he forgets about the matter. Then at work one afternoon, he picks up the phone to hear his friend asking him to meet him at the Parker House.

That evening, Hiroshi and Gotō take their time consuming the hotel's famous eleven-course supper, including scrod — the catch of the day — and the famed cream pie. Gotō is much impressed with the passenger elevator and the ten-storey annex, which looks like a huge French chateau, where he has a suite. Unlike Hiroshi, he is oblivious of the fact that this dining room was once the meeting place of the founders of the American literary Renaissance — Longfellow, Hawthorne, Emerson and Thoreau. He does not discuss such matters with his friend, nor is he aware that the actor John Wilkes Booth, who took target practice at a nearby shooting gallery, stayed there ten days before assassinating Abraham Lincoln.

Fun-loving Gotō has come to hate life in Japan. The army and the navy are in the ascendant. Soldiers crowd city streets. Young men want jobs with uniforms. If they cannot find jobs in the military, they become police officers. The Japan he and Hiroshi knew as young men has almost completely disappeared.

Hiroshi notices that Gotō has aged beyond his forty years. He tells Hiroshi that he is unhappily married, has three children and a troublesome mistress. Is Hiroshi married? No, Hiroshi informs him.

Does he have a mistress? No. He does not. He has had the occasional woman friend, but he has never had the inclination to deepen any relationship in which he has been involved.

Having brought Hiroshi up-to-date about life in Japan and perfunctorily exchanged personal information with him, Gotō renews his request for assistance. As it turns out, his command of English is not as bad as he feared. It is passable. However, he does not comprehend the American way of doing business. Does Hiroshi, by any chance, know Mr. Thomas Lawson of Dreamwold? Hiroshi informs Gotō he has met him only once.

"I was sent here from Japan to buy copper from Mr. Lawson. My instructions are unequivocal. I am to purchase as much as he will sell me at the lowest possible price. I must strike the best deal I can."

Patiently, Hiroshi tells Gotō that he is not a businessman. He does not think he can offer any pointers in completing such a transaction.

"That's not the point," Gotō replies. "Mr. Lawson refuses to conclude any transaction until we know each other better. I have spent hours at Dreamwold. I have examined his collection of elephants eight or nine times! I have been taken on a guided tour of the estate three times. I know the name of every horse and bulldog on the property. Mr. Lawson has confessed his great unhappiness to me. He built Dreamwold for his beloved wife, who then inconveniently died. He compares himself endlessly to Shah Jehan who built the Taj Mahal as a memorial to his beloved wife."

"Mr. Lawson must like you," Hiroshi observes.

"That's what I was beginning to think, and then, the other night, after we had consumed many glasses of whisky — a beverage I detest — he informed me there were four Thomas Lawsons and that I must know each of them if I expect him to sell any copper to me.

"There is Thomas Lawson the Connoisseur, who is desperately anxious to have all his furniture, paintings, sculptures, and animals admired.

"There is Thomas Lawson the Collector, who is a fierce opponent to anyone who attempts to outbid or outwit him in the acquisition of anything he desires.

"There is Thomas Lawson the Family Man, who is open, warm, affectionate, sentimental and loving.

"There is Thomas Lawson the Businessman who is shrewd, opportunistic, cruel and cunning."

Although the serious side of Hiroshi can see that Gotō feels trapped by all the layers of Mr. Lawson, he shrugs his shoulders: "He sounds a very divided man! A multiple personality."

Gotō appreciates the comic side of the situation, but he is flummoxed in dealing with the strange Yankee. Hiroshi does not consider himself the best observer of the secrets of the heart but nevertheless has an idea.

"I think you should tell Mr. Lawson that you have struggled all your life to be a good son to your father and that, unfortunately, you have never succeeded in that task. Tell him that the breach has deeply wounded you."

"If I told Mr. Lawson that, I would be telling him the complete truth."

"Exactly so. That is what he wants. No more and no less."

A somewhat mystified Gotō politely receives this advice. Their long meal finally completed, the two men shake hands, bow and take their leave of each other.

Two days later, a very happy Gotō telephones Hiroshi. "I am off to New York City tonight and my ship to Yokohama departs in a week's time. My deal with Mr. Lawson has been finalized.

"I followed your advice. I told Mr. Lawson that, unlike himself, I did not have four parts. 'I am, simply put, a wayward son trying to please a difficult father.'

"After staring at me for at least half a minute, Mr. Lawson grasped me by the hand and said that it was time we concluded our business arrangement. He sold the copper to me at what I consider a low price. At long last I shall be a hero to my father!"

Hiroshi congratulates Gotō at such a wonderful conclusion to his visit. In turn, he is offered his friend's undying gratitude. Once off the telephone, Hiroshi wishes that he could join Gotō on the ship back to Japan.

CHAPTER THIRTY-EIGHT

1912

RUSSELL HAS INSISTED that it is the "patriotic" duty of Hiroshi, LeB and himself to attend the very first baseball game at Fenway Park. Hiroshi informs him he would be happy to go to the much-anticipated event, but that for him the occasion could hardly be patriotic. His friend waves his hand in dismissal. "I didn't mean *American* patriotism. Baseball is the sport of the common man. The players are involved in a life-and-death struggle with the owners. The proles in a classic battle against the forces of oppression." Russell's recent reading of Marx and Engels has reinforced his conviction about the heroic struggles of the poor versus the rich. He has insisted that they sit in the farthest reaches of the grandstand so that they can be surrounded by the common man, the people who really love and appreciate the game.

This spring day is wintry. In fact it is so blustery that most of the fans are clad in heavy garments: thick coats, scarves, vests, mittens, gloves, and toques. The three of them — each taking refuge under heavy coats — make a strange grouping. Even on an outing to a base-ball game, LeB insists on dressing like a businessman: his three-piece suit may be frayed and torn, but it is the costume of a gentleman.

Russell, who refuses to recognize the unseasonable weather, bears an uncanny resemblance to a young Walt Whitman: his torn straw hat and straggly beard leave no doubt that he is of an artistic temperament. And then there is Hiroshi in white shirt and trousers under his long coat. My two friends, Hiroshi tells himself, probably represent the extremities in my own character, torn between convention and rebellion.

So completely surrounded are the trio by Irish lads, who have arrived inebriated and are intent on getting even more drunk, that LeB and Crook worry for Hiroshi's safety. Several of these louts are already pointing at him, whispering loudly to each other and then bursting into laughter. Things are on the verge of getting out of hand, when suddenly, Hiroshi turns around and asks the fellow directly behind him what position he plays. Taken by surprise, the young man admits to being a third baseman.

"You are what we call in Japanese a *saado*. I have not played in years, but I used to be a *sekando*, a second baseman."

"I didn't know Japs — I mean Japanese — played baseball," responds the startled young man.

"It's just about the most popular sport in Japan. When I lived in Tokyo, my friends and I played every week."

"Call me Tom," the fellow tells Hiroshi.

All of a sudden, the smirks have disappeared from the faces of the sea of men surrounding Hiroshi and his two companions. Hiroshi explains to the now-enthralled Irishmen that a double play is a *daburu pure*, a change-up a *chenji appu*, a grand slam a *manrui homa*. They bend over in laughter when he tells them a wild pitch is a *wairudo pitchi*. Hiroshi's listeners are impressed when he reveals that he fervently wants the Red Sox to crush the Harvard team; he is hoping for a *kaishoh* — a decisive victory — over the "swells" from Cambridge.

Hiroshi ascends even higher in his new friends' esteem when he displays an intimate knowledge of the history of the Boston Pilgrims, from their founding in 1901, the purchase of the franchise in 1904 by the owner of the *Globe*, General Charles Henry Taylor, their change of name to the Red Sox in 1907 and Taylor's decision to move the team from the Huntington Avenue Grounds. Now that he has confessed his proletarian sentiments and demonstrated his knowledge of local baseball history, Hiroshi has become for his new acquaintances a figure of almost heroic proportions.

While the *Star Spangled Banner* is being sung, Hiroshi borrows LeB's binoculars and begins to examine the occupants of the expensive seats behind home plate. Just behind the catcher sit the Spaulding brothers. They are there with a group of six or seven colleagues, who seem to be paying attention to the game. The two brothers scour their watches constantly, apparently wondering what the opportune time will be when they can depart without seeming disloyal to their civic duty of helping inaugurate the opening of the Park.

A few rows behind, Isabella Gardner and Okakura-sensei are huddled together; no one is paying them much attention. Today Okakura is in a Western-style business suit; the lady is dressed matter-of-factly, something Hiroshi has never seen before. However, the day is very cold, and she has likely dressed for warmth. Seeing the intensity in the lady's eyes and beholding a corresponding passion in the man's, Hiroshi further determines that the two are lovers, as he has long suspected.

Seven rows up from the couple Hiroshi spies Stuyvesant and Lawson together. Lawson is talking, Stuyvesant, who is listening intently, bobs his head up and down frequently in agreement. Mr. Stuyvesant knows how to attune himself perfectly to his clients, Hiroshi observes. Surprisingly, Wyman is nowhere to be seen.

The snow — as predicted in this morning's newspapers — arrives. At first, it is in the form of a fine, intense mist. Then it descends on them in large flakes. Next, a strong wind whips through the Park rendering the playing field invisible. In the midst of this turmoil, the

Red Sox manage to score two runs. That's what the scoreboard tells Hiroshi, who has not seen any players cross home plate.

Crook is in an exuberant mood. The swells from Cambridge are well on their way to defeat. LeB could care less who wins the game: he suggests that the three of them think of retiring to the nearest pub. Crook will have none of that. Hiroshi wants to stay, although the snow is refusing to melt and the air is freezing.

Suddenly, the area around the diamond clears. Harvard is on the field. According to the scoreboard, the game is now in the bottom of the eighth inning. The first two Red Sox batters, having great difficulty seeing the ball, strike out quickly.

Although he has lost interest in the game, Hiroshi uses his binoculars to study the batters, then the umpires, then the pitcher. All of them are stoic, given the horrible conditions under which they are labouring. So are the shortstop and the second baseman. When he focuses his glasses on the second baseman, Hiroshi is amazed to see Peter Wyman. Gone from his face is the scorn that has inhabited it when Hiroshi encountered him before. Wyman's eyes are intently fixed on the batter — ready to pounce on a ball heading his way. He is decidedly handsome in a refined, aristocratic way. There is something almost heroic about him, as if he might be a person with an interesting inner life. Hiroshi is caught unawares when a fly ball to the outfield ends the inning. Wyman is not one of the Harvard batters at the top of the ninth inning, all of whom quickly hit ground-ball outs.

As they are making their way out of the Park, Hiroshi asks Russell how someone like Peter Wyman can be playing for Harvard. He is told that the Cambridge cabal, anxious to humiliate the Sox, insisted on being able to call upon alumni that were particularly proficient in the sport.

This spring day is swelteringly hot and sunny. The snow of the week before has become a distant memory. Many aristocratic hearts in Boston have been saddened by the news of the sinking of the *Titanic* a few days before on April 15. Isabella Gardner had considered cancelling her reception, but finally decided, with a great deal of reluctance, to go ahead. In a letter Hiroshi received two days before, she told him it was important that people assemble even if all they could talk about was their losses and shared misfortunes.

When Hiroshi opens the door to the Eliot carriage that calls to take him to the Gardner estate in Brookline, he gazes in wonder at Kate's appearance. Her hair, normally worn down, has been taken up and luxuriously sculpted; the whole assemblage is held together by dark green ribbons that contrast beautifully with a new pale-green and cream dress, its bodice hugging her waist. The new costume and new hairdo have utterly transformed Kate. Hiroshi says not a word, but he knows, from the sly glance Kate casts in his direction, she is pleased to have taken him by surprise.

The truth is Hiroshi is a bit frightened. He hopes that Kate has not decided to compete with Mrs. Gardner, who, at such an event, will be wearing the most up-to-date and expensive frock on offer in Manhattan. He has not seen such a splendid dress as Kate's in a very long time, and she, who has always criticized those female denizens of polite society who must be clothed in the most recent fashion of New York or London or Paris, has certainly gone against her own principles. He had not expected Kate — who had no friends on the *Titanic* — to be in mourning, but she looks very different today. Kate may be without guile, Hiroshi reminds himself, but she is not without cunning.

Okakura-sensei had told Hiroshi of Green Hill's many delights. Today he sees it for himself. Low, wide and spreading, the house hugs the nearby landscape. Small balconies with low railings dot each side of the house. The large rooms are filled with Chinese wall paintings and Japanese screens. The accents in the garden are so subtle and gradual that they lead, effortlessly, from one place of mystery and surprise to another. Starry jasmine cross many of the paths, and for many visitors its perfume reminds them of moonlit fountains in Tuscany.

A sombre Isabella Gardner greets her guests this afternoon. Her tiny frame is accentuated by a maroon-coloured dress in which she seems enveloped, almost overwhelmed. Ignoring the Spauldings — one brother on each side of her — the hostess scurries over to Kate — whom she has met only twice, years before — and embraces her eagerly. In response to Kate's compliments about the beauty of the house and its surroundings, Mrs. Gardner throws her melancholy aside and becomes effusive: "I am delighted beyond words that the grapevine that holds this house in its embrace is in flower and that you can behold it today. Its odour is pervading, inebriating! It comes in at my window during the night and accompanies me into the arms of Morpheus!" Taking Kate's arm, Isabella tells her that they must inspect the orchids and the Parma violets — "the most lushly beautiful flower in existence" — in the hothouse.

Slightly embarrassed by his hostess's rhapsodic commentary, Hiroshi excuses himself and sets off to see the celebrated iris beds, which are heated in order to keep the flowers on display as long as possible. When he reaches them, he is so entranced by the sight and smell of hundreds of huge mauve, lavender, blue, cream, beige and brown blooms that he does not notice that Mr. Stuyvesant and Mr. Wyman are behind him. When he turns around, the older man grins at him but the other turns his back, cutting him.

Stuyvesant nods agreeably in Hiroshi's direction: "These Japanese irises must remind you of home."

Hiroshi replies that they do and begins to talk about the vast array of colours on display. Stuyvesant, whose knowledge of botany is extensive, is eager to discuss these "miracles of nature." While the two men exchange pleasantries, a stony-faced Wyman stands by, occasionally staring at Hiroshi as if examining an animal at the zoo.

What an amazing piece of work this Wyman is! Hiroshi tells himself. He has so many sides to him.

After twenty minutes, Hiroshi excuses himself. Mr. Stuyvesant extends his hand while Wyman once more turns away, as if to avoid even the slightest possibility of touching Hiroshi. Bothered yet again by Wyman's eccentric, hostile behaviour, Hiroshi decides to return to the house but keeps getting lost in the various twists and turns of the garden. He feels caught in a maze, always ending up at the spot from where he began. Finally, spying the tops of some women's heads at a bend in the path in the distance, he sets off in that direction.

Suddenly, he overhears the voices of Kate and Isabella in animated exchange. Any hint of hysteria in Isabella's voice has vanished; Kate is speaking in her gentlest way: "Your many kindnesses to my adopted son are much appreciated. You have fostered his talents in ways I cannot even begin to comprehend."

Isabella's voice is low, but Hiroshi hears each word clearly: "He is a remarkable human being. Mr. Okakura has spoken of him in the most glowing terms, and I am simply following his lead."

"I think there is much more kindness and gentle sentiment in your heart than you like others to see."

Kate's candour causes Isabella to burst into tears. Hiroshi now hears gentle sobbing sounds, and resolved not to be discovered by either woman, he doubles back on himself, promptly gets lost, waits twenty minutes and then heads back to where he heard the voices. Thank goodness, the path is now clear, and he can finally make his way back to the house.

CHAPTER THIRTY-NINE

1913

OKAKURA-SENSEI HAS abandoned Boston. Rumour has it that he is dying. This afternoon, while they are taking tea at Fenway Court, a despondent Isabella Gardner hands Hiroshi Okakura's most recent letter to her: "Ages have passed since I last saw you — are you changed any? I am afraid that you have made me homesick for Boston — I am enormously lonesome." To Hiroshi he had written the other day in his roundabout way: "There is great pleasure in the quest for the unattainable. You and I know that wonder is the secret of bliss and that with reason comes the death of the beautiful."

Just before his departure, Okakura had once again invited his subordinate to his flat. After dinner, a tipsy Okakura intimated that he knew full well the circumstances leading to Hiroshi's exile to America. This subject, which has never been broached by them before, pained Hiroshi because he has always assumed that his boss — fully aware of his past but himself far removed from such sordid circumstances — had decided, in the Japanese way of politeness, to make no mention of it.

Hiroshi is flummoxed when he realizes that Okakura has alluded to his sordid past in order to tell him about his own peccadilloes.

A decade earlier, on board a luxury liner carrying him back to Japan from the United States, Okakura had conducted a passionate affair with the wife of Baron Kuki, the Japanese ambassador to the United States, who had given his wife into his friend's care. A charming woman always dressed in the height of Western fashion, Hatsu in her youth had been a geisha in the Gion district of Kyoto. Eight months after the crossing, the Baroness gave birth to a son, Shuzo, obviously Okakura's son. After the voyage, Hatsu chose to live apart from her husband in a house frequented by Okakura. "My attachment to a beautiful woman is the real reason I am forced to live outside Japan; her husband, now my mortal enemy, has exacted a ferocious revenge on me."

In all his dealings, Okakura prides himself in speaking in circumlocutions. Putting things straightforwardly is for him a way of distorting them and, ultimately, rendering them prosaic and meaningless. This evening he speaks plainly. Okakura, certain that this young man is suffering needlessly, realizes he needs to know that others, whom he respects, have suffered similar catastrophes.

His boss's confession that he was led astray from the so-called path of righteousness touches Hiroshi, who is already certain that Isabella and Okakura are lovers. Hiroshi, recognizing that both he and Okakura are very detached from others, is sure that Okakura flirted with the possibility of loving Isabella Gardner — perhaps marrying her — and then withdrew. I do not love anybody and must not judge others, Hiroshi chides himself. He remains unsure what there is in him to love.

Takao's most recent letter tells of the death of the Emperor Meiji. The entire country is in mourning. Most shops are closed; all the kabuki and cinemas are shut. Hiroshi later learns that the house of the Emperor's chief physician had been stoned. If the doctor was at all competent, his persecutors reasoned, he should have been able to obtain eternal life on earth for the man who had done so much to alter Japan for the better.

Hiroshi's nightmares about his mother and father are so frequent and fierce that he deliberately keeps himself awake at night by reading. For reasons he cannot completely fathom, the story of the orphan boy Pip — especially his love for the elusive Estella and his championing of the escaped convict Magwich — moves him deeply. Perhaps I am witnessing my own past, he tells himself, especially my grandiosity and my desire to remove myself from the common herd. His mother's room may not have been filled with cobwebs, but, like Miss Havisham, she lingered in the past.

Hiroshi does not care for *Silas Marner*. To *Middlemarch*, Hiroshi is more strongly attracted although he finds the heroine Dorothea insipid. Of more interest to him is Lydgate, the highly flawed physician with "spots of commonness." This is a man with whom he can identify, and sympathize, since he himself is such a mixture of strange, disparate qualities.

Unlike milksopish Dorothea, the very flawed, money-hungry Gwendolen Harleth from Eliot's last novel appeals to Hiroshi, but he is most attracted to Daniel Deronda, the title character. Naïve and idealistic, Daniel, who does not know the identity of his parents, is overly zealous in his philanthropic pursuits. In the opening stages of the book, Hiroshi finds the protagonist insufferable, but the gradual revelation that Daniel is of Jewish, rather than Anglo-Saxon, ancestry rivets Hiroshi's attention. As someone of mixed race, he identifies with this tormented young man, who eventually decides to devote his life to the founding of a national home for his race in the Middle East.

The note pleads with Hiroshi to make his way to Fenway Court *"urgently ... Despair has me in his grip!"* As soon as he arrives, Hiroshi is told by Bolgi that the mistress is in the Gothic Gallery. He rushes up two flights of stairs, passes through the Chapel, and through the passage with the Japanese screens before reaching the inner sanctum, one of the galleries not open to the public.

The twilight, which makes it impossible for him to see anything clearly, gives a menacing look to the large beams on the ceiling. Along the edge, there are sixty-eight small heads — fifteenth-century portrait heads made into a frieze — staring down at him. The dark, muted colours coming through the stained glass add a further sinister touch. He looks up and down the room several times and becomes convinced that it is empty. He is about to search elsewhere when he hears a moaning sound coming from a bench along the furthest wall. He follows the wail until it brings him to Isabella, who is lying prone, her hands covering her face.

Kneeling down, he looks his friend in the face and then embraces her. He knows full well the sad news that is about to be imparted to him: "My dear Kakuzō is gone. I have not been so unhappy since I lost my dear, sweet Jacky." Isabella has lost a lover, Hiroshi a man whom he treasured as a friend and as a helper. He has no easy words for her, and — he is evermore grateful to her — she does not expect him to utter any meaningless platitudes.

Night has fallen. Isabella raises herself up and sits next to Hiroshi. After five minutes of silence, she takes his hands in hers. "It is the greatest possible comfort to have you with me at this awful moment. You who meant so much to Kakuzō. He told me you would find a way to continue his work. In young men like you, he often said, will be Japan's salvation. He will live forever more in you." Hiroshi nods acceptance of these kind words, but, in his heart, he doubts he is worthy of such fine sentiments. Perhaps I shall have to become so, he tells himself.

PART IV

THE ARTIST

CHAPTER FORTY

1917

BOSTON IS IN mourning. Many of its finest young men have died
in the trenches in France. Many doors — even in Back Bay — are
covered with black bunting.

Today, Hiroshi's own melancholic reverie is disrupted when he
receives a note from Kate asking him to call upon her as soon as
possible. When he arrives at Louisburg Square, Kate herself lets him
in. She indicates that they should go into the sitting room, where
the strong morning light fully reveals that some recent tears have
ravaged her face.

She has just received a telegram from Takao telling her that
Yoshiko has died. Since her return to Japan, Kate has gathered from
letters from Takao, Yoshiko had been more despondent than ever
before. About a year ago, Yoshiko had begun to waste away at an
alarming rate. She passed away quietly in her sleep.

Although Kate knows that any physician would scoff, she main-
tains that Yoshiko died of a broken heart, a heart further pierced by
some revelations Kate had made to her about Lieutenant Eliot on the
sea voyage from Japan to England thirteen years before.

This morning, Kate is filled with self-recrimination. Finally, Hiroshi tells her to stop berating herself. "As much as she could, my mother spent her entire life avoiding the truth. She protected herself from reality. Sooner or later, the truth insists on making itself known. My mother could not cope. All her self-imposed protections vanished."

A part of Kate agrees with Hiroshi, but she thinks he is a bit harsh. Sensing her disapproval, Hiroshi tells her that he considers himself a victim of what he terms "my mother's absence from life." Kate nods, not quite convinced that this is an altogether fair judgment on her friend and fellow sufferer at the hands of Stephen Eliot.

That night, when he is alone, Hiroshi's tears fall plentifully as he remembers his beautiful mother. With her, Hiroshi realizes, there was the chance of reinventing the past. He recalls her fondness for ukiyoe, but he also knows that she lived in the bygone times depicted in those prints. He does not wish to be trapped like she was. Despite her many frailties, he can now forgive her. Where there is love, there is always hope, he tells her spirit.

But his father? What a strange, cruel creature he was! Why should he harbour any good thoughts about him? Why should he seek any understanding with him?

That night he is visited in his sleep by the warrior Kato Sayemon, who, imagining that his wife and infant son were monsters, abandoned them to become a monk. Hiroshi's dream enacts the tale as told to him years earlier by Takao.

Mother and son, in an attempt to find out what had happened to the missing man, travelled far and wide to find him. One day they came upon the temple of Kongobuji, where no women were permitted. After an old man informed them that Sayemon now lived there, the son, Ishidomaro, ascended the mountain alone. There, encountering a monk, he beseeched him: "*Does a priest by the name of Kato Sayemon live here? I am his son; my mother is awaiting me in the valley below. Fifteen years we have yearned to see him again, and the love we have for him in our hearts aches.*"

The priest, who was none other than Sayemon, responded: "*I am sorry to think that your journey has been in vain, for no one of that name lives here.*"

Although he spoke with an outward display of coldness, there was a mighty struggle within the monk between love for his child and the way of life he had chosen separate from him. He was shaken to the core of his being, but he chose once again to crush those feelings.

Ishidomaro was not satisfied for he realized that the man standing before him was his long-lost father. "*Sir, on my left side there is a mole, and my mother told me that on the left eye of my father there is the same mark by which I would instantly recognize him. You have that mark.*" *The boy burst into tears, longing for the embrace that he knew would never be given to him.*

Offered a second chance, Sayemon did not seize it. "*The mark of which you speak is very common. I am most certainly not your father, and you had better dry your eyes and seek him elsewhere.*" *With that, the monk left in order to attend evening service.*

Hiroshi doubts his own father would have been shaken for even a moment by such a confrontation. After this dream, Hiroshi determines he must abandon the faint hope — in his imagination — of being a good son to Lieutenant Eliot, who was a monster after the insane monk's own heart.

Fiercer doubts than usual assail Hiroshi as he thinks about his future. He has to live in the here and now while at the same time he imagines a different life. He resolves to start drawing again.

CHAPTER FORTY-ONE

───

1918

A HOLY FRENZY drives Hiroshi. By candlelight, he draws incessantly. Rarely pleased with what he accomplishes, he turns the sheets of paper over and begins again.

Why, he asks himself, is he working so rapaciously? Unfortunately, he is a perfectionist who will not settle for anything second-rate. Now unwilling to look at the work of others in order to copy or steal from them, he begins, like a Van Gogh, to reduce his portraits, landscapes and flowers to their essence. Towards the end of his life, Hiroshi recalls, the Dutch artist, rapturous at beholding the forget-me-not blues, citron yellows, delicate pinks in the work of another artist, told his sister: "When one sees this picture, one gets the feeling of being present at a rebirth." That is my aim, Hiroshi vows.

He pines for his native land. Quite often, he is unsure whether it will ever be restored to him. For years his country has ceased to exist for him except in his imagination. Van Gogh, who had never been there, loved Japan — its landscapes and people — even though he had known them only through ukiyoe. In those woodblock prints, he had seen perfect earthly beauty. In his own art Hiroshi determines to recreate a Japan that may never have existed but should have existed. To this dream world he will devote himself.

The lines of Hiroshi's drawings become simpler and more refined. When he adds colour, it is cleaner and more distinct than anything he has done before. His art has become one of essentials purified of even a hint of excess.

The only reading these days that comforts Hiroshi concerns Vincent. As before, Hiroshi is touched by the love shared between the artist and his brother, the ever watchful and cautionary Theo. Strangely, Hiroshi's love for his own land is rekindled each time he reads of Vincent's affection for Japan. "The weather here in Arles remains fine," Vincent wrote his brother in 1888, "and if it was always like this, it would be better than a painter's paradise. It would be absolute Japan."

"Absolute Japan." What a curious phrase! Isn't that what I have been looking for all my life? Hiroshi wonders. The essence of Japan. Isn't that what he was unconsciously searching for when he redrew and then forged all those woodblocks years ago? Isn't what he admires about Sharaku is that artist's ability to go right to the essence of the Japanese personality? Its beauty, its fragility, its love of life, its world-weariness?

Once again, Hiroshi purchases paper and paint; he imports wood from Japan. He arranges to rent a small studio space two doors down from where he lives. Every evening he works there, sometimes until dawn.

There is no doubting, Hiroshi realizes, that his fascination with Sharaku is driving him in the resumption of his career as a woodcut artist. He does not wish to imitate Sharaku as much as he wishes to surpass him. That might well be a foolish and an impossible task, but he is going to take a stab at it. For the first time in a long while, Hiroshi feels himself consumed with ambition, an emotion he distrusts because it might master and, in the process, destroy him. It is now clear that he has been afraid to become an artist because he was a sham years before. He does not wish to be led into temptation once again. He is far too old to be an arrogant young man.

Hiroshi cannot erase from his mind's eye the self-portrait of Vincent Van Gogh dressed as a bonze, staring out glumly from the canvas, the epitome of self-imposed haughtiness. To Hiroshi, Van Gogh is daring him to follow in his footsteps.

The Dutch artist made his own versions of three ukiyoe prints. Those are not among his best paintings, but the portrait of Père Tanguy surrounded by woodcuts is a masterpiece. In the lower right corner is an *oiran* by Eisen; a depiction of Ishiyakushi by Hiroshige is in

the upper right corner; on the left is the courtesan Takao of the Miuraya. The old postal clerk is the real centre of attention. Here is a man who has experienced many of the miseries life can throw in one's way. Yet, his hands joined together, the old man, reflecting on the vagaries of existence, seems to have reached an understanding with the life force.

Even more to the point, Hiroshi is well aware, is how Van Gogh distilled the essence of his knowledge of ukiyoe into his landscapes, particularly the ones made at Arles. Hiroshi's admiration for the landscapes of Hokusai and Hiroshige is rekindled when he becomes aware of how Van Gogh looked at them and then transformed them to meet his own ends. These days

Hiroshi is drawn to the dreamy, wistful landscapes of Kuniyoshi, an artist usually associated with warrior prints.

Hiroshi recalls his childhood fascination with the magical plays of the kabuki, the subject matter of so much ukiyoe. Once upon a time, Hiroshi knows, he skated easily over surfaces in order to be a brilliant counterfeiter. He obviously cannot do that any more. He must use his eyes and his hands in a new way. He wishes that he had the transforming eyes of a Van Gogh. I must force my eyes to see in a new way, he instructs himself.

Hiroshi, having become acquainted with the work of the leading practitioners of *shin hanga*, the contemporary revival of ukiyoe, yearns to return the woodblock print to its important place in Japanese culture. The government in Tokyo, opposed to this revival, wants its citizens to produce oil paintings that can rival Western artists in that medium.

Although Hiroshi is convinced that *shin hanga* artists must be fully aware of the techniques used by their eighteenth- and nineteenth-century predecessors, he feels they must create a new, real Japan in their work. That is the challenge that confronts him. Okakura would be sympathetic to this movement, Hiroshi assures himself. This is the only way in which he can hope to follow his mentor's precepts. After wavering in his resolve several times, Hiroshi decides to visit Mr. Ikeda, another Japanese nationalist in exile in Boston, and to show him a sample of his work. Like his friend, Okakura, before him, Ikeda is a suspicious figure in Japan. So fierce was official opposition to his championing of *shin hanga* that he felt forced to emigrate. He is a publisher in exile.

Behind Mr. Ikeda's desk in his Western-style office are about a hundred masterpieces of ukiyoe of all sizes (*ōban, hosoban, aiban*) carelessly tacked to the wall. Hokusai's *Great Wave* is surrounded by *bijin* who seem to have no interest in the fishermen who might, in a moment's time, be flipped into the sea. Lovers about to commit suicide are placed next to children playing *go*. Warriors go off to battle while, by their side, some elderly gentlemen arrive at a house in the Yoshiwara. There is no rhyme or reason that Hiroshi can detect in the display. His years as a curator in Boston have made him uneasy with the way this collection is assembled. The fugitive colours in the prints are beginning to vanish; the prints have marks in their corners.

Hiroshi is doing his best to appear unperturbed, but he knows that he is doing a poor job of it. Mr. Ikeda, a friend of Okakura, probably knows of Hiroshi's disreputable past. That problem aside, he is known to castigate would-be artists who do not reach his high expectations.

Ikeda-san, an austere-looking man in his pinstriped suit, has a no-nonsense edge to him. His age is hard to estimate, but Hiroshi guesses he must be at least sixty. Ikeda, lighting cigarette after cigarette, never offers one to Hiroshi. Perhaps he instantly knows a non-smoker when he sees one? Without betraying a single fact about himself, Ikeda questions Hiroshi incessantly about his time in Boston, his knowledge of ukiyoe, his aspirations as an artist. He does not mind making his guest squirm when he asks why he decided only recently, in his early forties, to become an artist?

Hiroshi has not intended to make a complete confession of his life to his interrogator, but he talks freely about his childhood in the Yoshiwara, his wayward early life, his career as a forger, and his work at the Boston Museum. Ikeda shows absolutely no empathy, although scorn and dismay are also absent from his countenance.

Finally, Ikeda asks to see Hiroshi's portfolio, a mixture of drawings and prints. Holding his cigarette firmly in his mouth, Ikeda stands up and uses both hands to open and then inspect the contents of the box which Hiroshi deposits before him on his desk. An expressionless Ikeda looks at each drawing for a few seconds before going on to the next one. When he reaches the prints, he takes about half a minute scanning each of them.

His inspection completed, Ikeda sits himself down as if completely exhausted by his efforts. Lost in thought, he looks over to the open window on his left. Finally, examining his suit coat for any sign of a stray piece of ash, he looks in Hiroshi's direction. He studies Hiroshi's face for a moment or two and then, without any emotion in his voice, begins speaking. There is no doubt in his mind that the drawings show an intimate knowledge of the history of art in Japan and the West in the past two hundred years. He puffs several times at his cigarette. The prints are a completely different matter. Not raising his voice in the slightest or allowing even the semblance of inflection to emerge, he declares them to be masterworks.

Now, a slight display of feeling escapes Ikeda's lips. "The purpose of the *shin hanga* movement, of which I consider myself a — if not *the* — leading light is to build upon the past in order to transform the future. Perhaps your escapades — please forgive me if I'm using the wrong word — in the past have prepared you for the present? Your grasp of the woodblock medium is second to none."

Continuing in his dry, matter-of-fact way, Ikeda informs Hiroshi that time is of the essence. He would like to publish a series of, say, fifteen prints by Hiroshi. He offers excellent terms and asks when the entire sequence can be ready. When Hiroshi suggests six months, this is obviously the wrong answer. The great masters of ukiyoe, he is reminded, often drew twenty or twenty-five images in the space of a few days. Ikeda reluctantly suggests two months — aware that an artist like Utamaro only made the drawings and then approved the master blocks, whereas Hiroshi will be involved in every aspect of the production of his woodcuts. Hiroshi, a bit dismayed, agrees to have the series ready within that time, but he points out that he has pulled the prints by himself in the small studio space he has rented. He has no more room there. Ikeda immediately assures Hiroshi that there is plenty of studio space in the room above the one in which they are now meeting.

One of Hiroshi's strongest memories these days is of his conversations with Okakura-sensei, who has been dead for five years. What would he think of me now? He knows the answer: his late friend was so incredibly generous that he would have understood and approved all the twists and turns in his life.

Hiroshi's time in Boston passes quickly. He works long days at the Museum and equally long nights in his studio. Mr. Ikeda has sold a number of Hiroshi's prints in Japan. Hiroshi spends his weekends with Kate or with LeB and his family, who have now settled in Andover well outside the city. Every six months or so Russell Crook calls upon Hiroshi so that they can crawl from pub to pub, the American all the while lamenting the perils of the artist in the modern world.

With every passing year, the Van Gogh painting escalates in value. Negotiations have been at a standstill for a long time, mainly because Isabella Gardner cannot make up her mind whether or not to purchase the canvas, much to the disgust of Stuyvesant and Wyman who have asked what they term a modest fifty thousand dollars for it. However, Mr. Lawson has recently expressed an interest in buying the painting. The lady may finally have to make up her mind or lose out to a rival.

Hiroshi, who has made himself into an expert on the eccentric painter, hungers to see a real Van Gogh. When he can steal some time from his own department, he visits the office of the curator of Western art where he can read through all the scholarly magazines and newspapers that might contain a snippet of new information about the Dutchman. He is surprised when he discovers that Vincent began his working life as a dealer.

Hiroshi soon learns in detail about the reception of Japanese art in Europe. He is greatly amused to read that Monet, having created his famous painting, *La Japonaise*, which shows his wife clad in a kimono and holding a fan, later referred to it as a piece of trash.

Hiroshi also discovers that Van Gogh saw Japanese prints for the first time in Antwerp in 1885. He knows that Vincent — as he begins to think of him — lived in Montmartre next door to the Bing Gallery, where thousands of ukiyoe were kept in stock. He imagines the hours Vincent spent pouring over the prints.

Two years later, in 1887, Vincent made transcriptions in oil of two Hiroshiges: *Bridge in the Rain* and *Plum Tree in Bloom*. The perspective in both is Western; the colours are deliberately overdone. The artist told his brother: "I envy the Japanese artists for the incredible neat clarity which all their works have. It is never boring and you never get the impression that they work in a hurry. It is as simple as breathing; they draw a figure with a couple of strokes with such an unfailing easiness as if it were as easy as buttoning one's waistcoat."

Van Gogh's love for ukiyoe is palpable: "Come now," he asks his brother, "isn't it almost a true religion which these simple Japanese teach us, who live in nature as though they themselves were flowers?" Hiroshi laments he has never fully experienced the joy which filled Vincent's soul when looking at the prints: "You cannot study Japanese art without becoming much happier."

Towards the end of his life in the town of Arles, Vincent shaved his head in order to look like a Japanese monk. He no longer required any of his ukiyoe because "I am here in Japan. This is why I only have to open my eyes and paint the impressions that I receive."

Deeply attracted as he is to Vincent, Hiroshi comes to love even more his selfless brother, Theo, who did everything he could to make his brother's miserable existence bearable. Would that I could care for someone so selflessly, Hiroshi admonishes himself.

CHAPTER FORTY-TWO

1919

HIROSHI TAKES A month's holiday. He tells his colleagues that he is completely worn down. Freed from all usual responsibilities, he works eighteen-hour days on a new series of landscape and kabuki prints. The carving of the master blocks eats up most of his time; the colour blocks require less mental and physical effort; once again Mr. Ikeda — who has sold all of Hiroshi's first series of prints — has provided him with the finest inks and paper. On his third day, he pulls two prints and shows them to Ikeda, who pronounces himself pleased. A week later, Hiroshi has ten prints ready.

As the end of his second week approaches, Hiroshi is filled with joy. Finally, he is convinced, he has become an artist. This time, like Russell and LeB, he is a true one: these prints are profoundly original. Five of them are large portrait heads of imaginary kabuki actors. The ghost of Sharaku lingers in them. The other five are landscapes of scenes rendered by Hokusai, but these landscapes have the intensity and colour of a Van Gogh. From time to time, Hiroshi recalls the dire poverty in which the incessantly busy Hokusai existed.

For many years, Hiroshi has not thought of Yoshitoshi, the man from whom he learned so many practical things. Unfortunately, he sadly reflects, the disciple used The Master's teaching to become a forger. Of a sudden Hiroshi understands Yoshitoshi in a new way — his dreary shabbiness, his heavy drinking, his bad temper. The old man, despite frequent words to the contrary, had spent his entire existence trying to get it right, to make the one perfect image. Convinced he had never done this, he had come to despise himself.

Most often while working, Hiroshi thinks of Van Gogh in Arles, of the excitement that seized that poor man's desperate and lonely soul as he saw the colours and the forms emerging from within. No wonder he could not live anymore: he was torn apart by the outbursts of beauty that accompanied his feelings of self-loathing.

Quite often, Hiroshi sees Tedoya's name in the newspaper; frequently these are accompanied by photographs of him: Nikkei has raised new capital by trading its shares publicly; Nikkei might be merging with another, larger munitions manufacturer; Nikkei is moving to a larger facility on the outskirts of Tokyo. In all the photos, Tedoya's trademark smirk is in evidence.

Then, a year later, there are shorter pieces in the press, none accompanied by snapshots. Nikkei is badly undercapitalized, Nikkei has suffered a disastrous year. A month later, Tedoya's face, accompanied by headlines, occupies the front page of all the newspapers. The industrialist has gone missing. Foul play is suspected. Then silence.

Six months later, grainy, badly focused photographs of Tedoya's decomposed corpse, discovered in Ueno Park, occupy the front pages of the tabloids. Two eight-year-old girls, playing truant from school, had wandered into the middle of the park, got lost and finally managed to see the edge of it a considerable distance away from where they had entered. Walking uphill in that direction, they stumbled upon the corpse, its severed head, about eight feet away, staring at them with gaping sockets. Broken branches and dried blood stuck tenaciously to the ground testified to a mighty struggle. Terrified, the two youngsters made it out of the park and home to their parents, who telephoned the police. Hiroshi — remembering the dead body of the courtesan — is appalled at the amazing synchronicity between the past and the present.

A month later, a reporter from one of the newspapers, after what he claimed was a thorough investigation, was able to reconstruct what had happened. In order to keep Nikkei afloat, Tedoya had borrowed a large sum of money from an underworld boss. To secure the loan, Tedoya deposited with him a large number of guaranteed bonds. When Tedoya missed two payments, the bonds were presented for payment. Having decided to do away with Tedoya, the gangster paid one of Tedoya's mistresses to arrange an assignation with him in a remote part of Ueno, where he was butchered by two thugs.

LeB and Russell take Hiroshi on what they describe as a mystery ride to the town of Fall River, Massachusetts. The journey — long, cumbersome and fatiguing — takes most of a Saturday morning.

When their cab finally pulls up at the outskirts of the Reverend Arthur May Knapp's residence, LeB and Russell say they should go the rest of the way on foot. For about five minutes they walk up a slightly hilly incline before coming to a ridge where they can look down on the house, a recreation of a Japanese home. Hiroshi's eyes are drawn first to the magnificent irimoya roof and then to the deep, flaring eaves and curvilinear Tokugana gable piercing the front slope. For a moment or two, Hiroshi is back in Japan, but, on closer inspection, he becomes aware of all the adaptations that have been made to allow this house to weather a severe New England winter. There is a chimney and glass windows.

Inside the house are exposed beams and planks of beautifully marked black cypress. The windows are inserted in such a way that they can be, like *shoji*, easily removed. The recesses are Japanese, but the fireplaces are occidental. Western stairs with oriental railings lead upstairs.

Like Hiroshi himself, the house is a blend of East and West. An uneasy balance, he tells himself. Almost without noticing, he has fitted into his new life in Boston. He thinks of Japan all the time: his job demands that he do so. And yet for him his native land has become a place of dreams. We become what we pretend to be, he reminds himself. Does Japan really exist or is it a place that subsists only in my imagination?

Hiroshi expresses his sincere gratitude to the minister and his wife for receiving him and his friends. As is his custom, he is almost excessive in his thanks to his two good friends. Instead of giving him pleasure, however, the excursion to Fall River completely unnerves Hiroshi. The homesickness that invades him almost makes him physically ill. He can taste his desire to return to Japan.

LeB and Crook see an idealized Japan when they look at Hiroshi's woodblock prints. They praise their friend lavishly, but they have no conception of the real world in which the original ukiyoe was created. If, like himself, they had been brought up in the Yoshiwara, Hiroshi wonders, would they value these prints as works of art? Or would they see them as ephemera celebrating a sordid and degenerate way of existence? The Museum of Fine Art has received all manner of Japanese prints greedily accumulated by millionaires. Did those men have any understanding of that world? Or did they simply create a fantasy Japan full of beautiful women and gifted actors?

Hiroshi is well aware that, as far as Kate Eliot is concerned, he has become a complete triumph in Boston. She is correct to think that he is a completely reformed man. Now, he would never, under any circumstances, return to his crimes. He knows that she would be very reluctant to see him leave. He is the son she never had. But what exactly does life in Japan offer him? Could he fit in again?

He is, after all, only half-Japanese. He may avoid thinking of his American origins, but that fact is always at the back of his mind. It is the ghost haunting the precipice of his imagination and of his soul. Only one thing is certain: thinking of his father makes Hiroshi feel worthless.

CHAPTER FORTY-THREE

1921

FORMALLY DRESSED IN an old-fashioned white suit and a wide brimmed, pulled down hat, this fellow, who looks to be about sixty, has a high, broad forehead, small sharp eyes, a long pointed nose and a determined chin and jaw. He looks angry and a bit dejected. Hiroshi wonders if the man's face has settled permanently in this way?

Frank Lloyd Wright treats Hiroshi with disdain, almost as if he does not like anyone of the Japanese race. He had written ahead to ask about having two hundred prints evaluated during a brief stay in Boston. Delighted to comply, Hiroshi had hoped to exchange more than a few terse words with the famous architect.

I suspect, Hiroshi thinks, that he no longer appreciates anyone of my race. Here, in Boston, Wright does not mind making his feelings known. His involvement with fake prints has been as extensive as mine, Hiroshi recalls, and he was made to pay a bitter price.

Even before he began visiting Japan regularly to work on the Imperial Hotel, Wright has been buying and selling woodblock prints to finance his career as an architect. Some people had told Hiroshi that he really went to Japan in order to buy prints at low prices and sell them at exorbitant ones in the United States.

He also heard about what had happened the previous year when Wright's career as a vendor took a very unpleasant turning. Evidently, the print merchants in Tokyo and Kyoto, hating Wright as much as they had once despised Hiroshi, baited him. Through an intermediary in their pay, they let it be known that a huge cache of masterworks by Utamaro, Shunshō, Kiyonga and Toyokuni were in the possession of the eccentric widow of Baron Ito. An eager and anxious Wright, determined to be the first person on the scene, had taken a wide variety of conveyances — including a two-hour rickshaw ride — to her dilapidated country estate. The widow, surprised to see a white man demanding entry, told him she knew nothing of such a horde. Impatiently, Wright informed her that they were buried in the very room in which they were sitting. The widow, dazzled by the amount of money he offered to pay if he could but search, reluctantly agreed to have the workmen, who had accompanied Wright, dig up the floor of her principal sitting room. After about a half hour, the workers uncovered four large boxes. Moisture had got into one of them and destroyed its contents, but the other three were filled with the prints the architect sought.

Amazed and relieved, Wright offended the widow by offering her 25,000 yen. She was not the complete fool she seemed and balked at such a low offer, saying that she would like to place the newly discovered prints with some other dealers so that she could discover what they were really worth. Alarmed, Wright offered her 100,000 yen, the equivalent of $50,000. The lady was not pleased. She would, she informed him coldly, accept 200,000 yen if Wright would pay her that day and remove the prints. Reluctantly, he agreed.

Wright told the widow he was paying her far too much and was doing so because he wanted to rescue the prints for posterity. He did not inform her that he hoped to sell the prints for about $400,000. Upon his return to the States, Wright held one of his famous print parties, at which he took in that very amount from about six millionaire collectors.

All would have gone well except that many of the masterpieces were genuine prints in very poor condition that had been repainted with fresh colours, and such prints are virtually worthless. Upon discovering that his Kiyonga triptych, *Gentleman Entertained by Courtesans and a Geisha at a Teahouse in Shinagawa*, had colours of recent vintage, one collector demanded immediate restitution from the debt-ridden architect. The other customers, when they had their purchases authenticated by experts, demanded their money back as well. Wright had to have another print party at which he assuaged the angry buyers by giving them some genuine prints and promising them that he would eventually return their money.

Wright subsequently learned to his considerable chagrin and shame that there was no such person as Baron Ito and that the widow had been an ex-courtesan in the service of the consortium. An English expression comes to Hiroshi: "There but for the grace of God go I."

Hiroshi badly misses his old nurse and often thinks of returning to Japan in order to care for Takao. Rather than broaching that difficult topic, Hiroshi mentions to Kate that he has resumed his career as a maker of woodblock prints, and is careful to emphasize that he is not intentionally imitating or "stealing" the work of others.

Kate seems quite pleased by the revelation. "I'm not at all surprised. You are an artist, after all."

"I was exiled from Japan because I was such a successful imitator of ukiyoe. There is a great deal of difference between an artist and a copier."

"There is nothing wrong with imitation. All artists routinely copy each other. Your mistake was to represent your imitations as the work of the artists who actually designed the compositions."

"Exactly. I was both a thief and a liar."

"So that may be, but you were a very gifted woodblock artist. You have become one again. Perhaps having learned from the dead masters like Sharaku it is time now for you to go even further in inventing your own compositions?"

Kate has raised the very issue that has been hovering at the edge of Hiroshi's consciousness for some time. Now, he is able to ask himself: What is the difference between an artist and a forger? Both need to have excellent skills in anatomy, perspective and drafting; both must use their eyes carefully; both search for essential truths. Before, Hiroshi finally understands, he searched for truth in replicating the works of others. He never used his skills to unleash his own view of the world. Not a man satisfied with simple truths, he is staggered by this one. Ominously, another disturbing question intrudes: do I have something to give to the world and, if I do, am I prepared to pay for it in the hard currency of my own life?

CHAPTER FORTY-FOUR

1922

ISABELLA CONFIDES TO Hiroshi that the Van Gogh is to be delivered on Saturday. Mr. Stuyvesant has put a lot of pressure on this poor widow — as she sometimes labels herself. She has asked to see the canvas in situ, as it were, at Fenway Court and will then make her final decision. According to Stuyvesant, Mr. Lawson is now anxious to buy the picture. His late wife — never seen in public because she was always ill — was an avaricious reader; she had told her husband that Van Gogh was, as he puts it, "the coming thing." Hiroshi shudders, certain that the painting would have to share pride of place in the living room with the huge Frederic Remington bronze of bronco-busting cowboys.

If Hiroshi could call at Fenway Court at precisely two o'clock on Saturday afternoon, his hostess would be eternally grateful. If he is honest with himself, Hiroshi has mixed feelings about that event. He yearns to feast his eyes on his first Van Gogh; he has unpleasant memories of Stuyvesant and his lackey, Wyman.

A very elated Bolgi welcomes Hiroshi this afternoon. "Mrs. Gardner says this is a day for rejoicing. After eleven long years of negotiation, another masterpiece will soon be making its home here." He indicates that the visitor should make his way upstairs to the Raphael Room.

Isabella is pacing, so anxious is she to share her new treasure with a close friend. She takes Hiroshi by the hand as he approaches the door and leads him to where Stuyvesant and Wyman are sitting before an easel on which a large canvas is sheathed in velvet.

Stuyvesant, meticulously dressed as always, rises to shake hands whereas Wyman, keeping his seat, nods in an offhand way. In the years that have passed since Hiroshi eavesdropped on their conversation, he has seen Stuyvesant two or three times at Museum functions, at the ballgame, and at the summer party. It is now a decade since he saw Wyman at the ballgame and the summer party, athough he knows that he is reckoned a ne'er-do-well with a small private income; he has dabbled at becoming a painter but is evidently lazy. Gossip says that Wyman, very much in need of cash to support expensive habits, often acts as a henchman for Stuyvesant, who, in addition to his activities as a dealer, owns houses which he rents in Beacon Hill and the North End. When someone refuses to pay their rent, Wyman, gossip has it, requires them to do so with whatever means are appropriate.

A warm tender smile covers Stuyvesant's face. Wyman does not bother with any pleasantry, although he insists on doing the honours in revealing the Van Gogh. Without waiting for his hostess to invite him to do so, he walks casually over to the easel and rips the covering away.

Looking at the picture again, Isabella beams. This is a momentous event in her life as a collector. She lives for such moments. Expecting even a polite and restrained Japanese gentleman like Hiroshi to exclaim rapturously, when she does not hear any kind of sound from him, she looks in his direction.

Hiroshi is lost in thought. The colours are amazing, the composition extraordinary. The heads of the irises — blue with gold throats — are juxtaposed against the stark green of their foliage. So simple, so painterly, so extreme. The paint, thickly and vigorously applied to the canvas, calls attention to itself. This is not a picture showing flowers. This is a painting about the inner essences of flowers, a glimpse into their secret lives.

He is very moved by the painting and confesses his admiration to his hostess, who receives this communication rapturously. All four of them stand in silence for a few minutes, until Hiroshi calmly turns to his hostess. "This is a great painting, but it is most assuredly not a Van Gogh."

Isabella cringes, not sure of what she is hearing. Mr. Stuyvesant looks on the verge of collapse. Only Mr. Wyman can think of anything to say. "How have you arrived at such a preposterous conclusion?"

For the very first time, Hiroshi looks Wyman in the face. "I have been studying Van Gogh with great assiduity for the past few years. Although I have never seen one, as it were, in the flesh, I have poured over many reproductions, both in colour and rotogravure. The colours here are correct and the composition is accurate, but Van Gogh never applied paint to canvas in the way it is done here. In my opinion, we are looking at the work of a masterful forger who understands the essence of Van Gogh but is ignorant of his practices in the studio."

Isabella, having taken forever to make up her mind about purchasing the picture, is apparently the most upset of Hiroshi's listeners. Although she is always the perfect lady, she is angry. Stuyvesant interjects. "Madam, we shall simply have to have the painting authenticated by a scholar, perhaps someone from the Netherlands. I shall arrange for such a person to make the crossing within the month. At that time, we shall settle this matter."

Weighing his words carefully, he continues: "This painting was acquired by me in the Netherlands from a friend of the artist. I have provided you with all the relevant documentation. My integrity as a dealer has been brought into question by this gentleman who is no expert in this area."

Wyman says nothing. He does look Hiroshi directly in the face, but the only emotion registered is one of insolence.

Seeing that his presence is no longer required, Hiroshi excuses himself and makes his solitary way out of Fenway Court.

CHAPTER FORTY-FIVE

HIROSHI SPENDS THE rest of the day and Sunday in his room on Pinckney Street. He is tempted to call upon Kate to discuss the whole sordid situation that unfolded at Fenway Court but decides against it. Late on Sunday night, there is a rap on his door. He rouses himself and opens the door to a very haggard-looking Kate.

Although she has never been to this room before, she is not a bit interested in making even the most rudimentary inspection. Clothed in black, she stands before him looking like an avenging angel as the light in the room highlights her deathly pale countenance.

So there they are in the middle of the room: foster mother and adopted son. Hiroshi has been caught completely offguard, having not the least idea of why Kate has appeared. She seems not completely sure of what she is doing; she wrings her hands as if waiting for words to force their way of their own accord out of her mouth.

Finally, forcing herself, she breaks the bad news. "Mr. Stuyvesant was found murdered this afternoon. His assailant shot one bullet into his heart."

Hiroshi is unable to come to complete grips with the sorry event; he is not sure why the matter is so important to Kate, but he bows his head sorrowfully.

She continues: "The murderer was Mr. Wyman. After leaving Stuyvesant's home, he went back to his own lodging and shot himself in the head. He is also dead."

Hiroshi is beginning to fear lest these two deaths be somehow levied against him. "Everything about Peter was sordid," Kate goes on, "and his suicide note merely adds to the catalogue of infamies that was Peter Wyman.

"As a young man, Peter attempted to become an artist. He showed promise but when success and, thus, gratification, did not come at a rate that suited him, he abandoned that profession. In recent years, he served Stuyvesant as a henchman.

"A decade ago, the real estate market in Boston collapsed and so did much of Stuyvesant's fortune. Since his career as a dealer was in shambles, he decided to begin another one as a swindler. Wyman, who owed Stuyvesant a great deal of money, came up with the idea of marketing the first Van Gogh to reach North America to Mrs. Gardner. The painting, undertaken with considerable study and obvious dexterity, was done by Peter.

"The deception would have gone forward without a hitch had you not offered Isabella your opinion of the painting. Unmasked by what he considered to be Peter's bungling, Stuyvesant berated him as an incompetent. Peter has since boyhood been of an unruly and unpredictable temperament, and so he shot him dead. He then went home and took his own life."

Despite his difficulty in absorbing this information, Hiroshi cannot understand why Kate is so distraught about the deaths of people she did not know. Why does she keep referring to Wyman as Peter?

Hiroshi asks if Kate knew Wyman.

"Not very well. However, he was your half-brother — three years younger than you — the consequence of your father's liaison with Mary Wyman in the fourth year of his marriage to me."

Kate, having long been at pains to keep a great deal of information from Hiroshi, now completely lets down her guard. "Well before my marriage to Mr. Eliot, I had profound misgivings about entering into any kind of alliance with him. According to local gossips, Mr. Eliot had a Japanese wife. My own father inquired about my then fiancé and was told that he had, like many other men of his class, kept a mistress while in Japan. This information was never passed on to me.

"My own reservations were centered on what I could observe of Mr. Eliot's behaviour, which was frequently boorish. He drank too much, was habitually late for his engagements with me, and never seemed at all interested in anything I had to say. As you may know, he had a glass eye, the result of a brawl when he was a young man. To me, there was a Janus-like aspect to his face. Even before our marriage, I was under the impression that he fixed me with his blind eye while scanning the room with his good one.

"Forewarned should have been forearmed. I was at liberty to refuse him. I did not do so for several reasons. Despite his disability, he was a remarkably handsome man. I was also quite convinced that he was the type of person who required good management. I knew I could provide that in abundance. The truth is that I saw your father as a challenge, a project whereby I could rescue an impetuous man from certain ruin.

"Stephen Eliot may have been reckless, but he was also canny. When we married in May 1877, he had just about depleted the estate of his parents. Immediately, he attempted to do the same with the dowry provided to him by my parents. Luckily, he had no other money from my family.

"In the conduct of his business affairs, my husband was both mendacious and rapacious. He invested money in risky enterprises; when his bubbles were pricked, he lost a great deal of his own money and that of his clients. A merchant banker who acquires the reputation of being a thief is soon idle.

"When that occurred, Stephen closed his office and stayed away from here for long stretches of time. His mistresses were legion, but they soon deserted him when he no longer had vast amounts of money to throw in their directions.

"The life of Stephen Eliot had many strange slips and turns, but the manner of his death still gives me pause." Kate stops, rises and walks over to Hiroshi. Somewhat awkwardly, she sits down on the mat nearest him and takes his hand.

"In the last month of Stephen's life I was visited twice by a strange man. A cumbersome, hairless fellow of extraordinary height — he was almost seven feet tall; this giant, who looked to be in early middle age, first called on me to disclose that my husband owed his employer a considerable amount of money, just over fifty thousand dollars. At that point, I examined him even more intently. His hands looked like lion paws, his deeply recessed eyes were a cold gray, and his skin a pale white. He could have posed for a portrait of the incarnation of evil. His voice was high-pitched and feminine, as if another, more benign creature resided therein. He was a man of decided contrasts.

"Mr. Smith — that is what he called himself — had been instructed by his employer to inform me of this indebtedness. 'What was I going to do about this precarious situation?' — in employing the adjective 'precarious,' Mr. Smith was obviously quoting his employer.

"Without hesitation, I informed my caller that the problem originated with my husband and must stay with him. On that afternoon, my caller quickly absented himself. Two weeks later, although he came unannounced, I agreed to receive him. On this day, his cheeks were a bright red, as if he himself were agitated. His voice was even more falsetto than before. On that day he informed me that my refusal to settle my husband's account would cause him considerable distress, 'of a very personal kind.' Not sure what he meant, I told him that he must pursue whatever steps he thought proper to collect the debt. The elephantine Mr. Smith looked at me quizzically. I think he was surprised that I stood up to him.

"Two nights later, Stephen Eliot, who was taking dinner at the Parker House, walked to the roof of that establishment, where he fell to his death. The authorities and the newspapers were in complete agreement with each other: the inebriated Eliot, for inexplicable reasons, had walked up to the top of the hotel and had either lost his footing or decided to do away with himself.

"I have always known that my husband was murdered, and I must carry to the grave some of the responsibility for his death. I could have easily paid the debt but chose not to do so. At the time I saw Mr. Smith for the second time, I was fairly certain he was disinclined to commit homicide and was in hopes that I would release him from an act for which he might suffer a pang or two of bad conscience. Little did Mr. Smith know that a part of me would have gladly paid him to kill Stephen. As it turned out, I was rid of my husband without advancing a single cent in the cause.

"To this day, I do not mourn Mr. Eliot. But I was filled with a terrible anguish eighteen years ago when, through the agency of Mr. Wiley, I felt obligated to tell your mother the full story of the manner of his death. The news of how her husband had died filled your mother with rage against me. For several days, she refused to have anything to do with me. Finally, having decided that Stephen's life had gone out of control because he had abandoned her and Japan, she consented to speak to me again. Our friendship was resumed, although it never quite reached the intimacy it had once enjoyed.

"I did not bother to inform Yoshiko of the existence of Peter Wyman. I thought no good would come of it. Your father died in his forty-fourth year on January 12, 1890. Peter was fourteen years old at the time. Shortly after his death, the destitute Mary Wyman wrote me asking for an interview. At that meeting, she told me that she had been one of Stephen's many mistresses. Unhappily for her, she was the only one of them to become pregnant and bear a child.

"Since I had no reason to doubt her story, I provided her with money so that she and her son could live comfortable lives. I received them at my home, although I never had any discussion with Peter about his parentage. As a child, he was sober and dependable. In adolescence, he became difficult for his mother to manage. Although I remain on good terms with Mary, I have not seen Peter in the past decade. Since his mother no doubt informed him of the identity of his father, he would have known you were his half-brother.

"Before tonight, I had not anticipated any reason to make you privy to information which I thought you could live happily without." She begins to cry: "I never thought it would come to this."

As Kate had feared, her revelations fill Hiroshi with anguish. He had exposed his brother. Obviously, Hiroshi and Peter had inherited their talents as forgers from their father. His brother, knowing who he was, had hated him.

Before this evening, Hiroshi had attempted to remove his father from his consciousness. As a very young man, he had treated all things Western with contempt because of the man who had abandoned him and his mother. Now, he has much more psychic ammunition against him. Hiroshi finally understands the mysterious quarrel he witnessed between his mother and Kate aboard ship. He is poignantly aware that his mother never recovered from the shock of what Kate told her. Hiroshi is not certain that he can recover from what he has just learned.

Moreover, a sense of compassion for his dead brother overwhelms Hiroshi. If he had known Peter's identity, he could have approached him, tried to establish a relationship with him. Perhaps he could have assisted him to reform? Feeling that the bad seeds he inherited from the Lieutenant almost ruined his own existence, he wishes he could have helped his frail, anguish-torn brother. Why has my life been filled with so many missed opportunities, bad turnings and closed doors? Hiroshi asks himself. Unawares, he has helped to kill his brother. He is unlike the selfless Theo, who, as much as he could, shielded his brother from the horrors of life.

CHAPTER FORTY-SIX

1923

HIROSHI LIVES SIX months as a ghost in the aftermath of his brother's death. He sleepwalks through his job, eats only once a day, visits Kate once or twice a week, and sleeps a great deal. Over and over again, his mind reluctantly wanders back to the corpse of Taye that he discovered outside the Yoshiwara when he was a young boy. Now he dreams that the body he discovered among the bamboo rushes is that of his brother.

Isabella Gardner's influence is so considerable that news of the murder of Stuyvesant and the suicide of Wyman disappears from the headlines after two days. At the Museum, Hiroshi wonders if his fellow workers are privy to the blood tie between himself and Wyman? If so, they do their best to take no interest in the matter. On weekends, Hiroshi often stays with Russell Crook or LeB, who have wisely pretended not to know a thing about the two deaths. Isabella has written at length to thank him for his gracious assistance in uncovering the false Van Gogh — she does not allude to any of the consequences of the unmasking of the two villains.

The newspapers are filled with accounts of the earthquake that has shaken Tokyo to the grounds. Despite years of preparation and the construction of brick buildings, large parts of the city have been laid waste by fire. Cholera is rampant. Thousands have been killed. The city will have to be rebuilt, many parts from scratch.

A patriot such as Okakura would return by the next available boat, Hiroshi tells himself. That night he finds it difficult to sleep. Finally, he drifts off.

Hiroshi, who has been up since five o'clock this humid Tokyo Saturday morning, is about to stop for lunch when a feeble tremour shoots through his studio. Then nothing. A few seconds later, the tremour returns and the building begins to shake violently. The floor heaves and the walls and ceiling lurch drunkenly. The walls bulge as if they are mere pieces of cardboard. An incessant din assails his ears. For a half-minute, the walls hold against the onslaught before slabs of plaster fall from the ceiling. The air is filled with blinding, smothering dust. The walls spread and sag. Knowing that he will be safest at street level, Hiroshi makes for the staircase. Just as he reaches it, he is thrown to the ground and falls an entire storey. Getting up, he makes it down the two remaining flights to the entranceway. In front of him is an even thicker layer of dust. Hiroshi takes to the streets; it is like swimming through a thick river fog. Many of the buildings, including his, are still standing but the one across the street has been reduced to rubble.

His right arm is bleeding profusely, having been badly gashed in the fall. Only now does he realize that his right ankle might be broken. He hobbles along, able to see only a few feet ahead. Suddenly, the whiteness of the fog is interrupted by eruptions of red from the nearby fires.

His best hope, Hiroshi realizes, is to move away as much as possible from the wooden buildings that surround him. If he can just get two or three streets away, he might be safe.

Up till now, he has been the only person on the street. Then, he hears footsteps approaching him, but he cannot see anyone. When he looks down, he sees a boy of four or so about to collide with him. The youngster pulls to a stop when he beholds Hiroshi. He tells him that he became separated from his widowed mother in that empty twenty-five-acre track of land still called the Army Clothing Depot although the building has been long torn down. Could he help him find his mother? he pleads.

Hiroshi knows that the boy and he will be safe only if they move in the opposite direction, towards the river. He tells him that they will be in grave danger if the two of them return to the area of the Depot. The child insists on going back to save his mother. He breaks away from him, continuing in that direction. Hiroshi feels he has no choice but to assist him.

On reaching the main artery, they are confronted with a stalled trolley deserted by its passengers. At the next crossing, the street becomes filled with a crowd heading in the same direction they are. After an hour's march, Hiroshi and the child reach the entranceway to the Depot, which is filled with people and carts piled high with bedding, clothes, pots and pans, china, small pieces of furniture — even birdcages. Many of the women have babies tied to their backs. Near them is a group of schoolboys wearing black uniforms that looked brand new a few hours back. Patients from nearby hospitals have been placed on stretchers or are supported by nurses.

Panic has not struck. Used to fires ripping through their city, most people here are stoic, even though they know their homes have been destroyed and they will have to spend many nights in the open. There is almost no pushing. Everyone is resolutely polite. The ground continues to quiver, but most people are familiar with aftershocks. Strangers talk with each other, exchanging stories about their experiences that morning. Hiroshi over-hears an old man with a silvery goatee lamenting that he forgot to take his chess set with him. Photographers from the newspapers are taking pictures.

The child's mother is not to be found; the boy and Hiroshi have scoured the entire Depot. As the afternoon wears on, the bitter taste of smoke grows stronger. There are huge clouds in the sky which look like thunderheads. Perhaps a shower will put out the fire, Hiroshi tries to assure the child.

Suddenly, the entire depot is caught in a whirl. People start to fall down in piles. Caught in a shower of fire flakes, Hiroshi grabs the boy and makes for the entranceway. He pushes him in that direction but is startled when a

horse gone wild comes between them. A terrific wind blows him to
the ground. He stumbles to his feet and finds he is standing on a heap of
bodies. He falls again when someone runs into him. He can see the boy
stumbling along.

Almost blinded, Hiroshi looks into a solid wall of flame about to
consume him. Ghosts appear out of the smoke. He can just barely make
out a smile on the face of his beautiful mother, who rises out of the flames.
Then sweet Takao bows in his direction.

The fire begins to eat Hiroshi. As the pain sears through him, he looks in
the direction of the boy, hoping that he is safe. He sees that the boy has
reached the outskirts of the depot. He will be safe. The pain electrifies every
fibre in Hiroshi's body, but he does not mind. The child has been rescued.
Then, of a sudden, the child's face is there before him. It has become the face
of his half-brother, and it is clothed in a soft, gentle expression.

CHAPTER FORTY-SEVEN

———

ON THE DAY after his dream about the earthquake, Hiroshi is enervated. That night he goes to bed early, but, just as sleep is about to overtake him, he hears the soothing voice of Takao telling him a story.

After he slew Atsumori, Kumagai was disgusted with himself. His own son, sixteen years old, about the same age as the young warrior from the Taira clan, was also slain. Overcome with remorse, Kumagai renounced his life as a warrior. He could no longer carry on with his old way of life. He left his wife, his remaining children and his home, and became a priest. So filled was he with guilt and shame that he changed his name to Renjoh. He did not want such a person as Kumagai to exist.

For many years, Renjoh did everything he could to atone for the murder of the young soldier. He bestowed alms upon the poor, he nursed the sick, and he comforted the dying. He became famous for his renunciation of war. As the years advanced, he counselled many samurai to abandon their profession.

Still deeply disturbed by what he had done, Renjoh returned to the battlefield at Ichinotani to pray for the soul of Atsumori. There, he encountered some young men working as reapers on the nearby farms. He passed the time of day with them pleasantly until only one remained behind. This young man, of noble countenance and bearing, told him that he was a member of Atsumori's family and asked the monk to pray for the salvation of the fallen warrior's soul. The monk was overcome by the request. "I have spent all my life praying for him. I was the barbarian who murdered him." The young man looked him kindly in the eye and took his leave.

That night, during Renjoh's vigil, the ghost of Atsumori appeared to him. He reminisced about the golden age of the Taira clan, of the battle at which he was slain, and his own death. Very moved, Renjoh burst into tears and asked for forgiveness. The young man's dark eyes pierced those of his murderer: "You are no longer my enemy because you pray for me." After the ghost vanished, Renjoh was filled with the long-sought peace that had evaded him for so many years.

A change of name leading to the lifting of a heavy psychic burden. If it were only that simple, Hiroshi reflects. Yet, like Renjoh, Hiroshi has repented. He has attempted to erase his old life. He is that strangest of all creatures, a leopard who has lost his spots. The sense of guilt lingers, but, after all is said and done, he did not mean to harm his brother.

A new letter from Takao contains some disturbing news. She tries to conceal the worse from Hiroshi, but she cannot hide the obvious facts. The Yoshiwara is disintegrating. The statues in the park have weathered badly; litter accumulates everywhere; there are potholes in the walkways. She is much too old to run an establishment the size of the Chōjiya.

She has long harbored a wish to return to her birthplace near Arashiyama, a short distance from Kyoto. She has family there. In fact, she has just received news from a cousin the other day mentioning that a suitable house in that town is for rent.

As of old, Hiroshi sees the past through Takao's eyes. That sweet gentle woman had been the one who had trained him in the art of looking.

Of a sudden, Hiroshi's mind is made up. At the age of fifty, he will return to Japan, the place where he can forge his destiny as an artist. In so doing, he will continue the work of Okakura-sensei. He will settle in Arashiyama with Takao and take care of her.

When he breaks this news to Kate, she agrees to do everything in her power to assist him, but says her sadness at parting with her foster son torments her. She will be left all alone and might not see him again.

Within two days, Hiroshi's ticket on a steamship leaving Boston in a week's time is booked. He will be back in Japan in less than two months. Although he repeatedly refuses Kate's offer of money, he finally succumbs when she tells him she will be worried beyond distraction if he does not accept the very generous amount that she means to settle on him.

Afterwards, Hiroshi finds it difficult to remember the sequence of events in his final days in Boston, so strange is it to move out of a world of shadows into that of action. LeB is distraught to discover that his dear friend is abandoning him. He presents him with something to help him remember New England: a landscape tile with a pine tree at the centre. Russell Crook's farewell gift is a ten-inch tall vase depicting silver coloured carp swimming in and out of a bronze-flecked black background.

Two days before his ship sails, Hiroshi, by arrangement, calls upon Isabella. Today, Bolgi informs him, Mrs. Gardner will see Hiroshi in the Buddhist Room, a place at Fenway Court he has not visited before. Isabella's Anglo-Catholicism is well known to Boston's elite, but her devotion to eastern religions is something of a closely guarded secret. He is directed to walk through the Chinese Loggia and down into the darkness of the subterranean room.

Hiroshi is startled by all the statues of the great advocate of tranquility and wisdom. Some are tiny, a few inches high, but there are others that are as tall as himself. Some are encrusted with gold, others are unadorned. Isabella, wrapped in a pale-yellow robe, rises, kisses Hiroshi and asks him to sit next to her before the largest statue.

Without directly referring to the Van Gogh, Isabella tells Hiroshi that he has become, "like someone else who was very dear to me, a stalwart champion of truth." Although sad that she will probably never see him again, she knows that Hiroshi, in returning to his native land, will continue "the campaign." In that crusade, she assures him, he will achieve salvation. "Like the Buddha, you will become purged of all worldly ambition."

Russell and LeB say goodbye at the bottom of the gangplank. Kate, insisting that she be allowed to inspect his room, accompanies Hiroshi on board the ship. After pronouncing the room just barely of sufficient size, she walks out on deck with him.

Kate observes that they have become close, very much mother and son, in the nineteen years they have known each other. More than ever before, Hiroshi knows that, to her, he is her son — the child never born to her.

When she asks him to reserve a place in his heart for her, she breaks down, completely casting aside her Yankee sense of propriety, which has previously rescued her from public displays of emotion: "Before I knew you, I was not, to myself, real! You have helped me to become real!" As his eyes fill with tears, Hiroshi confesses to Kate that he has become, under her tutelage, a better man than he ever hoped to be.

ACKNOWLEDGEMENTS

PURE INVENTIONS IS a work of historical fiction that has been enhanced by my indebtedness to such excellent books as Cecilia Segawa Seigle's *Yoshiwara: The Glittering World of the Japanese Courtesan* (1993), Paul Varley's *Japanese Culture* (2000), and Wendy Kaplan's *"The Art that is Life": The Arts & Crafts Movement in America, 1875–1920* (1987). My understanding of Hiroshi's Japan was enhanced considerably by a visit to the Museum Meiji Mura, the 250-acre architectural museum at Inuyama City, near Nagoya. Takao's stories were often changed by her to suit her audience — the more historically accurate variants will be found in the forthcoming *Japanese Warrior Prints, 1646–1904* by Yuriko Iwakiri and myself. I have learned a great deal about Japan from three colleagues, Tsuneko Iwai, Yuriko Iwakiri, and Roger Keyes.

Donya Peroff copy-edited my manuscript with considerable acumen and great sensitivity. Attila Berki made many useful suggestions. Once more I have benefited from the inspired dedication Marc Côté brings to his twin roles of editor and publisher.

UTAMARO'S *COURTESAN HITOMITO of the Daimonji House* (p. 3) is
from the series *Kayoi Kuruwa Sakari Hakkei* (*Eight Views of the
Flourishing Activity of the Red Light District*) and is from about
1804. Eizan's weeping bijin (p. 26) was published by Izumiya Ichibei
circa 1809–13. Sharaku's portrait of Ichikawa Komazō as Chūbei and
Nakayama Tomisaburō as Umegawa (p. 30) is from 1794. Eizan's
Chūshingura Sibling picture showing a fashionably-dressed towns-
woman (p. 32) is from circa 1815–8. The image of Oniwaka/Benkei
(NOT Kintarō) (p. 65) is by Kuniyoshi and dates from about 1825–30.
Katsukawa Shuntei's depiction of the fight between Raikō (NOT
Kintoki) and Shūtendoji was made in about 1808–9 (p. 69).
Kuniyoshi's portrait of the archer Tametomo (p. 70) is from about
1845. Sawamura Tanosuke III (right) as Onzoshi Ushiwakamaru
and Bando Hikosaburo V as Musashibo Benkei in the kabuki play,
Wakaki hana shiki no furigoto (p. 72) was performed at the Nakamura
in 1862/03 — the artist is Kunisada. Katsukawa Shuntei's Atsumori
(p. 84) is from about 1810. Yoshitoshi's portrait of Kusunoki
Masatsura (p. 101) from *Selection of One Hundred Warriors* was published in 1868/12. Eizan's Kasumi of the House of Matsubaya (p. 112)
comes from the series, *The Six Crystal Rivers Compared with the*

Green Houses and is circa 1815. Yoshitoshi's depiction of Kiyotsune from the series *One Hundred Aspects of the Moon* (p. 118) is dated 1887/06. Toyokuni's portrait of Ichikawa Danzo IV and Iwai Hanshiro IV (p. 123) comes from about 1799. Gihachiro Okuyama's reinvention (p. 210) of Van Gogh's *Père Tanguy* is circa 1950.